SLEEPING WITH THE ENEMY

Senator Weatherford looked around the restaurant, pulling two envelopes out of his briefcase. He handed one to Muhammad and one to Tran. They opened them and saw glossy photographs of Major Bobby Samuels and Captain Bo Devore.

Muhammad said, "My people know who they are."

Weatherford leaned forward, whispering, "Some of my best contacts inside the military, especially in the army, are afraid of what these two could do to any or all of us. I have to quietly do everything I can to get them out of the way."

Tran grinned, saying, "They would not be wise to come to Vietnam or even close."

Muhammad also grinned. "I do not care where they go. If we must rid ourselves of them, then we will rid ourselves of them. You look troubled, my friend."

James did look pale. "It's not like I want you to kill two American army officers."

Muhammad grinned, "Yes, you do. You just do not wish to hear about it. My people have a saying, 'The sinning is the best part of repentance.' Think about that, Senator."

CRIMINAL INVESTIGATION DETACHMENT

BAMBOO BATTLEGROUND

DON BENDELL

BERKLEY BOOKS, NEW YORK

THE BERKLEY PUBLISHING GROUP
Published by the Penguin Group
Penguin Group (USA) Inc.
375 Hudson Street, New York, New York 10014, USA

Penguin Group (Canada), 90 Eglinton Avenue East, Suite 700, Toronto, Ontario M4P 2Y3, Canada
(a division of Pearson Penguin Canada Inc.)
Penguin Books Ltd., 80 Strand, London WC2R 0RL, England
Penguin Group Ireland, 25 St. Stephen's Green, Dublin 2, Ireland (a division of Penguin Books Ltd.)
Penguin Group (Australia), 250 Camberwell Road, Camberwell, Victoria 3124, Australia
(a division of Pearson Australia Group Pty. Ltd.)
Penguin Books India Pvt. Ltd., 11 Community Centre, Panchsheel Park, New Delhi—110 017, India
Penguin Group (NZ), 67 Apollo Drive, Rosedale, North Shore 0632, New Zealand
(a division of Pearson New Zealand Ltd.)
Penguin Books (South Africa) (Pty.) Ltd., 24 Sturdee Avenue, Rosebank, Johannesburg 2196,
South Africa

Penguin Books Ltd., Registered Offices: 80 Strand, London WC2R 0RL, England

This is a work of fiction. Names, characters, places, and incidents either are the product of the author's imagination or are used fictitiously, and any resemblance to actual persons, living or dead, business establishments, events, or locales is entirely coincidental. The publisher does not have any control over and does not assume any responsibility for author or third-party websites or their content.

CRIMINAL INVESTIGATION DETACHMENT: BAMBOO BATTLEGROUND

A Berkley Book / published by arrangement with the author

PRINTING HISTORY
Berkley edition / October 2007

Copyright © 2007 by Don Bendell.
Cover design by Steven Ferlauto.
Interior text design by Kristin del Rosario.

ISBN: 978-0-425-21631-6

BERKLEY®
Berkley Books are published by The Berkley Publishing Group,
a division of Penguin Group (USA) Inc.,
375 Hudson Street, New York, New York 10014.
BERKLEY® is a registered trademark of Penguin Group (USA) Inc.
The "B" design is a trademark belonging to Penguin Group (USA) Inc.

PRINTED IN THE UNITED STATES OF AMERICA

10 9 8 7 6 5 4 3 2 1

This is my twenty-fourth book, and I have dedicated previous books to my wife, family members, friends, the U.S. Army Special Forces, and even my horse. I told my wife this one needs to be very special, so I dedicate this book to all my fellow Vietnam veterans; army, navy, air force, marines, Coast Guard, reserves, National Guard, Air National Guard. This book is dedicated to all the grunts, jarheads, swabbies, privates, corporals, specialists, sergeants, warrant officers, and officers. It is dedicated to those who repaired helicopters as well as the crews. And dedicated to truck mechanics, drivers, clerk-typists, nurses, doctors, medics, supply clerks, MPs, finance personnel, dog handlers, FACs, pilots, forward observers, S1s, S2s, S3s, S4s, S5s, CSMs, first sergeants, cargo handlers, dental techs, radio operators, civilians, and the myriad of personnel, each an integral part, no matter what their job, who helped to make that one giant machine work. Most important, to all the wives, sons, daughters, and those loved ones left behind, and even more so, the widows and orphans. You are all the unsung heroes of the twentieth century. Thank you for your service risking your life to simply do what you believed in, whether drafted or enlisted. You did not run. You did not hide, and you risked your very life for your beliefs. We won all the battles, every single one, but somebody in a suit told us we lost the war. We did not lose the war. America lost its innocence, but we all did indeed win the war. If we lost, why does Vietnam beg us to do trade with them? More important, the groundwork you laid, the lessons learned have saved the lives of thousands of our brave, young fighting men and women now fighting in the War on Terrorism. For all Americans, even the ones who do not know any better, I say, "Thank you and welcome home."

ACKNOWLEDGMENTS

I want to acknowledge three very special people in particular:

Actress and superstar Bo Derek, without seeking publicity, but just being a good person, and on her own, started visiting wounded soldiers from Afghanistan and then Iraq, and especially the men of the U.S. Army Special Forces and family members of those killed in action. In 2002, at the Special Forces Association National Convention at Fort Bragg, North Carolina, we made Bo an honorary Green Beret. In tribute to Bo, and to my wife, Shirley, who I love more than life itself, I patterned the character Bo Devore as a cross between the two of them.

Second, I know he will try to take it out, but I will insist this gets left in, as I would like to publicly thank my editor, Tom Colgan, executive editor at Berkley. Tom has worked with authors, such as Tom Clancy, W.E.B. Griffin, Jack Higgins, and Ed McBain, and I am humbled to have him work with me, too. He is a proud father and loving husband, and has worked at Berkley since 1985, except for a short time at Avon/Morrow. A native New Yorker and a gentleman, Tom always makes me do my best and nothing less. Thank you very much, Tom.

Further, because of the extensive technical nature of this work, I referred to Wikipedia.org in many cases as well as government technical publications and wish to acknowledge such input.

Blessings,
Don Bendell

*Notice that the stiffest tree is most easily cracked,
while the bamboo or willow
survives by bending with the wind.*

— BRUCE LEE, 1973

HARDCORE

The woman could have been in her late twenties or early thirties and was a ravishing beauty. She was wearing a gray sweatshirt with the black letters "Army" and the shirt was too large for her. Nonetheless, her curves under it were obvious, and she had a natural sexiness and beauty that always revealed itself like a peacock trying to go incognito in a chicken yard. She wore black jogging pants and tennis shoes. Her eyes made her look like she might be a raccoon, as her mascara was smeared from crying, and her naturally curly long auburn hair always looked tussled, but perfectly fitting as a flame-like frame for the beautiful face. Holding a damp Kleenex, she sat cross-legged in the soft leather high-backed easy chair and appreciated its comfort.

"I was so innocent back then," she said, angry and weeping again. "How could that son of a bitch do that to me? He was my uncle."

The man in the other chair wore a U.S. Army class A uniform. On the collar was the brass indicating the Medical Service Corps and the distinctive gold oak leaf of a major. Dr. William Tewell was a good, caring psychiatrist with a

very successful practice in Philadelphia, but he felt unfulfilled. It was the first anniversary of September 11, 2001,
and he saw a special on television about the sneak attacks
on the United States. Dr. Tewell wept. And as clearly as
that, he understood why he felt unfulfilled. His father had
been an ROTC graduate platoon leader with the Big Red
One, the First Infantry Division in Vietnam. He had suffered an AK-47 wound in the right shin and received a Purple Heart, a Bronze Star with V device for valor, and a
Bronze Star for meritorious service in Vietnam. He came
back and never spoke about the war.

Bill Tewell's grandfather, his father's father, had been a
gunnery sergeant with the U.S. Marine Corps in the second
war to end all wars and served honorably at Bougainville.
He never spoke about the experience, either.

Dr. Tewell always seemed to notice that his father and
paternal grandfather both enjoyed tremendous respect
among their peers. He wanted that for himself.

Now, on the anniversary of the attack on the Pentagon
and World Trade Center, he knew that he felt a need to
serve in the military and make a contribution in his own
way. Because he was a shrink, the army inducted him as a
major, instead of captain like they did with medical doctors
and dentists.

From her soft leather perch, Bo Devore went on. "I can
still see the image of him panting over me and even feel the
pain of him tearing my vagina, Dr. Tewell. How can men
do that?"

Bill Tewell said, "What is more important is how you
feel about it."

Bo said, "I'm pissed! I wish he was alive, so I could cut
his balls off!"

The doctor said, "Is he the only one you are angry at?"

She thought for a minute and started crying harder, sobbing into her hands.

Bill Tewell waited patiently, smiling softly.

Finally, she raised her head, sniffling while she talked. "I
loved my mom and dad. Dad was one of the most respected

generals in the air force. He was a good man, but dammit! Dammit! Dammit all! Why did they let his older brother be alone with me? I was a teenaged girl, but my breasts had developed and boys were always staring. I know he fondled my mother one time when I was a girl! I want to know why, Doctor?"

Dr. Tewell said, "Captain Devore. Bo, I don't know why men do such things or why women do them, too. It is an insidious sickness, but it is very important for you to know that you did absolutely nothing to deserve it. Nothing! You were simply a young defenseless girl. But I do want you to look at something important that came out of this. How many captains are there in the entire U.S. Army who are CID agents?"

"Just me, and one major, my partner, Major Bobby Samuels. All other CID agents are enlisted men or warrant officers, but we are a special unit created after 9/11," she said, realizing what he was getting at.

He said, "Bo, what made you decide to join the army and what made you decide to become a detective?"

She thought for a minute and smiled. "My uncle raping me, although I did not even realize that was why until recently. I told you about it."

He said, "Think about the lives you have saved, the pages you have written in U.S. and world history, because you took a horrible, selfish act and turned it into a triumph. You are indeed a survivor."

Bo felt uplifted and much better.

She smiled, a tear forming in her right eye, saying, "Thank you, Doctor, for putting it that way, but why do I feel such a need to cry now and I feel so sad? Please don't ask how I feel, tell me."

The doctor smiled softly again, saying, "You are grieving."

"Grieving?" she asked. "Grieving for who?"

He said, "Grieving for that little girl who lost most of her childhood innocence and you kept hidden away for so many years inside your safe, little protective cocoon you wove for her."

"Why did she come out now after all these years?"

The doctor said, "Because you have so much strength, spiritually and emotionally, that you finally, subconsciously, felt it was safe to bring her out. You cry for the little girl whenever you feel like it, but keep on doing what you are doing. And don't ever stop being a survivor."

Bo said, "Don't worry. I will always be a survivor."

2

LEFT COAST

Her father was born in Paris, and her mother was the only daughter of two Chinese immigrants. Her hair was all the way down well below her waist and was very shiny jet black. Her television series had been at the top of the Nielsens for three years running, which was the major enabling factor when she beat out an Oscar-winning actress for the lead role in the biggest box-office blockbuster of the previous year. The superstar was "the" fantasy woman for literally millions upon millions of men around the world.

Even with his loose-fitting, oversized white shirt, she was aware of the muscles rippling underneath. He was so tall and handsome, he could easily play a leading man in any of the films or TV shows she appeared in. What really impressed Pacific Cartier, though, were his honest talks, his sensitivity, and the passion with which he had loved his late wife.

Pacific had never seen him at any functions and everybody had been trying to get him to talk about his work, but he had never mentioned it or anything professionally that he did. She figured he must be a model, as she simply could not think of any time she had seen him at the Emmys, Oscars, or at any of the L.A. hot spots.

Pacific had always had any boy, and then any man, she wanted and decided she had to make a move now. She walked over and sat down next to him.

She stared into his eyes, as he smiled at her and nodded.

She said, "Hi, Bobby."

Bobby replied, "How are you today, Pacific?"

"Lonely."

"I'm sorry," he said. "We can talk if you want."

Pacific did a fake pout, saying, "Just talk? Why don't we go to my room and share a deep conversation?"

He said, "Oh, I am enjoying the sunshine right now and relaxing out here on the grass."

She said, "Oh, I'm sorry. You're not gay, are you?"

He chuckled, saying, "I don't think so. Do I look gay?"

"No." She laughed. "You look fabulous! You have never spoken of women or about your job. Are you a model?"

Bobby said, "Yes, I am. I'm a 1963 split-window Corvette model with a complete engine."

He chuckled at his own joke, which took her a couple of seconds to understand. Then she laughed.

Bobby said seriously, "First of all, thanks for the compliment. You are extremely beautiful yourself, but just because I don't speak about women does not make me gay, Pacific, and I am not a model. You have heard me talk about my late wife."

"Well, gee, Bobby," she said, "you are such a man of mystery. What kind of work do you do?"

Bobby said, "It would probably bore you. I just poke into things a lot. Look up records. Ask questions. Things like that."

Pacific got upset, saying, "I should have known. I knew you were too good to be true. You are an investigative reporter, aren't you, just looking for a celebrity-trashing story?"

Bobby fell over backward laughing.

As if it was scripted, two psychologists walked by and one spotted Bobby and kept staring. He broke into a big smile and said something to the other one.

They walked over and Pacific said, "Busted. I was hoping people would not spot me here."

She and Bobby stood. The smiling doctor nodded at Pacific as he stepped past her, his hand extended to shake with Bobby, and the other doctor followed suit. Only then did they acknowledge Pacific and even commented on her acting and awards. Now, she was really puzzled.

The smiling doctor said, "My God, I am so honored to meet you. I read all about you in *Newsweek, Time,* and in *Army Times.* My name is Gunther Swenson, Dr. Gunther Swenson. I had no idea you were staying here. May I come back and get my picture taken with you?"

Bobby said, "Sure, Doctor, if it is only for your personal use. I do not want my picture in the news, at all."

Swenson said, "I'll be right back," and he headed for his office.

The other man said, "I'm a doctor here also. We're both shrinks. My name is Albert Finnegan. Can I get your autograph for my son?"

Bobby said, "Sure, Doctor. Pleased to meet you, but I do not know why you would want my autograph."

He signed, and then the doctor turned to Pacific and asked, "May I get yours, too? We are all big fans of yours."

She was feeling some flames of jealousy. This just never happened to her except once when she was at the Oscars and Lauren Bacall came backstage and people just flocked around her.

Dr. Swenson returned and asked his friend to take pictures of Bobby and him and then Bobby and Pacific and him.

Bobby shook hands with all and left, leaving the astonished beauty even more perplexed. She asked the two doctors to remain.

Pacific said, "Bobby and I have been together in here

for four weeks, but he has never spoken about any women or about his work. Is he in the business? I mean is he in film or TV? Oh, I know. He's a famous athlete."

Dr. Swenson said, "Ms. Cartier, do you remember when the large commercial airplane crashed in the Rockies in Colorado a few months ago?"

She said, "You mean with the Muslim terrorists on board who were going to blow it up over the L.A. area?

He said, "Exactly, and do you remember there was an undercover military policeman and policewoman on board who saved just about all the passengers and crew and helped everybody survive a raging blizzard for some days before they could be rescued?"

Pacific said, "My God. Is he that soldier?"

Dr. Swenson said, "Not only that. Do you remember the former Green Beret army major who was captured and held by the al Qaeda in Iraq last year, and he was going to be beheaded on videotape, but he thwarted their plans and fought his way to freedom?"

Pacific said, "Oh my Lord. Are you telling me that is Bobby?"

The other psychologist said, "It sure is, Pacific. A true American hero. He got the Distinguished Service Cross for that, the nation's second-highest award for heroism."

Pacific had chills all over.

Then she remembered going to some antiwar rally her publicist told her to go to, so she might be seen with Susan Sarandon, George Clooney, Martin Sheen, and others. She did not know anything about the War on Terrorism and whether it was right or wrong, but now she felt guilty about going to it.

What if she ended up with Bobby, as a lover, or even a husband, and she had gone to that stupid rally? she thought. Now she really had to land him. He was so dangerous, but so sensitive, and so damned handsome. Pacific never wanted a man so much in her life. She could not help but think how she might have a shot at landing some roles meant for Angelina Jolie, Reese Witherspoon, or Julia

Roberts maybe, if she just had America's ultimate warrior on her arm, and hopefully in her bed.

The other neat thing was that here they were at the Betty Ford Center together, and maybe he would help her maintain her sobriety. God knows she had tried, but this was her third time at Betty Ford. She just could not seem to get it right, but did not realize it was actually because so many studios or producers would always bail her out of trouble.

He certainly seemed to be taking his sobriety very seriously. He was working his twelve steps and did speak in generalities in regard to his life, but was not afraid to open up. She remembered how touched she was when he spoke one time about being married and his pregnant wife being killed by a drunk driver. It was quite obvious he really loved the woman, and he wasn't afraid to let the tears run when he spoke about her.

Dammit! Pacific thought, she was letting herself fall in love again. Why did she do that so much?

Pacific first went into the women's restroom inside just off the main lobby. She redid her mascara and lipstick, and checked her hair and the rest of her makeup. Looking carefully in the mirror, the superstar made sure everything looked right, and she cupped her breasts with both hands to make sure they were properly seated to present the most attractive presentation for her prey.

Bobby had a deal with one of the workers in the cafeteria. She would always stop at the local convenience store and buy two French vanilla cappuccinos, one for her and one for Bobby. He would meet her after she came on shift, and he would reimburse her for her own morning cappuccino and his. One day in the cafeteria where she worked, they had gotten into a conversation and found they both loved frosted chai teas and those machine-made French vanilla cappuccinos. Bobby always laughed when he would buy one, because he thought about the USAF's ability to drop a 2,000-pound smart bomb from a stealth fighter, have it drop thousands of feet and cover several miles, and put it right down through the air-vent shaft on a building's roof, yet it seemed like every convenience store cappuccino machine he would find had a little handwritten cardboard sign on it, reading: "Stop pushing button when cup is two-thirds full."

As just about every SF (Special Forces) operator or every experienced cop in the world does, he found a corner table where he could sit with his back to the wall and face the door. This is not paranoia, but a very common tactic of most cops and combat-oriented military men and women. It is simply a psychological thing about being prepared to meet emergencies head-on and see trouble coming in the door, so to speak.

Bobby saw Pacific walking into the cafeteria. He could not help but see her. Not seeing her would be like missing spotting a swan flying through a flock of mud hens. He also, with hidden glances, noticed her eyes sweeping the room and focusing on him.

Cup of tea and glass of water in hand, she was soon at his table, and Bobby rose, holding the chair opposite for her. Pacific made a mental note that that usually only happened to her in romantic dramas she would be in because the script called for it. In real life, she hardly ever saw men rise when a woman sat, much less hold her chair.

"Bobby," she said, "I am so glad I found you again. Can you talk for a few minutes?"

He smiled. "Sure, what's up?"

Working on her best feigned victim posture, she said, "I have really been having some issues, and they have been incredibly hard to deal with."

Pacific paused for effect, like she had learned in acting classes, then continued, "I had a party at my beach house in Malibu, and there were stars from all over Hollywood."

Bobby was unimpressed, but she could not tell as he listened politely.

Trying to work up tears like some actresses could produce so easily, she went on, "Well, anyway, you know what our drinking is like when we drink alcoholically. I remember being with a couple that you read about in all the gossip magazines, but she is drop-dead gorgeous, and he is considered one of the world's sexiest men."

Pacific paused here to sniffle a little, so Bobby would picture her and the other sexy actress and the hunk all drinking together. Her hope was that Bobby would imagine himself as the hunk.

"Well," she continued, "what is eating me up is I remember being a little flirty and joking around with them at the party, but that is all I remember. The bad part is I woke up the day after the party. Well, I have this king-sized poster bed and a deck off my bedroom that looks out over the ocean. I had the door open to let the ocean breezes in."

She could not tell if this was making him dream or fantasize.

Pacific went on with the tale, hoping it would capture his imagination. "So, I looked down at the ocean outside and the curtains blowing, and I looked at myself, and I was totally naked."

Pause for effect.

She continued, with a forced cry, "Then I saw both of them, the two stars, and they were naked, too, and I was lying between them. They were up against my body on both sides, Bobby! The three of us must have made love, and I cannot remember a thing."

Bobby remembered back to his old flame, a beautiful and famous national network news reporter named Veronica Caruso. She was sexy, gorgeous, and the most manipulative woman Bobby had ever met. Until now, he thought.

He handed her a napkin for her tears and said, "Pacific, you are such a good star, I imagine they pay you very well, and you should invest in a really good counselor so you can work these things out. You ought to get yourself a good woman you have confidence in to be your sponsor in AA and share this with her."

She was frustrated. This was not working.

"Bobby," she pleaded, "I really want you to help me, please?"

He smiled softly, saying, "I am really sorry, but that

would be the blind leading the blind. I have way too much on my plate, Pacific. I cannot help you. I'm sorry, I have to go."

He stood, and she jumped up, touching his arm and saying, "Look, can't you tell when a woman is hitting on you?"

Bobby smiled and nodded.

She said, "So what's up? Why are you rejecting me? Are you in love with somebody else?"

Without thinking, Bobby said, "Yes, I am. Very much so. I have to go."

Bobby walked away briskly, leaving one of the most beautiful women in the world standing there bewildered and upset. He was in shock. What had he said? He felt guilty. He had loved his wife so much, but now he realized he was in love with another: Bo Devore. He didn't even know if he could trust himself. He had gotten drunk and fondled Bo's breast in a restaurant. That was what made him finally hit his bottom, just seeing that hurt in her eyes. He had betrayed a trust. Bo was his subordinate, his friend, his partner. He could not let her know he loved her, but he did know his love for his late wife was tearing him up emotionally and contributing to his own drinking. That would have to be reconciled.

Easy does it, Bobby thought. One day at a time.

What seemed to him like oversimplified AA slogans now made perfect sense to him. He would be leaving the Betty Ford Center in a couple of days and would have to deal with the real world. Little did he know, he would be soon facing his toughest challenge ever.

3

JUNGLE SECRETS

The Lacrosse satellite passed overhead, 400 miles overhead, in fact, and looked down through the dense foliage of the jungles along the border of Vietnam and Laos. Y-Ting Tran felt a chill and noticed some of his men did, too. He felt the presence of the enemy. Without giving hand signals of any kind, he dove into the thick jungle undergrowth and so did all his men. Bobby Samuels had explained this to Bo before. Real warriors, such as many American spec ops types, Vietnam's Montagnard tribesmen, Laotian Hmong, Australia's aborigines, Native Americans, and similar would "feel" or "sense" the presence of the enemy. Bobby's feeling was that this is a sixth sense, a sense of "knowing" that is undeveloped in most people, but more pronounced in warriors. When she scoffed at the idea, Bobby asked her if she ever got chills down her spine when someone stared at her back. That made her a believer.

A *Quân Đội Nhân Dân Việt Nam,* Vietnam People's Army (VPA), patrol appeared walking along the trail in eastern Laos. There were twenty in the patrol and all carried a variety of small arms, AK-47s, SKSes, RPGs, and a

7.62-millimeter Chicom (Chinese communist)-made machine gun. The combined patrol of Vietnamese Montagnard tribesmen and Laotian Hmong tribesmen listened intently as the patrol stopped.

The leader of the patrol, a captain that one of the soldiers called Dai-uy Hoe dialed a satellite phone:

"Chao Ong. Co chuyen gi moi khong?" (Hello, sir. Anything new?)

There was a pause and then they heard, *"Toi manh jioi. Cam on, Ong. Khong co di dau het. Bay lau nay may o dau?"* (I'm fine. Thank you, sir. I didn't go anywhere. Where have you been?)

Another pause and then the captain spoke again. *"Khong, Toi di choi thoi. Lau lam roi toi khong thay may."* (No, I'm just hanging out. I haven't seen you in a long time).

There was another pause, and he chuckled, saying, *"Do xao ke! Toi di bo chi huy . . . Khong, Hanoi. Toi cung doan vay. Chao, Ong."* (Bullshit! I'm going to the headquarters . . . No, Hanoi. I guess so. Good-bye, sir.)

He hung up, turned, and stepped forward right into the big blade of Y-Ting's knife. It entered the man's stomach, and he looked down and was fascinated by the water buffalo handle held firmly in the Rade Montagnard's grip. He looked at the two little brass inlays in the back of the blade and the little swirl engravings on what he could see of the side of the blade now sticking into his midsection. He saw the blade twist and turn and in slow motion saw bright red blood spurting out all over the handle and Y-Ting's hand and forearm. He also now felt the most excruciating pain he had ever felt in his stomach. Dai-uy Hoe saw all his men now being repeatedly stabbed by other Montagnards who just seemed to appear out of the jungle floor. His eyes rolled up, and he saw the leaves above as he fell backward and felt the back of his head hit the ground, and then his sight ended. He heard distinct screams of pain, and realized some of the men he saw were not Montagnards. They were Laotian Hmong warriors. He wondered why they were with Montagnards, and then he thought nothing. He was dead.

Without a hand signal, the others joined Y-Ting in dragging the bodies deep into the undergrowth. They went through the pockets and packs of each dead soldier first and armed themselves with the new weapons and equipment as well as the food the soldiers carried.

The satellite overhead was the size of a bus and was now looking at the several truckloads of VPA soldiers just nine kilometers away, and the satellite could see the bodies of the dead VPA hidden in the undergrowth.

Lacrosse satellites are built around a synthetic aperture radar (SAR), which can see through clouds and send down photographic-quality images. Each satellite has a huge wire-mesh radar antenna and 150-foot solar panels to generate all the kilowatts of electricity required by its powerful radar transmitter.

Further, each Lacrosse passes over its assigned observation target on the ground twice a day, peering down through bad weather to show military commanders elsewhere on the ground where to strike and what damage was caused by air or artillery strikes. Lacrosse satellites can show objects as small as a foot across at night and in bad weather. Big objects on the ground, like tanks or surface-to-air missiles (SAM), can be seen even if hidden in the woods, or in this case in a tropical rain forest, especially still-warm bodies giving off thermal signatures.

A specialist at the NRO, or U.S. National Reconnaissance Office, called a number at the Pentagon and relayed the information about the killing of the communist Vietnamese patrol.

Several spec ops (special operations) intelligence analysts sat around a table wondering how they could warn this patrol to get out of that area quickly. One of those specialists was M. Sgt. Manual Garcia, on loan from the Seventh Special Forces Group at Fort Bragg, North Carolina. Manny started out as an 11Bravo, an SF weapons sergeant, but he switched to operations and intelligence shortly before he made E7. He attended a number of schools and applied his skills in Colombia, Argentina, and Chile. Most important, he was a Green Beret, so he personally knew how to think outside the box.

Manny said, "Was anybody listening in when the VPA commander was on the phone?"

A young woman got up and ran to the phone and made a quick call, returning in two minutes.

She said, "Manny, the NSA recorded his call."

Manny said, "Can they trace the commander's sat phone number?"

She went to the phone again and returned with a number written down.

Manny dialed the phone, and it rang seconds later in the midst of the jungles of Laos along the border of Vietnam. Y-Ting looked at the phone display and saw the 202 area code. A big smile crossed his face, and he answered.

"Allo," Y-Ting said.

Manny said, "Hello. This is Washington. You have a VPA patrol nine clicks southeast of you. Get your men out of there. If you head west or northwest, you won't run into any more patrols."

Y-Ting repeated what he was told in Rade, and his man who spoke Hmong repeated it to the Laotians.

Y-Ting enthusiastically said into the phone, "Thank you, sir. Thank you. God bless America!"

Manny said, "You're welcome, buddy. Get out of there."

"Yes, we go now," Y-Ting said. "Thank you. Good-bye."

They headed due west at a fast pace, and three hours later, turned north walking through a jungle stream for forty minutes. They stepped out and Y-Ting Tran was almost bitten by a bright green bamboo viper. American GIs during the war in Vietnam referred to the deadly little snake as a "step and a half," saying that is how far you will get before you die if one bites you. The neuro-hemo toxic snake has a very deadly bite, but Y-Ting grabbed it after it struck, catching it just below its head, which he lopped off quickly with his Montagnard knife. He then stuck the body in his pack to be cleaned later and eaten for dinner.

They were headed toward Mukdahan near the Thai border to meet with their American friend, who was referred to by the CIA not as a friend but as an "independent contractor." This twenty-man squad was a first. Laotian Hmongs and Vietnamese Montagnards, both very similar in appearance and racial and societal characteristics, had joined forces together to fight against not only the communist government in Hanoi but also the new menace, the al Qaeda .

Contrary to the reports of international news media, government officials, and other major sources, the largest al Qaeda training camps in the world, for several years, have not been in the Mideast, but in the Philippines. A large contingent of al Qaeda moved into the southern part of Thailand, Indonesia, and were now secretly building facilities in Laos and Vietnam.

The Hmong tribespeople in Laos are very similar to the Montagnard tribespeople in Vietnam, and both groups are horribly discriminated against, especially by the governments in Vientiane and Hanoi. In fact, the situation in Vietnam was really bad.

There are thirty-one different tribes of Montagnards (a French word meaning "hill people") and each has its own language, customs, and tribal mores. Malayo-Polynesian in appearance, the Montagnards live in the mountainous Central Highlands region of Vietnam along the borders of Cambodia and Laos. Many Vietnamese call them *moi*, which means "savage," but in English translates to "nigger." They use the slash-and-burn method of raising mountain rice, wear loincloths, bracelets, necklaces, and little else. They eat rats, monkeys, and other animals from the jungle.

The Hmong are very similar, living in the mountainous jungles of Laos along the Vietnam border. Although some tribes of Montagnards are Malayo-Polynesian in their ethnic backgrounds and others are Mon-Khmer, the Laotian

Hmong are actually Chinese in origin. The Chinese refer to them as *mieu*.

Both groups worked extensively and became very close during the Vietnam War and the secret war in Laos with U.S. Army Special Forces, the Green Berets. With this relationship in mind, the CIA sent independent CIA contractors who were retired Special Forces into the area to unite both groups into a cohesive unit that could provide humintel (human intelligence) on VPA forces, Cong-An (the deadly Vietnamese secret police), and most important, the burgeoning al Qaeda involvement in the most mountainous areas of Laos and western Vietnam

While international news media directed all their attention at the al Qaeda in the Mideast and even Europe, they were building their largest training camps in the Philippines. They also were building a presence in southern Thailand, Indonesia, and now Hanoi, wanting to use their oil money for a new sanctuary and fertile ground to spread *Dar el Islam.* Not wanting to get attacked later by the al Qaeda, the communist officials of the Hanoi government secretly invited the jihadists to use their vast triple-canopy jungle areas to hide away their training camps and headquarters from the pesky U.S. satellites constantly overhead. They encouraged them to mingle in their cities to relax, to spend money, and in the back of their minds, of course, was the naïve belief that "sucking up" would spare their lives and country. They did not realize that they were simply making the al Qaeda's world expansion goals easier to accomplish in the Pacific Rim area.

The other problem in Vietnam and other communist countries was simple. Even in areas where the Hanoi government did not concern itself, bribery worked. The communist society does not work, so it is rife with corruption. Province, district, and individual city and hamlet chief political officers all over the country of Vietnam are for the most part corrupt. Their hands are out for any funds that can enhance their personal wealth and power base in any way possible.

Hanoi desperately wanted the perks, and billions of dollars of income, from a world free-trade agreement. Many strides had been made with the United States and with Europe, but not enough. Paranoid about every resistance group meeting in Vietnamese neighborhood garages or family rooms in America, Hanoi could only visualize numerous conspiracies ready to overthrow their government and "pay them back for the U.S. embarrassment" called the Vietnam War.

Because of wanting a new budding fiscal relationship, Hanoi learned, years before, to open their airports and ports to allow American tourists, but there was one big problem. They had been methodically defoliating the interior Central Highlands region for decades to make way for new coffee, tea, and rubber plantations. They also had deposed the Montagnard tribesmen, for decades, targets of a horrible discrimination and, in some cases, genocide program. Many Montagnards were forced into slave labor gangs, and the feared and hated Cong-An terrorized Montagnard villages throughout the mountainous regions. Additionally, the Vietnamese had been, for decades, moving large numbers of lowland Vietnamese into the mountainous region and had also forced some young Montagnard women and girls to intermarry with Vietnamese men in order to further decimate the race. Children, in fact, were only allowed to learn to speak Vietnamese and were forbidden to learn their own tribal languages.

Because of the oppression, Hanoi had steadfastly refused to allow Americans or other tourists to enter most parts of the Central Highlands region, except the most carefully monitored and sanitized areas, so the apartheid-like conditions would not be exposed to world media. Because of this, the Hanoi-based al Qaeda appeasers figured they could easily allow the terrorists to build a few training camps in that area or just across the border, which they pretty much controlled anyway. Work had already begun. The world's largest al Qaeda training camps had already been functioning for years in the southern Philippines.

Now, construction was under way building several large terrorist training camps along the Laotian-Vietnamese border. Everything was covered with thick jungle canopy and where clearings were made, using some of the old Ho Chi Minh Trail tricks from the war in Vietnam, the VPA construction crews would climb high up and swing large growths of bamboo across the clearings and then tie the tops of them together, forming a large green archway. Also, using tricks learned fighting against the Americans years earlier, and the French before that, most classrooms, meeting rooms, and walkways in between were underground. Unlike the previous wars, however, they now employed earth-moving machines and not shovels to construct these, and cement mixers and rebar to provide fortification, not just root-crossed sod.

The al Qaeda gladly footed the highly inflated bill for all the construction. Nguyen Van Tran was the powerful deputy prime minister of the Socialist Republic of Vietnam. He had also, over the past couple of decades, developed a very deep, very secret fiscal relationship with powerful, empire-building U.S. Sen. James Weatherford, who was on the Senate Armed Services Committee and cochair of the Senate Intelligence Committee. Besides billing the al Qaeda for the clandestine camp construction, they also double-billed the senator's secret entity that had a hand in much of Vietnam's construction endeavors.

The senator was very active in the background when Senator John Kerry chaired the Senate Select Committee on MIA/POW Affairs in 1992, helping convince Kerry to ignore 42,000 pieces of evidence about live sightings of American POWs and end the investigation. Not much later, in February of 1994, President Bill Clinton removed the trade embargo against Vietnam. Then in 1998, President Clinton signed the Jackson-Vanik waiver, and on December 10, 2001, the U.S.-Vietnam Bilateral Trade Agreement entered into force. Although Vietnam still continues to suppress and harass its minorities, such as the Montagnards and the Cham, relations with the United States and others have continued to progress, and by 2004, direct flights were started between Ho Chi Minh City and San Francisco.

All the control, however, for this Far Eastern faction of the al Qaeda came from one man located on a small resort island in southern Thailand called Koh Samui. Muhammad Yahyaa was from Saudi Arabia and was close with al-Zawahiri back in the early nineties and had won the confidence of the al Qaeda leadership.

He oversaw the training camps in the Philippines, Laos, Indonesia, and Vietnam, as well as overseeing all tactical operations of the al Qaeda in the Pacific Rim area. He previously had communicated directly with al Qaeda's number one and number two men located in Pakistan, not far from the Khyber Pass, bin Laden and al-Zawahiri, using satellite phones, but a couple of close calls by U.S. air strikes stopped that. Muhammad now had to use the internet to communicate with designated intermediaries, couriers, if you will. They carried messages back and forth from the central al Qaeda leadership.

Y-Ting and his men arrived at the designated meeting place not too far outside Mukdahan, on the Thai-Laos border, on a 1,000-foot-tall mountain overlooking the region near the Phu Mu Forest. They were met after crossing the Mekong River by another patrol of Thais who had a camp prepared for them under the cover of a large rock overhang, one of many in the area.

Shortly after dark, while the men sat around several cooking fires, thousands of feet overhead a B-1B bomber passed through Thai airspace and a small black dot appeared from the bomb bay underneath. The American CIA contractor the Montagnards and Hmong liked so well was dropping at 220 miles per hour in a military freefall through the night sky. Breathing O_2 and wearing night vision, he clearly saw the strobe lights from the three of the Hmong from Y-Ting's patrol below marking his very small landing zone.

He would soon be joining them on the mountain, and the Montagnards were all excited about seeing this man who fought alongside some of their fathers. The smiling American they called Boom.

4

DELTA CHARLIE

Bobby Samuels and Bo Devore were both refreshed. They had both spent time at Bethesda Naval Hospital in private rooms getting treated for the wounds they incurred first crashing in a commercial jet liner and surviving a mountain blizzard, then fighting in a shoot-out with al Qaeda members trying to destroy the Glen Canyon Dam, then more fighting in Mexico and Texas against a Brazilian street gang called O Grupo Grande and the al Qaeda, and finally, they both stopped two al Qaeda terrorists from simultaneously detonating backpack nuclear bombs in Miami and New York City. Their biggest cheerleader happened to be four-button Gen. Jonathan Perry, chief of staff of the U.S. Army. He wanted them to get the best treatment possible, some rest, and then a thirty-day convalescent leave for each, and in the army, convalescent leaves do not go against your allotted thirty days leave time per year. They needed the rest, and got it, but now they had their biggest test yet ahead of them.

Bo sat down at her desk, wearing a tight black body shirt, tan jacket, faded blue jeans, and running shoes. She went to the automatic coffeemaker and wondered if Bobby, her partner and boss, had returned.

It was ten until seven in the morning. After five minutes, General Perry's limousine driver, a nice-looking sergeant first class, showed up and knocked politely on her office door. He was wearing class As.

"Sergeant Fisher, please come in," she said politely, taking a sip of coffee the exact same color as his skin tone and as shiny on this humid morning, "Want a cup?"

"No, thank you, ma'am," he said, standing at attention. "I am here to drive you somewhere."

She said, "At ease, Sergeant, please."

He relaxed. "Thank you, Major. I am under orders to drive you somewhere, if you will accompany me, Major."

"Of course," she said, as he snapped back to attention while she walked out the door, followed by the well-built, handsome sergeant.

Walking down the hallway, she asked, "Where is the general taking me, Sergeant?"

The sergeant got a door for her, replying, "The general is not coming, Major Devore. He lent out his car and me for this mission, which I am not allowed to discuss, ma'am."

"I'll respect that," she said and wondered just what in the heck was going on.

He drove her uptown toward the White House and actually drove her to Old Ebbitt Grill just around the corner from the White House. It was Bobby and Bo's favorite restaurant and world famous for its oysters and other meals. The sergeant pulled up in front of the restaurant and let her out, opening the brass door for her. The restaurant had just opened. She walked up to the maitre d' station and spotted Bobby in a booth near the back. He waved, and she smiled. Oddly enough, he, by coincidence, also wore faded jeans, running shoes, a black tight turtleneck, and a tan sport coat. The only difference between the two was the snug, hard-leather shoulder holster snuggled up next to her left breast, quite capable of hiding and camouflaging such an accessory, while Bobby was wearing his holster under his jacket on his right hip over his right hip pocket.

Both holsters firmly encased a high-polymer space-age plastic-and-steel Glock model 17 9-millimeter semiautomatic loaded with full metal jacket hollow-point Corbon bullets. Each pistol had a round in the chamber, and the very reliable safety on each gun was on the trigger itself, mounted on the front of it. When the safety was depressed, the weapon was ready to fire its deadly contents.

Bobby smiled, waving to her. She nodded her head and walked to the table. As she approached, she could not help but notice his broad smile, and as she got even closer there was a healthy glow he had not had in a long time.

Bobby hugged her, holding her tight, and then handed her a dozen roses as she blushed and sat down.

Bo did not know what to say. This was really startling to her.

Finally, she said, "Thanks, Bobby, the roses are beautiful, but what's the occasion?"

Bobby smiled, saying, "Bo, you are my partner, and I missed you. Simple as that."

They both ordered frittatas described on the menu as "open-faced omelets topped with mushrooms, onions, diced tomatoes, Cheddar cheese, served in an iron skillet with home fries and whole wheat toast."

"How was your leave?" he asked.

Bo said, "It was wonderful and relaxing, but apparently not as good as yours. You look relaxed, healthy, the best I have seen you."

He hesitated, then said, "Bo, you are not only my partner but my closest friend. This has to remain only between you and me."

She said, "Of course. What's up?"

Bobby said, "Bo, I got drunk and grabbed your breast, and even worse, in a restaurant. It devastated me to know I disrespected you like that."

She got tears in her eyes and remained silent.

Bobby drank all of his water and orange juice, then went on, "That more than anything is what made me hit my bottom. I am an alcoholic and can never ever drink any alcohol again. I just spent thirty days at the Betty Ford Center, Bo, and I learned more about myself than I ever knew I could."

Bo could not help it. She stuck her face into her napkin and silently wept. Bobby reached out and touched her arm.

She stopped and raised her head, dabbing her eyes.

Bobby, reading her mind, smiled softly and said, "Your mascara is okay. You do not look like Ricky the Raccoon."

She smiled. "Thanks. Bobby. I have prayed for this conversation for ages. I forgave you for the groping incident, but I knew you had a drinking problem and had to hit your bottom. I am so happy."

Bobby said, "I'm glad you are. Personally, I'm scared."

They brought the food while Bo kept herself in check, then she burst out laughing.

"What's so funny?" he asked sincerely.

Bo laughed even harder, finally saying, "You saying you're scared of anything. You have a DSC, Silver Star, Purple Hearts, earned a Green Beret, master blaster jump wings, Ranger tab, were in Delta Force, the HALO committee at Fort Bragg, and you are scared. If Bobby Samuels is scared, then we're all in trouble."

Bobby shook his head, not understanding the humor in her statement.

Deciding it would be smart to change the subject, Bo said, "The flowers are really beautiful. Thank you. All of this is such a nice surprise."

Bobby said, "Bo, I told you. You are my partner, my friend, and I have an awful lot of trust to earn back."

She smiled softly.

"No, you don't," she said. "I believe you. I believe in you."

Bobby looked up at her and stared into her eyes. It took her breath. Then, he shocked her even more. He leaned across the table and lightly kissed her. She subconsciously reached up and gently touched her lips with her index and middle fingers.

Snapping back to reality, she said, "Wow! Would you do that if your partner was a male?"

Bobby smiled, saying, "I hope not. But you know what? If I felt about him like I do you, I might consider turning gay."

Then Bobby laughed like he was making a joke, and she chuckled, but inside she hoped it was not. Bobby now knew that indeed it was not a joke.

They had a long, leisurely breakfast and Bobby ordered another order to go. He paid, and they went to the limo, where he gave the take-out breakfast to the driver.

Bobby and Bo returned to the Pentagon and were summoned to General Perry's briefing room. He was not there, but his aide was as well as the J-2 general, Maj. Gen. Andrew Beck. There were also some other high-ranking officers and senior NCOs.

For the next hour, Bobby and Bo listened to an eye-opening briefing on the al Qaeda situation in the Pacific Rim region.

U.S. Army Special Forces operators from the First Special Forces Group–backed offensives have decimated some established camps in the Mindanao region, killing and capturing some al Qaeda-backed Indonesian Jemaah Islamiyahs with Pilipino militants setting up classes and plotting attacks, kidnappings, and executions through the island complex for a number of years.

Previously, Abu Sayyaf Pilipino rebels had used small arms and simple hand and rocket-propelled grenades to attack civilian targets in the island nation. Al Qaeda's Southeast Asian ally from Indonesia, however, for some years, had been sharing bomb-making expertise with radical Muslims in the Philippines. Humintel sources stated that a dozen or more designs and chemical recipes of explosives had been taught to assist local ragtag insurgents become deadlier.

In 2005, in one terrorism attack alone, 116 people were killed with a series of high-tech explosions. There had been now for several years some very close cooperation among local and foreign militants using the southern Philippines as a training ground following the loss of al Qaeda camps in Afghanistan after the American invasion there in 2001.

According to the briefing officer, even a 2005 Associated Press article quoted one Philippine security official who said Mindanao "is like a terrorist academy" with trainees taught how to make bombs, plant them, then set them off in test missions designed to help militants perfect their techniques to complete the course.

Jemaah Islamiyah militants appear to be continuously testing new designs and explosives mixtures, said officials, who spoke on condition of anonymity because of the secretive nature of the information.

When they investigated the Sunday bombing of a passenger ferry while it was boarding passengers on Basilan island, injuring thirty people, it seemed to be designed more to produce panic and terror instead of killing people.

The briefer said that the evidence of al Qaeda and Jemaah Islamiyah "training and technology transfer" in bomb devices had been going on for more than six years for members of Abu Sayyaf.

The most shocking fact to come out of the briefing was that the largest al Qaeda training camps in the world were located not in Afghanistan, Iraq, Iran, or Somalia, but in the Philippines.

The briefer read a statement from the Council on Foreign Relations about Jemaah Islamiyah: "Also known by the initials JI, it is a militant Islamist group active in several Southeast Asian countries. The primary objective of the group is the establishment of a pan-Islamic state throughout the area. In August 2003, Nurgaman Riduan Ismuddin, a.k.a Hambali, the operational chief of the organization was captured by anti-terror forces in Thailand. It was thought at the time that this would spell the end of JI. However, attacks against western targets continued. The most recent was the bombing in Bali on October 1, 2005 in which nineteen were killed and over one hundred wounded.

The worst attack perpetrated by the group was the October 2002 bombing of a nightclub in Bali. In all, two hundred and two innocent people were killed in the blast. Over two hundred members of JI were arrested in connection with this attack, and three leaders were sentenced to death."

Then they turned their attention to Laos and Vietnam where Bobby and Bo learned of the several joint Vietnamese Montagnard and Laotian Hmong operations to spy on the blossoming al Qaeda training centers and activities there. They were also briefed that the al Qaeda had slowly been sinking their hooks into the drug trade from that part of the drug-rich Iron Triangle region.

The group finally broke for lunch and Bobby and Bo returned to their office to start catching up on all the mail and emails they had piling up while they were on leave. It was enough to make anybody cry.

5

WEST BANK

The Honorable James Weatherford walked into the quiet restaurant on the corner at 75 Avenue des Champs-Elysées in Paris. The famous and recently renovated thoroughfare with new granite sidewalks and even more shade trees, also named *la plus belle avenue du monde*, "the most beautiful avenue in the world" in French, stretches from the Concorde square to the Arc de Triomphe.

Ladurée Tea Room, a high-class restaurant founded in 1862, also had a world-famous bakery and was well known for its pastries. The famous "macarons" (biscuits) were a real specialty of this establishment. It was equally famous for its raw and cooked vegetable salads.

When the senator walked in, he was immediately taken to a large table in the corner, where he was greeted by a broadly smiling Nguyen Van Tran, one of the key bureaucrats with the Communist Party of the Socialist Republic of Vietnam, the SRV, or as they called themselves Cong Hoa Chu Nghia Viet Nam. In fact, his title was deputy minister of agriculture and rural development for the government and, a teenaged member of both the Red-Scarf

Teenagers' Organization and the Ho Chi Minh Revolutionary Youth League, he grew to become one of the thirteen permanent members of the very powerful Political Bureau. Muhammad Yahyaa, the powerful al Qaeda coordinator, had traveled from his posh beach villa at Koh Samui, Thailand, and was also there to greet the U.S. senator.

The three shook hands and smiled, while a camera started clicking pictures one after another, shooting through the windowpane. Mounted on the shoulder of the faux artist with easel and large canvas under a tree along the far side of the Champs-Elysées, the long-range surveillance telephoto camera was comprised of a high-quality Zenit 122S SLR camera with Super-3S telephoto lens, MC Helios-44m-6 interchangeable lens, and accessories. A well-known sniper camera, it was originally developed for Soviet KGB surveillance operatives. It's a unique configuration of a 35mm camera with a powerful 300mm telephoto lens and an ingenious integrated stabilization system similar to the Hollywood Steadicam system. Instead of needing a tripod, the camera and long telephoto lens were mounted on a special metal alloy rifle-type stock, which had a built-in trigger-activated shutter release and focusing mechanism. The camera was aimed as a rifle or shotgun would be, and the trigger was pulled to take the photograph. Focusing is achieved by using a control knob located on the stock. The camera's split-image focusing allowed for excellent image sharpness under varying conditions, and its multicoated achromatic lens provided for optimum light transmission and exceptional photographic imagery. Shutter speeds on the long-range camera ranged from 1/30 second to 1/500 second.

The modified digital film camera, besides taking shots to be developed, also took instant digital shots that were transferred to the laptop sitting next to the painter's easel. From there the photos were transferred to a repeater a mile away, which transmitted the images to a U.S. Milstar satellite miles above Paris. Milstar satellites like that one make up the most advanced military communications satellite systems to date. From a stationary orbit 22,000 miles above Earth, they provide secure, jam-resistant worldwide communications, linking command authorities with ships, submarines, aircraft, ground stations, and in this case a spy for the Central Intelligence Agency.

Each giant Milstar is really more like a smart switchboard in the sky, directing encrypted voice, data, teletype, and fax message traffic anywhere on the Earth and each one can link up with other Milstars to forward messages.

Each one of the Milstar satellites is about as big as a semitrailer rig.

An intelligence analyst received the shots on her computer in Langley, Virginia, and they were immediately burst to several other computers by her at various locations, all within taxi-riding distance of the U.S. Capitol building.

Copies of several of the photographs along with a top secret brief were immediately hand carried into the briefing room and shown to Bobby, Bo, and the others after a quick explanation by a military intelligence chief warrant officer 5.

Bobby and Bo heard all about Weatherford's underhanded political tactics for the past several decades and his presidential aspirations. Of particular concern to their briefers and to General Perry were two men who belonged to the Defense Intelligence Agency. These men were frequently assigned to Senator Weatherford's intelligence committee and FBI information, both electrical and humintel, had indicated they had been promised lucrative positions with Weatherford after their retirement.

One man was named Lt. Col. Julius Brock, and the second was named M. Sgt. Darellus Parker. Both men were black and each had less than a year to go to retirement. Listening to Weatherford's promises of riches and his supposed caring about the plight of minorities in America, along with an excessive amount of greed, the two soldiers would be shocked to know that with his white cohorts in the Senate he referred to them as his "twin army niggers."

They both started out two years earlier just trying to please the senator, following orders and being loyal, but slowly they allowed themselves to become corrupted. The senator effectively used them as his spies into the military, and for the most part they were always at his disposal.

It was made clear in the briefing that this was not a witch hunt to attack a future presidential opponent, but a determined effort to fully investigate someone who really seemed to have no concept of true patriotism or loyalty, beyond self. Senator Weatherford was ruthless, crooked, shrewd, wealthy, and for years had collected indebtedness from our other congressmen on both sides of the aisle. He also was a major campaign contributor for many of the other politicians in congress, including Republicans in his opposing party that had something, maybe a future vote, he wanted.

He was already quite wealthy when he entered congress due to inheritance. After a divorce from his first wife and the death of his second, he married a filthy rich heiress who had been the only child of one of the major bubble gum makers in the world.

The first wife was simply dumped for the second who was the daughter of a renowned brain surgeon. After the old doctor got to know James Weatherford, his respected son-in-law, he offered his daughter a choice: Dump the good senator and receive a million-dollar gift from Daddy, or be taken out of his will.

This came about because the surgeon and his sweet but very meek wife held a large party to celebrate St. Patrick's Day at their sprawling estate in upper New York state. Senator Weatherford, a junior senator at the time, started pumping hands and charming folks before the food was even served. He constantly went over to his wife and gave her a loving hug or nuzzled her cheek, and folks noticed. The word at the event was that they were a wonderful loving couple just made for each other, but he was after all a politician.

He, however, had his eyes on a blonde voluptuous

woman who was introduced as the head of radiology at not the surgeon's hospital, but at the hospital across town that seemed to be a bit of a competitor.

What James Weatherford did not know, after an hour of covert flirting back and forth, when he finally invited the young lady to look at his father-in-law's stables, was her little secret. In the stable, one thing led to another, and they soon were tearing each other's clothes off and made mad, passionate love in the tack room on a pile of horse blankets.

Her little secret was the fact that she and the surgeon had been having an affair for the past eight months. Two weeks after that, when she caught the surgeon having another affair with one of his nurses, she blurted out about her whirlwind tryst with his son-in-law in the stable.

Now, he was stuck. He could not tell his daughter what he knew about her wonderful husband, but he absolutely did not want her married to the scoundrel. He could not believe that, of all women the man would cheat with, he chose the doctor's girlfriend.

It really surprised her to have her father pop in at their house in Arlington out of the blue, saying he was there for a medical conference. While she ran to the deli to get them some fresh-cut meat for sandwiches, he planted his card.

He had carefully copied his son-in-law's printing and on the back of one of Weatherford's business cards, he had spent a full afternoon writing the radiologist's name and phone number on the card, along with a note to himself saying, "Great blowjobs." Sneaking upstairs to the master bedroom, he carefully made the card look accidentally dropped into the dirty clothes hamper. The surgeon knew his daughter was very finicky about washing clothes, insisting on doing all laundry herself.

She found it and made the call after two days of thought. The radiologist readily admitted to her sexual escapade with Weatherford, but did not spill the beans about Daddy, as she was trying to get back into a newer, better affair with him. She did apologize profusely and explained that James had pursued her all that night and was appealing to her because he seemed so loving and tender with his wife.

That night, she tossed down the gauntlet with the errant senator, and he cried, he begged, he apologized literally on his knees, and he started plotting. She seriously considered her dad's offer.

Henry Alcala was a bodyguard hired by the senator at that time, referred to him by his younger brother, the would-be felon of the family. He had befriended Henry, a large, overmuscled bouncer who only the most radical drunks messed with, when he met him at his favorite nightspot. While at a White House event, the senator's poor wife unfortunately died when her Mercedes crashed into a bridge abutment. The autopsy could not detect where her skull had been caved in earlier from the bodyguard who sent her car into the bridge.

The $10,000 he was paid by the senator went up his nose in months, and he died a year later of a drug overdose.

After a reasonable time of fake mourning, Senator Weatherford started dating Hollywood actresses, singers, society dames, and various celebrities, looking for the one who had enough millions and enough charisma to help him campaign and get elected president. She would also have to be passable as a First Lady. Finally, he met the bubble-gum heiress and commenced his best seduction techniques, honed to a fine art after years at the best country, polo, and yacht clubs on the East Coast.

They had now been married for over a decade. It was stormy but he had learned all the buttons to intimidate her and totally controlled her now.

Now, the good Senator James Weatherford was seated in a French restaurant in Paris meeting with a communist leader and an al Qaeda leader making sinister plans.

"Chao Ong Tran," Weatherford said, priding himself on learning a Vietnamese phrase.

"No, Jim, *Anh Tran,*" the communist leader said.

"What?"

Nguyen Van Tran went on, *"Anh Tran. Anh* means

'friend' maybe, like 'my friend,' and *Ong Tran* means 'mister.' It is not same as friend."

"Oh," Weatherford said, and then looked to Muhammad, saying *"Asalakalakum."*

Muhammad said, *"Lakum Salam,* Senator."

The three shook hands and sat down.

After ordering drinks and food, they started discussing business.

Muhammad said, "Today your food and drink is my treat, and I have two beautiful women for you who will join us before we leave."

"Thank you, Muhammad," the senator said. "I love the food here, and I always love beautiful women."

Tran laughed and said, "Yes, me, too. Thank you, Muhammad."

Muhammad said, "My associates want to give you, Senator, a campaign contribution, and we want to give you a gift, too, Deputy Minister."

Weatherford said, "Thank you, my friend. How much do you want to donate?"

Tran added, "Yes, thank you very much. What kind of gift?"

Muhammad smiled, saying, "We give each of you ten million U.S. dollars. It is for each of you personally as a gift of appreciation."

James Weatherford had been dealing with Muhammad for two years now and with Tran for much longer. He was in way too deep and had crossed way too many lines long before. He now no longer made a pretense of trying to be honest.

Weatherford was shocked at the amount and said, "Thank you very much, my friend, but I have been around long enough to know that you do not get such gifts for nothing. You must want something major from me and from my friend Tran."

Sipping some wine, Muhammad, justifying that by thinking he must drink wine while with his enemies who were doing so, said, "This is true, my friend. We want you, and we want Tran to make a lot of money. We want you to achieve your goal of completely open trade and commerce with the Socialist Republic of Vietnam. We want Hanoi to make lots of money. In order to do this, we must make a bold statement to help sway world opinion to listen to our cries."

Tran said, "I do not understand this you say."

"I am not clear, either," James added.

Muhammad grinned and looked around nervously. "When I attended Harvard University in your country, we had a professor who used to always say, 'You must break some eggs to make an omelet.' "

"I have never heard such a saying." Tran replied. "What does it mean?"

"An omelet is a dish made with eggs, where they are mixed up," James Weatherford responded. "It is an old saying in my country."

Muhammad went on, "As you know, my friends, if we can influence the news media in America to sympathize with our position, they can influence the people to understand we do not want to kill Americans, but to be respected in the world community."

"What about September 11, 2001, the World Trade Center?" Weatherford asked.

Muhammad said, "I know that was a sad time for your country, but nobody knew that the buildings would come down. When the director, when Usama bin Laden and Sheik al-Zawahiri were planning the attacks, it was just to get America's attention. We had no idea, well, I mean they had no idea those two buildings would come down."

Weatherford said, "Yes, I don't think anybody did. But what do you plan now?"

"Nothing really, but we do want you to use your influence next month to keep the coast guard and navy from patrolling the Port of Los Angeles heavily," Muhammad replied.

Weatherford said, "I hope you do not think I will be a party to another 9/11 attack on my own country!"

Muhammad smiled. "Relax, my friend. We just want to make a statement. Yes, maybe a few fishermen or what do you call boat loaders, ah yes, longshoremen, might be lost, but as the saying goes, 'You have to break a few eggs to make an omelet.' You will have more money for your campaign to become president and when you are elected, then we can make a lasting peace treaty with your country. You are the only one who is not a fool."

"Hmmm," Weatherford said. "That is true."

Muhammad had once again pushed the right button: James Weatherford's greedy ambition to become president.

Tran asked, "How do I become a part of this?"

"You are a big part, Tran," Muhammad answered. "You are helping provide us with safety for our new training camps for our trainees in your part of the world, like our men in Indonesia, Thailand, and the Philippines. We will take over much of the drug trade in the Golden Triangle, and we will share our proceeds with Hanoi, and we will make more donations to you, Senator."

James Weatherford's face reddened.

He looked around and whispered, "Wait, you are talking about making money selling drugs. I am a U.S. senator."

Muhammad started laughing.

He said, "Mr. Senator, we control most of the world's opium trade in the Golden Crescent region—Pakistan, Afghanistan, and Iran. We produce about eighty-five percent of the opium trade in the world, and we share with many in government. Almost all of the other fifteen percent comes from the Golden Triangle—Thailand, Laos, and Burma. Do you know how much money you will make, Senator?"

"Millions?"

"Billions!" Muhammad said, "And billions for the SRV, too, Tran. We are talking about the al Qaeda controlling close to one hundred percent of the world's opium production, and you both are our silent partners. When you are president of the U.S.A. you will go down in history, James. You will have wonderful treaties with Afghanistan, Iran, Pakistan, Iraq, Lebanon, Egypt, Syria, Saudi Arabia, Somalia, Dubai, Yemen, the SRV, Laos, the Philippines, Indonesia, Thailand, and by then we will have Cambodia, and maybe more. In the meantime, my friend, you will get much richer, and that is okay because you are helping your country."

Muhammad was a very clever and convincing liar. The al Qaeda leadership believed they were divined by the almighty to spread Islam throughout the world. Unlike the seventh-century mind-set they had been emulating, the al Qaeda had a goal to further *Dar el Islam,* the Nation of Islam with little or no concern for borders, but there was a big difference between the seventh century and now. In the seventh century, conquering Muslim sheiks would allow those conquered to convert to Islam, unless they were Jews or Christians. In that regard, they became automatic third-class citizens. Others could maintain their own religions but would be considered second-class citizens. The al Qaeda, however, would allow no such quarter to modern-day Christians or Jews. The fatwas declared they were to be exterminated, period.

Contrary to naïve liberal thinking, influenced heavily by the U.S. news media, the al Qaeda was not jealous of America or Americans. Their feeling is and was that Jews and Christians, all of them, are to be killed all over the world, period. They are also supposed to spread Islam and not stop until *Dar el Islam* is realized worldwide.

So now, the al Qaeda had a wealthy U.S. senator in their hip pocket, and when he ran for president, and before he ran, they would manipulate the world and U.S. media as best they could to influence the election. They were absolute experts at it.

The divide-and-conquer lessons had been effectively learned during the war in Vietnam and elsewhere since. The strategy of tension, *strategia della tensione,* is officially defined as a way to control and manipulate public opinion using fear, propaganda, disinformation, psychological warfare, agents provocateurs, false-flag actions, and terrorist actions.

Knowing that the American left oft goes overboard to prove that Americans are fair and unbiased, the al Qaeda following in the footsteps of the communist party and other insurgency movements had learned to prey on the generosity and open-armed hospitality of the Yankee infidels by playing the U.S. news media like Yo-Yo Ma vacationing in a cello factory.

One most recent tactic was to send AQ terrorists or terrorist sympathizers into airports worldwide, train depots, and the like and push the envelope on security, praying loudly publicly in front of other passengers, traveling in groups but acquiring seating separately in tactically superior seats, and causing minor disruption. A Muslim attorney would be ready to defend the actions of the travelers immediately and go on the attack about civil rights violations and bias by the travel industry, airlines, and anybody else who needed molding into the pro-terrorist target fit. This tactic was meant to test security and loosen up security for Muslim travelers, cause discomfort with the populace, and provide more headaches for the government.

Senator Weatherford looked around the restaurant, then pulled two large envelopes out of his briefcase. He handed one to Muhammad and one to Tran. They opened them and saw glossy photographs of Maj. Bobby Samuels and Capt. Bo Devore.

Muhammad said, "My people know who they are."

Weatherford leaned forward, whispering, "Some of my best contacts inside the military, especially in the army, are afraid of what these two could do to any or all of us. I have to quietly do everything I can to get them out of the way."

Tran grinned, saying, "They would not be wise to come to Vietnam or even close."

Muhammad also grinned. "I do not care where they go. If we must rid ourselves of them, then we will rid ourselves of them. You look troubled, my friend."

James did look pale.

"It's not like I want you to kill two American army officers," he said sheepishly.

Muhammad grinned evilly, saying, "Yes, you do. You just do not wish to hear about it. My people have a saying, 'The sinning is the best part of repentance.' Think about that, Senator."

Muhammad laughed at his own saying, and Tran joined in, but Weatherford shook his head and thought how far he had sold himself to the devil, and then laughed out loud at the Arabic proverb, and then started laughing harder, until all three were laughing heartily.

They toasted with glasses and Weatherford said, "I guess I am a coldhearted, tough son of a bitch."

Muhammad stroked his ego even more, adding, "One must be to be a powerful world leader."

James Weatherford liked that. He had never been a shrinking petunia, and a president had to make really tough decisions, sometimes sacrificing a few lives for the good of all. It was settled in his mind; Bobby Samuels and Bo Devore had to be eliminated. They were too tough and making too much of a name for themselves in the inner circles in D.C. He would have them stopped now, and anybody else who got in his way.

6

LIFE OF A WARRIOR

In Texas, Bobby Samuels and Bo Devore made a clever infiltration, thanks to General Perry, with a pair of German-created stealth wings. More had been secretly secured for use by certain CIA and spec ops personnel.

The lightweight carbon-fiber mono-wings would allow an operator to jump from high altitudes and then glide 120 miles or more before landing—making them almost impossible to spot, as their aircraft can avoid flying anywhere near the target.

The technology was first demonstrated in 2003 when Austrian daredevil Felix Baumgartner—a pioneer of freefall gliding—"glided" across the English Channel, leaping out of an aircraft 30,000 feet above Dover, England, and landing safely near Calais, France, twelve minutes later.

Wearing an aerodynamic suit, and with a 6-foot-wide wing strapped to his back, Felix soared across the sea at 220 miles per hour, moving 6 feet forward through the air for every 1 foot he fell vertically—and opened his parachute 1,000 feet above the ground before landing safely.

Military scientists saw the massive potential for secret military missions. Currently special forces and spec ops, such as the SAS, whom this was initially proposed to, rely on a variety of parachute techniques to land behind enemy lines.

Existing steerable square parachutes, or parafoils, are used normally, but when opened at high altitudes above 20,000 feet, jumpers have to struggle to control them for long periods, often fighting very high winds and extreme cold, while breathing from an oxygen bottle.

They can also free-fall from high altitude and open their parachutes at the last minute, but that severely limits the distance they can "glide" forward from the drop point to just a few miles.

But the German company ESG developed the strap-on rigid wing specifically for special forces and spec ops use.

Looking like a six-foot-wide pair of F-15 Eagle wings, the device allows a parachutist to glide up to 120 miles, while carrying up to 200 pounds of equipment. Not only that, the stealth wings are fitted with oxygen supply and navigation aides. When they would approach their landing zone, the jumper would pull their rip cord to open his parafoil canopy and then land how he normally would. The manufacturers claimed the ESG wing is "100 percent silent" and "extremely difficult" to track using radar.

Bobby and Bo had told Boom Kittenger how effective the stealth wings had been and were very enthused about how well they could infiltrate a hot situation like they had in southern Texas a little northeast of El Paso, a shoot-out with members of a Brazilian street gang called O Grupo Grande as well as elements of al Qaeda.

He was wondering what he had been thinking, wearing a set of stealth wings, now looking out at the night sky over northern Thailand from the back ramp of a giant C-130 Hercules. He was breathing O_2, oxygen from a bottle built into the right wing, and pulled his night vision optics on over his face. He looked at his Global Positioning System tracker in his right wrist and shook hands with the Special

Forces master sergeant jumpmaster watching the red light to the side of the big ramp.

In less than a half minute, the red light went out, the green light came on, and the big Green Beret slapped a beefy palm against the back of Boom's right shoulder and yelled, "Go!"

Boom, instead of jumping, turned his head, removed his O_2 mask, and grinning, yelled above the prop roar, "Naw! I wanna go home, sit on my couch, eat bonbons, and watch *The Jerry Springer Show*."

Quickly, he replaced his mask, and waving, he went out the back door diving off the end of the ramp in a crab position. Laughing and shaking his head slowly, the SF sergeant backed up and returned to his seat on the side of the aircraft, while the ramp and door electronically closed.

Boom had to drop tens of thousands of feet and was going to travel laterally for over 100 miles. He was very excited. This was a new adventure, another adrenaline high. He would be working again with Vietnamese Montagnards and Laotian Hmong, was serving his nation in an important function, and was making an absolutely immoral amount of money as an independent contractor for the CIA.

On the ground, Y-Ting lit a strobe light in the middle of the large clearing, which had been a mountain rice field, and also placed a radio transmitter that sent out a homing signal to Boom's receiver perched above his reserve chute. When he soared into range, a small green light would start blinking over and over and a small LED screen would show him which way to steer to effect his descent toward the drop zone.

The joint patrol waited and watched, patiently. Suddenly, they saw a laser light come from the sky and as quickly went out. Seconds later, in the moonlight they made out the outline of a large parafoil chute. Excited whispers went back and forth between the oriental fighting men. Minutes later, Boom glided into the drop zone, and at the last second, he seemed to lift up and set down with an easy stand-up landing.

The patrol left LPs out to watch for enemy approach, but for the most part they gathered around the tall American and his parachute and equipment were quickly rolled up.

Y-Ting, with right hand outstretched, grabbed his own left forearm and Boom did the same and they shook hands smiling.

The Ede, or Rade, Montagnard said, "Hello, Boom. We are glad you are back here with us."

"Suaih asei mlei mo ih?" Boom said.

The warriors whispered excitedly among themselves.

Y-Ting replied, *"Kao suaih moh. Lak jak a ih liu?* You speak our language very good."

Boom said, *"Suaih moh."*

After exchanging greetings and inquiring about each other's health, Boom was supposed to immediately cache it but knew how these resourceful little warriors were. During the Vietnam War, he remembered how thrilled a Montagnard man with a family could be with one piece of tin. He would dig a large bunker in the side of a hill, use the tin for a roof, cover it with layers of dirt and that was considered a mansion for many.

With a parachute and its suspension lines and risers, a Montagnard or a Hmong could create a variety of resources.

With the Stealth wings, one of them could just about create a multiroom mansion for their family.

There was no talking until they reached their G-base, or guerilla base, one hour later. Here things were more secure, and a large cooking fire was on as well as several smaller fires. As soon as they arrived, several men offered Boom food and rice wine.

Boom politely declined and said he had his own food and was ordered to eat it, this time. He said his commander knew they did not have much food, and he was to decline any offers for foods or drink, or he would be court-martialed. He knew that they understood chain of command and would not want him to break most direct orders, although they also learned that most Green Berets would defy orders to accomplish a mission if the order did not make any sense.

In actuality, the retired command sergeant major was the man Bobby Samuels called when Bobby hit his bottom and realized he was an alcoholic. Boom dropped what he was doing and left his ranch in Colorado, flying cross-country to Washington, D.C., where he rented a car and forced Bobby to go with him to his first AA meeting, something Bobby would never regret. Bobby had a mission to accomplish then, so he put off going to the Betty Ford Center but made as many AA meetings as he could. Boom had been a recovering alcoholic and had even accompanied Bobby's father to AA meetings. Bobby did not even know his dad was an alcoholic growing up or that he went to AA. He just knew he could never recall seeing his father drink.

Boom, who was now in his late fifties but was in such good shape everybody thought he was in his forties, had drunk plenty of rice wine with the Montagnard warriors and the Hmong warriors during his tours in Vietnam and in Laos. He knew that drinking the smooth but potent beverage was a major part of both warrior societies. He also knew the little men lived very simple, uncomplicated lives, so he did not want to go into a ten-minute dissertation about alcoholism, so he simply said he was ordered not to drink or eat with them. This the Montagnards fully knew and understood, so it kept him out of trouble drinking and not having to explain himself, either, without insulting them by a flat refusal.

The tall, graying SF engineer-demolition specialist pulled several small green plastic bottles of U.S. Army insect repellent from his pack and handed them to Y-Ting and several of the patrol members. They got excited and started talking rapidly with each other. Small pieces of cotton were passed out from an old first-aid kit and pieces of cotton were wedged onto the ends of small sticks. The Montagnards squirted a drop or two of repellent on each cotton swab and then started touching them on the engorged bodies of the large leeches all over their legs, feet, and other parts of their bodies. When the insect repellent touched the leeches' bodies, they would immediately back out of the skin, leaving a tiny blood hole where their heads had invaded the hiker's body traveling through the damp, dark jungle.

Boom was hungry, so he got an MRE from his rucksack and put water on the small cooking fire provided for him. Y-Ting and two others came over and squatted by his fire.

Boom smiled at the warrior leader, saying, "Tonight, we should relax, eat, sleep, talk a little, and wait until tomorrow to speak of the enemy."

Y-Ting said, "We must tell you about the tiger."

"What tiger?"

"Ooh, he was bad," Y-Ting said. "He ate his wife. He ate my cousin. Ate two more people from my village."

"What?" Boom said.

"You know my village in Vietnam near Buon Ale A?"

Boom said, "Yes, I know where you mean."

Y-Ting responded, "We had a tiger and it would watch the village. When the villagers go to river for water or wash clothes or fish, it would follow. When the women go to the rice field to harvest rice, it would circle the field and kill villagers and eat them."

Boom said, "What happened to the tiger?"

One of the patrol members, not even looking up from his bowl of rice he was busy devouring, said, "Y-Ting kill," with Boom a little surprised that the man even spoke English.

It was in fact the first time Boom had even heard the man speak.

Boom said, "Cool, Y-Ting. How did you kill him?"

Y-Ting said, "I go out after him and find tracks outside village, maybe ten clicks. He goes far. I see he goes to another village and kills people. Maybe still there only one day.

"Next day, I go to rice field where women die," he went on. "I take stool with me and sit on it."

Boom laughed and interrupted, "A stool?"

He was surprised that Y-Ting knew the word and why he would do such a thing.

Y-Ting said, "Yes, I take stool and sit there. Maybe three hours, I sit, then I see tiger's shoulders in high grass. He comes for me."

Boom asked, "What if you had faced the wrong way?"

Y-Ting said, "Oh, I would not do that. Wind must blow into tiger's face or he think me smell him coming and run away."

Boom knew better and wondered why he even asked such an obvious question.

"So tiger comes slow, what you say?" the strong little man went on. "Squatting? No, crouching. Tiger comes slow, crouching. He thinks me no see. He gets closer and closer."

"So did you have your sights on him that whole time?" Boom asked.

"Oh no," Y-Ting said. "I did not want Cong-An to come see me with a rifle. I just had my knife."

"Holy shit!" Boom countered. "You faced a five- or six-hundred-pound tiger with a Scrap Yard knife?"

Y-Ting laughed, saying, "No, I was trained number one by Boom Kittenger."

"What?" Boom said, surprised and humbled.

Y-Ting said, "Tiger attacks and runs at me. I drop down, cover my head, and his legs hit trip wire. I have trip wire across path and have wooden clothes pin with positive wire to one battery attached to screw through end, and negative wire on other side with screw, and wooden plug in between and they go to basting cap inside bamboo tube I fill with C4 I steal from SRV. Have blasting cap in end, and I wrapped with many stones inside tape."

Boom said, "I'll be damned."

Y-Ting replied, "Legs hit trip wire and screws in clothes pin hit each other and explosion. Blew shit out of tiger."

"Sure glad you paid attention when I gave you guys classes on demo."

"Me, too," Y-Ting added. "Thank you. We must learn. Our

enemy has tanks, planes, guns, bombs. We have maybe more . . ."

He looked for a word and hit the left side of his chest with his hand, smiling and saying, "Heart."

Boom clapped a hand on his friend's shoulder.

Boom Kittenger had served with both Bobby and Bobby's late father, Command Sgt. Maj. Honey Samuels. Boom himself was a legend in Special Forces, the spec ops community, and the CIA; his legend was only overshadowed by retired Command Sgt. Maj. Billy Waugh. Billy Waugh had been face-to-face with Usama bin Laden four times working for the CIA, had served seven and a half years straight in MAC-V/SOG during the Vietnam War, and was the man who literally tracked down and led the French police to capturing the infamous Carlos the Jackal. He had served either the Special Forces or the CIA in fifty-five foreign countries. Billy had in fact authored a book about his adventures called *Hunting the Jackal.*

Special Forces engineer/demolition . specialists are trained to expertly build a bridge or blow one up. And of these men, Boom Kittenger was one of the very best. After retirement, Boom was called upon by the Department of Defense, DEA, and CIA to perform difficult missions.

The stories about Boom during the Vietnam War and all the decades in between were many and most were not embellishments, although many hearing them might think they were.

One of the simplest and most clever was the story about Boom when he was on an RT, or Recon Team, out of FOB (Forward Operating Base) 1 in Phu Bai. MAC-V/SOG or Studies and Observation Group was a top secret unit in the Vietnam War manned primarily by Green Berets who would conduct cross-border operations, usually in three-to-nine-man RTs, which almost always were comprised of six men, with two being Americans; the others were four mercenaries, and most of them were Montagnard warriors.

They went on long-range patrols conducting direct-action missions in Cambodia, Laos, North Vietnam, and even in China. Obviously, many, many Americans went home in body bags.

On this particular mission, Boom, as well as a young gung-ho first lieutenant and four Montagnards of the Bahnar tribe, were inserted by helicopter into North Vietnam.

The ASA, the Army Security Agency, had top secret units emplaced around Vietnam then with radio equipment that was directional finding and could also read the power of enemy radio transmissions. At the same time, they had a fleet of twin-engine propeller-driven Mohawk aircraft with the same capabilities. The planes would fly around, shoot an azimuth on an enemy radio transmission, and then ASA operators in an office miles away would intersect the azimuth between both radios and pinpoint the enemy radio. Also, by determining how powerful the radio transmission was, ASA analysts could determine the size and type of radio and determine if it was one with an enemy company, battalion, regiment, or division headquarters.

In this case, for Boom's team, a North Vietnamese Army (NVA) division had been emplaced near the border of Laos where the main tributaries flowed into North Vietnam aimed toward Hanoi.

Operation Tailwind was going on down south with Prairie Fire team insertions as a diversion for a big operation further north in Laos called Honorable Dragon. Because so many teams were being inserted into Laos and engaging NVA units, G2 (headquarters intelligence) wanted to know why this division was sitting tight.

Boom's team was inserted to infiltrate into the NVA divisional staging area, take plenty of photos, reconnoiter, and then create some "silent sabotage," as Boom called it, and sneak away and call for pickup.

With the young lieutenant leading, the whole team took hours to low crawl into the division ammo supply reserves. There, they hid for two hours and quietly removed the copper-jacketed bullets from 7.62-millimeter rounds, used in their AK-47s, SKSes, and light machine guns. They then poured out the gunpowder from each round and replaced it with C4 plastic explosive, then put the bullets back together and replaced them at random among the stockpiles of ammunition. In so doing, the NVA would later distribute the ammunition; at some point, while fighting, each of those rounds would explode in somebody's rifle and take most of the soldier's head along with it. This would create a tremendous psychological deterrent to good aiming at American soldiers. Literally gun-shy, NVA soldiers would then start shooting from the hip or holding the rifle up very high or next to tree trunks to try to save their heads from shredding, thus ruining their aim at American soldiers.

Following sabotaging the small-arms ammo, Boom took two 82-millimeter mortar tubes for the supplies, and working quickly, and using a length of bamboo, he tamped C4 plastic explosive at the bottom of the tube all around the firing pin. When firing rounds from the 82-millimeter mortar, NVA soldiers would drop a round down the tube and duck. At the bottom of the tube was a firing pin that would detonate the blast that would propel the explosive round out the tube and towards the enemy. When a round was dropped in with the C4 around the pin, the mortar tube itself became a giant bomb and would explode, also detonating the round. The bursting radius would be quite large and many casualties would be inflicted. In a much bigger sense than the exploding bullets this would have a tremendous psychological effect on soldiers firing the mortars.

Boom and the team successfully exfiltrated the division headquarters area with plenty of photographs and worked their way to a jungled ridgeline ten kilometers away. The next morning they were extracted on Stabo rigs, or harnesses kind of like horse collars on a cable where the men had hands free to fire weapons, which hoisted them up through the triple-canopy jungle and into the confines of one of the Greyhounds, a Huey helicopter unit that bravely flew support for MAC-V/SOG.

In the morning, the patrol set out for a hidden valley ten miles distant. They moved rapidly, and the men chatted with each other incessantly until they had gone five miles.

Suddenly, just like Boom had witnessed during the Vietnam War, these warriors simply "sensed" the near presence of the enemy. They stopped talking, and rifles came off their shoulders and were carried at a modified port arms position.

They moved off the trail and slithered into the trees, waiting. Soon an LPA (Lao People's Army) patrol came by, heading in the opposite direction, the men talking and laughing as if they hadn't a care in the world. The Montagnard-Hmong guerilla unit waited unmoving in the jungle for ten more minutes. Then, as one, they came out of the trees and reassembled on the trail.

Boom Kittenger could not ever get over that. It was the same way in the Vietnam War decades earlier, working with the parents and uncles of some of these very men. That uncanny knowing sense they possessed that warned them of the enemy presence. It was incredible to Boom.

The patrol kept moving steadily and quietly toward the objective, which they reached by afternoon. The patrol went up a ridgeline and down the other side. Halfway down, they dropped to their bellies and low crawled, pulling themselves along the damp rain forest floor. They came out at the edge of a large valley and Boom could finally see for the first time.

Before them were numerous buildings, barrack-type buildings, and all made of rattan on raised stilts, holding them several feet off the jungle floor. Under a large—very large—camouflage netting was an obstacle course.

There was a large water tank, and it, too, was suspended on a high stilted platform, the stilts actually trees that had been cut off and leveled. Above it, too, was camouflage cargo netting with many jungle branches and greens woven into the netting. To any aircraft flying over, it would look completely innocent.

There was what looked like a stilted rattan building with classrooms inside and there were numerous men going in and out of all buildings. There was also something very interesting to Boom, another building perfectly square, also rattan, also camouflaged, but it was obviously a Muslim mosque.

There were guard towers and machine guns emplaced, as well as an antiaircraft position, ammunition bunkers, and various training emplacements and devices.

Boom got a digital camera out of his backpack and plugged it into a digital bursting device that would immediately transmit the video and/or photographs he was about to take via satellite back to Langley with a feed going into the very bowels of the Pentagon.

While the rest of the patrol took up defensive positions along the jungle fringe, Y-Ting escorted Boom, and they crawled around the training camp perimeter taking video and digital stills, transmitting it back stateside immediately. This process took them until well after dark, but they simply donned the night vision devices Boom brought for most of the patrol.

At one point they stopped, as an apparition seemingly rose in front of Boom, but they quickly saw it was the hood of a large cobra. It swayed back and forth, but the former Green Beret grabbed a stick and tossed it aside. They went on. It took two more hours to gather the rest of the patrol and get out of there.

By midnight, they were far enough away that they could set up a night location. Boom spent some time on a satellite phone telling about the number of Laotian, Thai, and Arabic Muslims he saw in the camp. Y-Ting told him that there were also several Pilipino and/or Indonesians in the group.

7

BACK IN DELTA CHARLIE

It was during the workday in the United States, in Washington, D.C., in fact, and the J-2 of USARPACOM, or the chief intelligence officer for the U.S. Army Pacific Command, concluded his briefing to the Senate Intelligence Committee about the Laotian al Qaeda training and operations of Boom Kittenger and his patrol.

Sen. James Weatherford asked more questions than all the others. He was deeply troubled and knew he must get word to Nguyen Van Tran and Muhammad Yahyaa immediately. He headed for his office and called the Vietnamese embassy in Washington, which was located in a suite on Twentieth Street northwest.

He said, "I am sorry. I meant to get the number for the Viennese Orchestra. Wrong number."

As soon as the operator got the coded message, the information was passed on to Nguyen Van Tran.

Tran moved quickly to a private office and unlocked a drawer. He checked out a cell phone that had never been used and headed for an Oriental restaurant a few blocks away.

By this time, he knew that the senator had time to leave the Capitol building, so he dialed the senator's cell phone.

James Weatherford answered, "Hello."

Nguyen Van Tran said simply, "Thai restaurant we meet at before. Twenty-third Street."

The senator said, "In ten minutes."

Instead of taking his limo, he hailed a cab and headed toward the restaurant. The cabbie wore a turban on his head and was dark-skinned. Weatherford wondered if he could even speak English, but the man said in very broken English, "Where go?" The Middle Easterner had been waiting there for over an hour when he spotted Weatherford looking for a cab.

The congressman told him the restaurant and the man nodded, pulling away from the curb and forcefully inserting his taxi into the constant flow of traffic.

They were there in minutes, and he pulled roughly up to the curb, looking at the meter and saying, "Figh dollors fifty, please."

The multimillionaire senator handed him a five-dollar bill and a one-dollar bill, brusquely saying, "Keep the change," as he quickly exited the cab and entered the restaurant.

As soon as he entered the establishment, the turban-clad cabbie put the meter down and picked up the microphone, saying, "This is Agent Fernella. I transported the suspect to target restaurant number three one minute ago, over."

A voice on the other end of the scrambled radio transmission replied, "Good work, over."

Fernella said, "The cheap bastard only tipped me fifty cents, over."

The voice chuckled, "What did you expect from him? Class? Move a block away and maintain surveillance. Do not pick him up again. Smith will bring his cab into position. Over."

Fernella said, "Wilco. Out."

The FBI agent pulled his taxi down the street, made a U-turn, and pulled up next to the curb, parallel parking it facing back toward the Thai restaurant. Inside the senator ordered Tom Yung Goon, a Thai shrimp soup with straw mushrooms specially seasoned with lime juice, lemongrass, and hot peppers. The man with his back to him at the next table, Vietnamese in appearance, ordered Tom Kha Gai, also a soup of southern Thailand made with slices of chicken in coconut milk flavored with Thai herbs and seasoning.

A few minutes later, another man came in who looked Middle Eastern and sat down across from Nguyen Van Tran. Muhammad Yahyaa ordered a plate of drunken noodles.

With inconspicuous whispers, James Weatherford sold out his fellow countrymen, Sgt. Maj.-ret. Brandon "Boom" Kittenger, U.S. Army Special Forces, a man who had dedicated his entire adult life to the service of the United States of America, risking his life for the country for close to forty years, as well as the two premiere CID spec ops agents, Maj. Bobby Samuels and Capt. Bo Devore.

Nguyen Van Tran whispered, "Need photographs, papers about dis Boom and operation."

James said, "Tran, you be here eating tomorrow at one p.m. sharp. Wear a blue suit and maroon tie. Do you have them?"

"Yes."

Weatherford went on, "An army sergeant will come in and set a valise down by you. Pick it up when you leave. I'll have a set for you, too, Muhammad. You can get it later from Tran."

Muhammad said, "Okay."

Nothing else was said by any of the men.

In the FBI surveillance van, a man dialed a cell phone; in the restaurant, a teenaged boy and girl waiting for takeout hugged and cuddled, until the boy's phone rang.

From inside the van, a voice said, "The directional mike is not working. Do you have the bottom of the fake schoolbooks pointing toward them?"

The juvenile-looking special agent replied, "Yes, Mom. Of course. I'll be home as soon as my order gets here."

He gave the female agent a look like he was getting a lecture. She giggled and pulled out her lipstick. While she placed the glossy red on her lips she snapped ten photographs from the bottom of the tube. The three plotters paid no attention to the teenagers up at the counter, until their order was delivered, and they paid and left. Muhammad stared at the rear end of the female agent and had his usual lustful thoughts.

In the van, the FBI technician called it into headquarters that the mike in the restaurant was not working. This was shared with Langley, the National Security Council in the basement of the White House, and the Pentagon. There was a lot of cursing going on.

Outside the restaurant cameras were clicking from three different locations as James Weatherford was picked up by another FBI agent in a different taxi. Muhammad and Tran were both followed by surveillance teams. All three men were now on twenty-four-hour-per-day surveillance, and now associates and assistants were starting to be watched.

Bobby and Bo left work and contemplated their new assignment. They would be part of the massive task force to take on the al Qaeda expansion operations into the Far East, the Pacific Rim, or Papa Romeo, as the briefers were already referring to the area of operations. The problem was that the senator James Weatherford also knew about the task force and knew that Bobby and Bo were involved.

He also knew that Bobby, an army major, was singularly in charge of a multiagency task force earlier that year in pursuit of two al Qaeda operatives who had smuggled two suitcase nuclear bombs into the United States, transporting one to Miami, Florida, to detonate and the other to New York City to detonate simultaneously. The task force was comprised of agents and operatives from the Department of Homeland Security, the Department of Health and Human Services, the Treasury Department's Secret Service, the Federal Bureau of Investigation, the Defense Intelligence Agency, the Central Intelligence Agency, the Department of Defense, the Citizenship and Immigration Services, the

Miami-Dade Police Department, and the New York City
Police Department, as well as several other agencies.

The plans the al Qaeda made for that operation were
even more complex than that on 9/11. The bombs dropped
on Nagasaki and Hiroshima were fifteen kiloton nuclear
bombs; and in Nagasaki a brick building, albeit a very well-
built brick building, a little over 200 yards from ground
zero essentially survived the atomic blast without being de-
molished.

The al Qaeda had purchased, it was reported, over
twenty backpack nukes on the world illegal-arms black
market.

The Soviet RA-115 backpack nuclear bombs only
weighed just over fifty-seven pounds each and could fit not
in a backpack but a large suitcase, so they could be carried
and hidden almost anywhere. The al Qaeda operatives'
challenge was to put them where they could rain fire and
fear on the U.S. populace.

With a nuclear bomb, over 50 percent of the damage
done and lives lost is from the initial blast, then over 35
percent is from the radiation wave, and then all the rest is
from fallout and residual effects. The blast from a 1-ton
backpack is considerably less than the 15-kiloton bombs
that hit the Japanese cities in World War II, but the falloff
with nuclear bombs is not really that great as the size de-
creases. For example, the ground-zero blast from a 1-
megaton nuke, which would be like 1,000 backpack nukes,
has only a 70 percent increase over a two hundred kiloton
nuke. So with nuclear bombs, it is like comparing a hole in
the ground seven to eight miles across, as opposed to four
to five miles across.

An airburst nuclear bomb could spread radiation over a
very large area, but would do significantly less blast damage, as almost all explosions blow up and out.

The attack on the World Trade Center was indicative of
and was supposed to be a symbolic gesture of attacking
America's enterprise system of capitalism, and the attack
on the Pentagon was obvious. Flight 93 was intended to

strike the White House and would have made bin Laden
ecstatic. Neither he nor any of the al Qaeda leadership had
any idea that the World Trade Center would collapse from
the intense heat. They had hoped for the death of hundreds,
but when they collapsed, they thought Allah was indeed
blessing them.

Now the al Qaeda had counted on two RA-115 backpack nuclear bombs to create more damage than Hiroshima and Nagasaki with one-fifteenth the blast power of
each.

The AQ figured that by bombing halfway up the Empire
State Building, they would achieve bin Laden's goal of attacking a major American landmark, but from a practical
application, they would destroy most of the building, sending pieces of brick, concrete, metal, desks, chairs, computers, and other items in a hail of destruction with all of those
items becoming falling deadly pieces of shrapnel spread in
all directions. Additionally, the upper half of the building
would be gone and all the people within, many below
would die, and the radioactive fallout from the blast being
raised high above the ground would spread over a large
area, especially if prevailing winds were not blowing out
toward the ocean. Had they blown the building lower, much
of the shrapnel falling would not be deadly, but from that
elevation, they reasoned even a falling coffeemaker could
become a deadly weapon.

Usama bin Laden had long dreamed and spoken about
an American Hiroshima, wherein they would detonate two
nuclear devices simultaneously during daylight hours for
maximum terror effect in two American cities with large
Jewish populations. So while Bobby went to New York
City to thwart the effort there, Bo had gone to Miami,
Florida, the other target city of the al Qaeda plot.

The metropolitan area of Miami had a population of 5.5
million people, many celebrities lived there, and most important, the Miami metro area had a very large Jewish population so most of the al Qaeda leadership saw it as a
no-brainer.

There was no Empire State Building in Miami, but there was the Four Seasons Hotel and tower on Brickell Avenue in Miami, which had a height of exactly 788 feet 9 inches, making the tower the tallest U.S. building south of Atlanta and tallest U.S. residential building south of New York City. So it was much more than the tallest building in Florida. It also had office space for lease and hotel rooms, which would more easily facilitate unencumbered bomb emplacement. The construction of the sixty-four-floor high-rise was a reinforced concrete structure incorporating core shear walls, post-tensioned slabs, and perimeter columns with spans between the columns that reached forty feet. It would work.

Bo and Bobby both had been very successful in killing the two al Qaeda operatives before they even had a chance to emplace the nuclear devices in the buildings.

This really upset the al Qaeda leadership headquartered in Pakistan at the time. They decided now because of Bobby and Bo to try a new approach. They were going to try to bring a large ship into the port of Los Angeles carrying tons of radioactive "yellow cake" nuclear waste seated atop a ship-sized explosive charge, which when detonated would send millions of tons of radioactive dust into the air over Los Angeles and surrounding communities.

Sen. James Weatherford had no clue that the al Qaeda really planned to kill millions in southern California and with burning radioactive material, no less, but with his mind-set, it may not have mattered to him anyway. He just was driven to become president, as he felt he was the one with the answers.

The al Qaeda planned to detonate the "mother of all dirty bombs" in the Los Angeles basin, and a self-absorbed, self-centered, egomaniacal, totally immoral U.S. senator was unwittingly, but also uncaringly, going to be the man to pull the trigger.

Bobby and Bo finished work and were going to head home to their respective town house condominiums, but Bobby asked her if she wanted to go to dinner and discuss plans. They had been told they would be going west, very far west, so they knew they had to start making plans.

They hopped on the metro and went to Crystal City to go to a restaurant Bo liked. Instead of taking a taxi from their stop, they decided to just walk as the day was so unusually nice for that time of the year.

The two were always aware of their surroundings, but did not pay much attention to the slight man who got on at their stop at the Pentagon and stepped off at their stop in Crystal City. He stayed far behind them, busily engaged in directing his accomplices to the scene.

When they entered the restaurant, he breathed easier, sitting down on a bus bench to be even less conspicuous. A large SUV filled with Vietnamese hoodlums showed up outside the restaurant about the time Bobby and Bo's food was served. Nguyen Win Hoi, who was no relation to Nguyen Van Tran, went over to the car and pulled out a photo of Bo and a photo of Bobby to show the men.

The leader was a large scar-faced man with an everpresent scowl on his face, who was half Vietnamese and half Chinese and named Vang Duc Minh. Minh came from a sexual tryst between a Red Chinese officer and a married schoolteacher in Hanoi. Her husband was a Communist Party official in the giant bureaucracy, and when he learned of her infidelity, he kicked and beat her horribly, tossing her out of his house. She ended up as a street prostitute to support herself and the damaged baby growing in her womb.

Because of one of the kicks delivered by his mother's husband, Minh's face was slightly distorted due to broken and improperly healed cheekbone and eye socket fractures.

They originally were going to attack by executing a drive-by, but these men were from the SRV army and not really gangbangers. They were well-trained, hardened killers; however, most of their experience had been in the Central Highlands region of Vietnam killing innocent Montagnard villagers or closer to Ho Chi Minh City killing Cham women and children mainly. Now, they were going up against DSC recipient Bobby Samuels and Silver Star recipient Bo Devore. Had they known the capabilities of the two, they might have requested reinforcements.

Minh sent two men into the shadows of the barely-lit parking lot, each armed with Uzi submachine pistols, and something Muhammad would have been furious about since the deadly .45 automatic guns were made in Israel.

Two more were placed on the street, but strategically it was an ignorant move, as one was up the street from the restaurant and the other down the street, so if Bo and Bobby came out between the two, they could shoot each other in the crossfire. Each of them was equipped with .357 Magnum revolvers. Two more with folding stock SKS rifles that were equipped to fire automatic were hidden behind a van a short distance from the restaurant entrance. The driver of the SUV would sit down the street with the engine running waiting to pick up the ambushers as soon as the trap was sprung. The nasty Vang Duc Minh would wait just outside the entrance of the restaurant armed with a giant .44 Magnum automag Desert Eagle in a shoulder holster, but inside his long, dark green trench coat was a Mossberg 12-gauge pump shotgun loaded with double-aught buckshot Magnums. The barrel was only eighteen inches long and the shotgun had a pistol grip handle.

The men all nervously waited in the dark street, shivering against the chilly evening. This was their first shoot-out against people not armed with bamboo-made crossbows and spears, but possibly with guns themselves. Each man was very nervous and wanted to make sure they made the first shots count.

Inside, Bobby and Bo spoke across a candlelit table, each eating delicious lobster tails.

Bobby said, "Bo, I have really been wanting to have a long, very important talk with you ever since I got back from California, but they keep us so doggoned busy."

Bo said, "We can talk right now, or do you want to wait?"

"It is too important to discuss here," he said, "and we are going to be shipping out any day for the PR. How about we get out of here, Bo, and head to my place or yours so we can talk privately?"

Bo's heart started pumping wildly. Was he going to talk about love? She hoped and prayed. Bo was deeply in love with Bobby, but she always knew she could not compete with the memory he carried of Arianna, his late wife. She had seen Bobby shed tears over the woman more than once, and she had been dead for well over a half a decade.

He was indeed going to talk to her about love, because Bobby finally understood about the self-imposed psychological Armor All Protectant he had worn over his emotions for years now. His time at the Betty Ford Center not only helped him understand the disease of alcoholism that afflicted him and his late father and made him realize that, like a diabetic avoiding sugar, alcohol was poison to him that he must avoid at all costs. It also clarified something to Bobby very plainly: He was, despite his strong posturing to avoid ever getting hurt again, very much head over heels in love again with his partner, the very voluptuous and beauteous Bo Devore.

Because they worked together and their jobs were so dangerous, he could not just be a romantic. They had to really discuss issues, so they could still work effectively.

Bo said, "Why don't we go to my place?"

He smiled and nodded, reaching for his wallet and removing a platinum credit card.

She asked, "Can you give me a hint about what this is about? I am a cop, you know."

Bobby grinned, saying, "Sure. I'll be right back."

Now her curiosity was really piqued, as she saw him go up and pay the bill, then leave for the entrance foyer. When they came into the restaurant, Bobby noticed there was a coat check room and a large machine with a steel claw and numerous stuffed animals inside. When he paid his bill, he got change for a ten-dollar bill, and he now smoothed one out and inserted it into the slot of the machine.

It took the bill and indicated he would have two plays. He grabbed the joystick and looked over the many varied

colored bunnies, bears, dolls, and stuffed cartoon characters. He saw what he wanted, a fluffy, bright blue teddy bear
holding a red heart with the words "I love you!" in white
script. It was partly covered by an official Bugs Bunny character, and Bobby decided to hook it out of the way first, and
he caught Bugs under one arm on the first try. He was
amazed, as he watched the claw, in its always fragile grip,
move the character across the other stuffed toys and drop it
into the bin in the front left corner of the machine.

Bobby pushed the hinged door in the front, and he
reached in the machine and pulled out Bugs Bunny, dis-
playing his ever-present bucktoothed grin despite his being
taken from his comfy home. Bobby tucked Bugs under his
arm and turned all his attention to the blue bear. He figured
if he could manipulate one of the pincers in between the
red heart and the bear's paws, it should be easier to lift it
out. It took two more dollars to accomplish it, but his theory proved correct.

With the blue bear in his right hand and Bugs Bunny in
his left, he headed back toward the table. Bo saw him enter
the room with the two animals and she blushed. Halfway to
their table, he stopped and looked at a cute little eight-year-
old girl eating with her parents.

Bobby said, "You sure are cute. Do you ever watch
Bugs Bunny on cartoons?"

She said shyly, "Yes."

The mother corrected, "What do you say? The nice man
said you are cute."

She said, "Thank you."

Bobby winked at the father and handed the bunny to the
little girl, who smiled broadly. He said, "Now don't ever
take gifts like this unless Mom and Dad are with you,
okay? But I want you to give Bugs a good home, will you?"

She nodded enthusiastically, saying, "Thank you very
much! Bugs will stay in my room."

The mother enthusiastically said, "Thank you so much,
sir."

The father shook hands with Bobby, smiling, and softly

said, "Thank you," probably embarrassed that he had not won a gift for his little girl.

Bo was so impressed with the generosity and niceness of Bobby Samuels, who was also the most dangerous man she ever knew.

He walked up to her and sat down, saying, "You asked if I could give you a hint about what we are going to talk about, so here it is."

Bo received the blue bear and looked at the heart and the three magic words she had only dreamed about, and tears flooded her eyes as she looked up at a smiling Bobby. He leaned across the table and touched her cheek, gently guiding it toward him. Their lips met softly, and he lingered there, kissing her gently, but with soft passion. As their lips parted, he pulled back slowly, smiling into her eyes with a penetrating stare that said clearly, "I want you."

Bobby stood and reached out for her hand and lifted her to his side.

Bo looked up at him from under his steely arm and said softly, "Thank you, Bobby. I will keep this always."

They headed for the door, arms around each other, feeling the warmth of each other's bodies and both wondering what it would feel like to be against each other in the nakedness and full vulnerability of love.

Bo and Bobby stepped out the door just when Minh had taken his hands off the shotgun long enough to light a cigarette with a butane lighter. It would be the split second they needed to even hope to have a chance to survive.

Bobby saw the look on Minh's face and the big man's hands reached under the long coat, and he didn't even try for his weapon. He dashed forward and reached for the big man's wrists. His right hand hit the handle of the Desert Eagle, and Bobby simply drew it from Minh's holster and flipped the lever off safe, aimed at center mass, and squeezed off two quick shots, as the big man started to bring up the sawed-off shotgun.

Bo was drawing her Glock 17 while this happened, and suddenly, before Bobby shot, felt something slam into and

glance off the ceramic heart plate of her IIIA Second
Chance Kevlar vest. She also felt the round tear through
her blouse and jacket, and immediately spotted the Vietnamese shooter to their right, who had just nailed her in the
area of the heart with his .357 Magnum. Once again, her
vest had saved her life, and as Bobby boomed twice with
the Desert Eagle slamming Minh backward through the
front glass of a curbside Cadillac, she fired a double tap as
well into the chest of the shooter to their right.

Before the shock even cleared, Bo heard Bobby yell,
"Down!" and she dropped to the sidewalk, bruising both
kneecaps, as bullets tore over her head from behind, and
she heard the giant Desert Eagle boom, twice more. Bo
looked behind her, seeing the other punk with a .357 Magnum spin with Bobby's first round and his head literally
explode with the second round.

Bo felt something slam into her thigh from her right and
bullets cracked around her in steady staccato, as she rolled
forward over the curb into the street under the Cadillac.
Bobby rolled on top of her protectively, and she heard him
unload the Desert Eagle in the direction of the automatic
weapons.

"Let me out," she screamed, pulling Bobby's Glock, as
she quickly rolled under the large car and out onto the
street.

She saw the SUV's lights come on, and jumped up behind the Cadillac body with her Glock in one hand and
Bobby's in the other. She spotted the Uzi shooter and opened
up with both weapons spitting fire. In the meantime, Bobby
grabbed Minh's body and grabbed a new magazine for the
Desert Eagle, which he slammed into place, and opened fire
again. Bullets in the street rattled like a symphony of hate
and bad guys fell in place. Bobby stood with the sawed-off
shotgun in one hand, Desert Eagle in the other, and all were
down. He could see Bo's face was ashen. She had been hit.
He also saw the SUV bearing down on her, and Bobby
dove across the hood of the Caddy, landing on his feet, protectively standing between Bo and the oncoming car. He

dropped the .44, lifted the Mossberg shotgun, and pointed at the hood of the SUV and opened fire, knowing from training and experience that aiming at the hood should put the pellets through the windshield. Bobby did not wait to find out, as he quickly ejected spent shells and jacked new rounds into the chamber of the black shotgun. He ran out of ammunition as the vehicle seemed to swerve, and he turned and wrapped his arms around Bo protectively and threw both of them onto the trunk of the luxury car a millisecond before the SUV crashed into it and exploded in a ball of flame. The impact sent Bobby and Bo through the air, but he kept his arms protectively around her.

The air left him as he hit the pavement twisting his body to take the impact while Bo landed on top of him, her fall cushioned by his body. He quickly looked down to see where she was hit.

He put her palm against the wound and commanded, "Push down hard, Bo."

Bobby reached inside his jacket and pulled a loaded 9-millimeter magazine out, inserting it into his Glock, which he took from Bo. Sirens approached rapidly, as Bobby checked all would-be assassins, pointing his weapon. All were still; he glanced quickly at Bo and noticed she was hugging her blue teddy bear.

Bobby looking around and pulling his badge out, said to her without looking down again, "Bo, you okay?"

She said, "Yeah, I think I'm shocky, but I did not lose much blood, and I know it missed the bone. It burns like hell. It feels like it went into the muscle on the back of my thigh."

Numerous police cruisers pulled up, sliding to screeching stops, as Bobby held up his badge for all to clearly see. He used the barrel of his Glock, indicating the fallen would-be killers lying all around the street.

Officers were out all over, guns drawn, with two pointing at him.

"U.S. Army CID," he yelled. "My partner is down! She needs an ambulance ASAP!"

No sooner had the words left his mouth than an ambulance pulled up and next to one of the shooters, and two cops ran over and directed the vehicle over to Bobby.

Bobby spotted a sergeant who seemed to immediately take charge and yelled, "We were ambushed when we came out of that restaurant. None of them are checked. The driver in the SUV tried to run us down! Check the SUV!"

Walking toward Bobby and looking all around, gun drawn, he nodded to two officers who checked the inside of the SUV. They both made faces.

One yelled, "The guy don't have a head, Sarge!"

The sergeant came to Bobby and Bobby presented him with his and Bo's badges and IDs. He looked at them while Bobby turned and watched while the paramedics worked on Bo. They started to put her on a gurney, and one attempted to take the blue bear, but she jerked it back, holding it firmly.

"Ma'am," the EMT said, "we can't take that in the ambulance. I'll give it to your partner for safekeeping, and—"

Bo interrupted, "You'll get your fingers broken trying to take it from me. I appreciate your help, guys, but nobody touches this bear."

The paramedic looked at the other, who grinned and nodded.

The first one said, "Yes, ma'am," and they loaded her onto the gurney.

Bobby looked at the sergeant, explaining, "She's my partner. I have to ride with her, Sarge. Can you have someone interview us at the hospital?

The police official said, "Sure, Major Samuels. Of course. Just, do you think there are any more?"

Bobby said, "No clue. Never saw them before, and we don't have a clue why they attacked us."

Later, Bo opened her eyes and saw sunlight streaking through the window of the hospital room. She blinked and yawned and saw an IV attached to a plastic needle going into a vein on her left arm. She turned her head to the right and saw her hand was being firmly held by Bobby, who was wide awake in a chair next to the bed.

Bobby smiled at her, leaned forward, and kissed her forehead. She noticed a splint on his left forearm. He, too, was dressed in hospital clothes. Bo looked straight down and saw that the blue bear was resting in the crook of her arm.

Bo said, "Bobby, what happened to your arm? Why are you wearing that? Why are you in a hospital gown and robe?"

Bobby said, "Nothing. Just got scratched."

A laugh from the doorway turned both of their heads, as a distinguished-looking doctor entered the room. "Because he has a greenstick fracture and severe bruising of the forearm, and two bullet holes in him."

Bo said, "What?"

The doctor said, "He didn't even speak to anybody about it until he was sure you were being treated. He had his upper thigh and lower thigh on his right leg torn open by bullets that apparently creased him pretty good. You had a bullet enter the back of your leg and tear out a little muscle and tissue, but fortunately it passed through your thigh without mushrooming at all. You will be sore, but I think fine."

Bo asked, "Why aren't you making him stay in bed, too, Doctor?"

Again the doctor laughed, saying, "This man is your partner, Captain. Do you want to tell me that anyone is going to make him do what he doesn't want to?"

Bobby gave her an impish smile. Bo started laughing.

There was a knock on the door and the chief of staff of the U.S. Army, Gen. Jonathan Perry, entered the room, and Bobby, moaning, stood at attention.

"Sit your ass down, Major," Perry commanded and stuck his hand out.

Bobby complied, saying, "Yes, sir," and shook hands with him.

The doctor and general also shook hands and introduced themselves to each other.

The general then leaned over Bo and kissed her on the forehead and handed her a dozen white roses. Bo smelled them and sighed.

She said, "Thank you, sir. They are beautiful."

He said, "The doctors here said it was better to treat you here and not transfer you to a military hospital. How long will they be in the hospital, Doctor?"

Bo said, "Until today, sir. We are going home today."

Bobby added, "I agree, sir."

The doctor said, "Actually, General, they both will be in pain, but nowadays, we like for people that are healing to move around and exercise their bodies more. I would say they are both limited to whatever pain they can endure."

The general raised his eyes, saying, "God help us."

All in the room laughed.

Bobby said, "Sir, if we can just go home to rest today, we will be at work tomorrow."

The chief of staff said, "Day after tomorrow, Major, and that is not up for debate."

Bobby and Bo said, "Yes, sir."

"Do you two have to always kill everybody you have a disagreement with?" Perry asked.

"No, sir," Bobby countered quickly. "The man at my corner deli argued with me the other day about how thick to slice my lunch meat, and I never even pulled my Glock."

They all laughed again.

Bobby got very serious. "General Perry, that was a lot of assassins and a planned ambush. We have no idea who was behind it."

Perry said, "We cannot talk here, son. We'll talk day after tomorrow."

"Do you have any clues about it, sir?" Bo asked.

"Yes, but for now, you two rest for forty-eight hours," the general replied. "Don't say anything else here. Operational security."

Bobby said, "Yes, sir."

Two hours later, after a lengthy lecture from the doctor and from two nurses, Bobby and Bo were released. They were wheeled to the hospital exit in side-by-side wheelchairs and at the exit were greeted by four MPs.

The staff sergeant in charge of the detail told Bobby,

"Major, we have been detailed to drive and protect both of you. Where to, sir?"

Bo said, "My place, Sergeant," and she gave him the address.

The MPs drove them in a sedan with another following behind them. Bobby noticed a tail and told the sergeant in charge. The MP looked behind them and grinned.

"The FBI, sir," he explained. "They are assigned to watch over both of you, too."

Bobby said, "Sergeant, I appreciate you gentlemen doing this. I also need to ask you to detail someone to go to our armory in the basement of the Pentagon, and check out a pair of CAR-15s for Captain Devore and me, a good supply of magazines, and tell them we want them with flat receiver groups, tactical handles, lasers, and holographic sights."

"Absolutely, sir," the noncom replied. "I assume you want plenty of 5.56 ammo?"

Bobby said, "Yes, thanks. Captain, anything else you want?"

Bo said, "Yes, sir, flash-bangs and some smoke grenades."

"Good idea," Bobby said.

The sergeant responded, "I have a bunch of flash-bangs in the trunk of this vehicle, sir, and I'm signed out for them. I can give you plenty. We'll have the smokes brought out from the Pentagon with the other ordinance."

Everybody wondered about the blue teddy bear the captain was carrying, but nobody asked. The MPs stationed themselves outside the condominium complex where Bo lived after Bobby assured them he and Bo would clear the house for intruders. The FBI sedan pulled up down the street about a block away and Bo and Bobby gave the two agents within a slight wave, which was returned by small waves from them.

They both limped inside, laughing at themselves, as they both moaned in pain.

"Coffee?" Bo asked, as soon as they entered her kitchen.

"Please," Bobby said.

Bobby went to the restroom while she made coffee for both of them, and they moved to the living room so they could sit or half lay on softer cushions. They both sat on her large overstuffed sectional sofa facing each other. Bo had finally put her bear down, setting it against the pillow on her bed earlier.

"Now, it is early afternoon," she said. "We have the rest of the day to talk and all day tomorrow. Why don't we have that discussion?"

Bobby said, "My thoughts exactly."

He paused to gather his words, and went on, "Bo, you and I are partners and that is extremely important to me."

"Me, too," she interrupted.

"We have been through so much together, it has just been incredible," he continued. "And there is no man or woman anywhere who I would rather have as my partner."

Bobby paused, so Bo responded, "Bobby, I cannot even fathom thinking about anybody else being my partner."

He went on, "Well, that is just so important to me, and I think to our mission. I think you and I make the very best team available since our mission has evolved more into a spec ops specialization."

"So why are you telling me this?" she asked.

He said, "You gotta bear with me. This will take a while."

"I'm right here, Major," she said. "You want some more coffee?"

He stood and said, "Yes, but I'll get it. You rest your leg."

Bobby took her cup and his and went to the kitchen. He could not believe how hot her condo seemed. He was sweating. He poured two cups and returned and sat down again with a moan.

Bobby went on, "That day when I learned I had gotten drunk and fondled your breast in that restaurant and embarrassed and disrespected you so, that—"

Bo interrupted, "I forgave you for that."

"Bo, I know," he said. "But you have no clue what I had

to go through emotionally to forgive myself. It was the second lowest point of my life. It was definitely my bottom."

"I am sorry it ever happened," she replied. "I am sorry you had to feel so badly, but I'm glad that you cared so much about what I thought."

Bobby responded, "When I went to Palm Springs, I finally had to face some issues that I had avoided or had been in denial about for some time."

He drank some coffee and continued, "I did a lot of soul-searching and worked a lot on taking my own personal inventory. Bo, I am a one-woman man, and I really loved Arianna. I was dedicated to her."

Bo said, "I know. I have always been jealous to think a woman could be loved that much."

He paused for a long time, then said, "Well, you shouldn't be jealous. You see, I was being a one-woman man to someone who was gone, long gone. I have been faithful to Arianna for years, but she isn't coming back. I never really buried her, emotionally, I mean."

Bo felt her heart leap.

She said, "I am glad. I think it will be healthier for you."

"Well," he said, "that's not all. I have been in denial for some time, now."

Bo asked, "You mean about Arianna?"

"No, about you."

"Me?" she replied. "What do you mean?"

Bobby thought for a minute and said, "Bo, you know some of the crazy things I have done, almost getting killed."

"No, being very brave," she corrected. "What about them?"

He said, "Do you know the main reason I ever do any of those things?"

She said, "To do what is right and brave and heroic?"

"No," Bobby said and stared into her eyes. "To show off for you. Just about everything I do is to simply make you proud of me."

Bo could not speak. Tears welled up in her eyes, and she just looked at him.

"What do you mean?"

Bobby said, "I am your boss. We are partners. I really loved my wife, and always will, but, Bo, I am so in love with you, I just cannot help myself."

A sob escaped her lips, and she threw herself forward and into his arms, saying, "Oh, Bobby."

They kissed long and hard and then their faces parted slightly, and he smiled, staring into her eyes, and she his. Their lips came together softly now, and he lifted her right hand, kissed her palm slowly, and then the inside of her wrist.

She whispered with a husky voice, "Make love to me."

Bobby smiled and said softly, "No."

She was taken aback, but he quickly explained, "You have stitches in the back of your thigh and I have a few my-self. Let's go into the bedroom and take a long nap, if you don't mind sleeping with your head on my chest and my arm around you."

She moaned, standing, and said, "I have dreamed about it over and over."

Surprised, Bobby replied, "You have?"

She said, "Yes, Bobby Samuels, I never believed I could love any man as much as I love you."

He swept her into his arms, and they kissed long and hard again. Then he held her a long time, just stroking her hair, saying nothing.

Bo turned on the CD player with several albums of soft love songs. They each went to bathrooms and went into her bedroom and slowly removed each other's clothes. They marveled at each other's incredible bodies and lay down on the bed, doing nothing but looking at each other and occa-sionally touching each other, all over, a cheekbone, lips, hair, shoulder, a hip, everywhere.

Then, both moaning in pain and chuckling about it, they lay in each other's arms, doing nothing but sometimes smiling. They finally drifted off to sleep and awakened three hours later to a knock on the door.

Bo jumped up and tossed on sweats, grabbing her Glock. She went to the door and looked out the peephole. She opened the door and the MP staff sergeant entered carrying a bag, followed by two other MPs carrying Bobby and Bo's weapons.

"The major is in the latrine," Bo explained, feeling her face flush.

Bobby already had his clothes on when she said this, and he snuck into the bathroom and then opened the door and flushed the toilet. He walked out into the room and greeted the MPs.

"Thank you very much, Sergeant," he said, admiring the weapons.

He and Bo both sat down at the coffee table and started loading 5.56 rounds into the CAR-15 magazines. The CAR-15 was first developed during the Vietnam War and is simply an M16 or AR-15 rifle with a telescoping stock and much shorter barrel, as well as a different receiver and forward stock configurations.

Bo said, "Sergeant, it is painful for both of us to get up or down, but there is a full pot of coffee in the coffeemaker by my sink and there are mugs on the rack near it. You and your men pour yourselves some coffee and relax."

The sergeant said, "Thank you, ma'am, but we have our orders."

Bo smiled. "I know and your immediate orders are to relax and enjoy some coffee. Stakeouts and surveillance are a bitch."

The men all laughed and headed for the kitchen, thanking them. One half hour later they left and Bobby and Bo headed back to bed, where they stayed simply talking half the night away.

Finally, at 3:30 in the morning, they went to sleep. Bobby awakened several times, and he just stroked Bo's hair, looking at her. She smiled but breathed like she was asleep.

He felt so renewed and unburdened and so much in love, again.

Bo opened her eyes and saw that it was morning. She ached, probably worse than the day before. She looked under her satin sheets and saw she was naked, and stretched and yawned. She realized she and Bobby had not even made love yet.

She wondered where he was and got out of bed, tossing on a nightgown. She made her way to the kitchen smelling several enticing aromas.

He had the small kitchen table set by the kitchen window. There were some red roses in a bud vase in the center of the table, and on the table was service for two, a platter with golden French toast, and another with strips of crisp bacon. There were two bowls with pink grapefruit halves in each and cups of steaming hot coffee poured out already.

"Oh my God!" Bo exclaimed. "This is wonderful, darling!"

Bobby said, "Well, get used to it, girlie, because if you're going to be my wife I plan on spoiling you the rest of our lives."

"Your wife?" she said, smiling. "Are you proposing, Bobby Samuels?"

"No," he responded quickly, "I am not. I will never try to control you except on this one thing. You and I are meant to spend our lives together, and I expect you to be my wife, soon, very soon. I am not asking. I am agreeing that it is something that must happen. It is God divined."

Bo laughed, munched a strip of bacon, and said, "My, how romantic, Casanova!"

Bobby laughed at himself, his face turning red. He limped out of the room and returned holding the blue bear and walked over to her at the kitchen table.

Bobby dropped in front of her chair on both knees and said, "Blue here does not want you sleeping alone with him ever again. I don't either, because I cannot imagine my life without you, Bo. I want to love you and make love to you. I want to be your best friend ever. I want to laugh with you, cry with you, argue sometimes, but enjoy making up. I want to make you proud of me. I want to hold you and write you love poems, and work with you, and play with you. I am a half a Bobby without you. You make me whole. Please, Bo, tell me you will marry me? Tell me you love me half as much as I love you. Tell me you will marry me soon?"

Bo laughed and grabbed his head in her hands.

"How could I ever say no? I love you, too, Bobby, and want to be your wife more than anything in the world," she responded.

Bobby and she kissed again. He started to stand, but stopped.

He said, "You are not going to believe this, honey. This is an unforgettable proposal, because I cannot get up off my knees."

Bobby moaned and lay facedown on the floor, laughing at himself and his pain. She pushed his chair to him, and he grabbed it, slowly rising up while moving hand over hand up the chair.

"What a romance, huh?" he said after he was seated at the table.

Bo said, "You know what? We have been wounded so many times, it's probably very appropriate."

"And I have another proposal," he said.

"What?"

Bobby sighed and said, "I feel our relationship is so special and being married is so special and permanent, and I cannot believe I am saying this, but I think we should not make love until we get married."

Bo smiled and said, "I cannot tell you how many times I have dreamed of lying in your arms, and how many times I have dreamed of you being inside me, but I think that is totally cool. We're too beat up to do anything anyway."

Bobby grinned, saying, "Anything? What did my parents call it, heavy petting?"

He lifted her good leg and softly kissed her foot, then kissed the inside of her ankle. He pulled a rose out of the vase and pulled the petals off and slowly dropped them on her leg going up under her robe. Then he kissed from rose petal to rose petal, softly and tenderly.

Bo moaned, but not from pain, and whispered, "I love you, Bobby."

The next morning, Bobby and Bo arrived early at the office as usual and were immediately summoned to Gen. Jonathan Perry's office. They sat in the outer office speaking to his aide-de-camp, recently promoted to full-bird colonel. Both limped into his office, dressed like two undercover cops, and snapped to attention, saluted, and spoke simultaneously, with Bobby saying, "Sir, Major Samuels reports!" and Bo saying, "Sir, Captain Devore reports!"

He returned their salutes and said, "Sit down, you two. Coffee? I'm having some."

Bobby said, "Thank you, sir. One with cream and one black."

The general was visibly upset, looking like he may have been crying previously, or had a head cold. He ordered the coffee and did not speak.

A minute later, a specialist in white mess duty uniform entered pushing a cart with cups, cream, sugar, and a large coffeepot. He poured coffee for all three and left.

The general said, "There is never any easy way to say this. CSM Boom Kittenger is dead."

Bo gave out a loud whimper and started crying. Bobby instinctively reached out and put his arm around her, and she leaned against his chest and sobbed.

It was all Bobby could do to keep from crying. His jaws tightened together so firmly, he was worried he would crack his teeth.

"What happened, sir?"

"He jumped into Laos with those new experimental stealth wings you two used in Texas and married up with a combined patrol of Laotian Hmong and Vietnamese Montagnards. They went to a large al Qaeda training camp north of there and Boom took some amazing video and did a complete reconnoiter of the facility," the general said.

"We saw satellite images of it in our briefing, sir," Bobby said. "Did he get caught?"

The general said, "That's just it. They got away clean

and did not leave sign, but they were totally surrounded by SRV troops the next morning at daybreak."

"How was Boom killed, General?" Bo asked.

General Perry said, "He called on his sat phone immediately and gave a quick report as the troops closed in. He gave his laptop and other important materiel to the Montagnard leader of the patrol, a guy named Y-Ting, and said for him to get that patrol out of there and call us, while he covered for them. He would not let them argue."

Bobby said, "He fought the SRV troops?"

Perry said, "Not just them. The al Qaeda from the camp joined in. He threw a bunch of smokes and the Yards and Hmong low crawled the hell out of there. They said he fought like a man possessed and was yelling, whooping, and taunting them like crazy."

"Was he shot?" Bo asked.

"He was wounded, multiple times," the general said sadly, "and had his sat phone dialed and at his side. Our analysts say the sounds sounded like they hacked him to death with machetes. Then . . ."

Then the chief of staff of the U.S. Army got choked up and stopped.

"Do you know what he did, Major?"

Bobby was afraid to ask, but he said, "What, sir?"

"They heard him screaming, as those little bastards chopped him up," the general said. "Then he started singing "God Bless America." Can you believe that?"

Bobby said, "Absolutely."

The general paused again and finally added, "Then they found his phone and somebody spoke into it in a thick Mideastern accent and said they had cut off his head and would display it in their compound."

Bobby choked a sob, and Bo started crying again.

The general said, "His body is on its way back here thanks to some very brave, very loyal Royal Thai Army troops. They got the patrol out of there, too, and it is back in Bangkok at our embassy. His funeral will be held in Colorado where he lived."

Bobby said, "He always told me if he ever died, I was to scatter his ashes up in the Sangre de Cristo Mountains near his home. He loved them."

"His sister already called the Pentagon with that request this morning," General Perry said. "Chapter 4/24 of the Special Forces Association headquartered in Colorado Springs is spearheading the funeral planning. Tenth Group at Fort Carson is providing an honor guard of Green Berets and are providing bagpipers and a bugler. I guess Boom had two ex-wives and both wanted his flag, so Tenth Group is bringing extras."

Bobby said, "He even mentioned that to me. He told me if he died and was not married that he wanted his flag to go to his oldest daughter."

"Fine," the general said. "Because I already asked to deliver his eulogy, I will personally present her a flag from here that flew atop the Pentagon."

Bobby clenched his teeth, saying, "General, please, sir, I want to go to Laos."

General Perry said, "You might, Bobby, very soon, and you, too, Bo, but first we will honor this very brave soldier and patriot. He deserves not only the payback we all want but he has earned our deepest respect and honors, too."

"Absolutely, sir," Bo said. "I just can't believe he's gone."

"At least he died a warrior," the general said, "He would have written that script, and in total service to his nation."

Bobby asked, "Sir, when will the service be?"

The general said, "Later in the week, but they haven't set the day yet."

Bobby said, "Sir, if you don't mind, Captain Devore and I might want to go to Las Vegas and then we will go to Colorado from there."

He glanced over at Bo, and she smiled broadly, nodding yes.

The chief of staff asked, "Las Vegas? Why?"

Bobby said, "It is unreal having joy mixed with so much sadness, but I guess it is to be expected during war. I have asked Captain Devore to marry me, sir, and she said she would."

The general broke into a big smile and walked over to Bo and gave her a big hug.

"It's about damned time!" he roared.

He shook hands with Bobby and said, "Well, we have not totally unfolded the mystery of your would-be assassins, but we are positive it is all tied in. You can go but not on commercial air. We will have an air force jet take you to Nellis Air Force Base and MPs will accompany you."

Bo said, "Sir, thank you, and we understand the air force jet, but, General, we are MPs ourselves. We are cops, sir, and we are soldiers. We do not need babysitters, with all due respect, sir. We want a quick wedding and a short honeymoon, but we want to have some time alone, General. You have been in love, sir?"

He grinned, then said, "Bobby, you better not ever try to boss her around. Very well. We'll have a talk and then you two will take off for Nellis. It won't count against your leave time. We'll say it's convalescent leave, which both of you ought to be getting used to by now."

The general called in his aide and told him to get a jet standing by to take them to Las Vegas, and also said he needed his office marked with a sign for a top secret briefing. The efficient colonel jotted notes in his BlackBerry and took off.

Minutes later, his secretary buzzed him, and she told the general that his office was properly marked for a TS briefing.

He said, "All right, you two, you know all the security warnings about a TS briefing, so we will dispense with that."

Bobby said, "Yes, sir," while he poured more coffee for all three of them.

Jonathan Perry said, "The Department of Homeland Security has been spearheading a very secret multiagency investigation of U.S. Senator James Weatherford. We cannot prove it yet, but we think he is behind the attack on you two and the killing of Boom Kittenger."

Bo said, "A U.S. senator?"

"A U.S. senator and about the biggest scoundrel in Washington, D.C.!" General Perry responded.

Bobby said, "Talk about an investigation. I bet everybody involved has had to walk on eggshells."

"My boy," the old man replied, "you have sure hit that nail on the head. One leak, one peep, and every apologist for the senator, every reporter, every person who is honest but has been taken in by his deceit, will swear that we are all stooges of the president cooking this up as a political gimmick, because he is in the opposite party from the president. I don't give a rat's ass what his politics are—he is a traitor, a crook, and an accomplice to murder, and a Benedict Arnold as far as I am concerned."

Bobby whistled.

The general said, "We have surveillance tapes, photos, and video of him meeting on a number of occasions with a deputy minister from Hanoi who is also a major official in the Communist Party named Nguyen Van Tran, and a major al Qaeda cadre member who you have already heard about, Muhammad Yahyaa, who operates out of Koh Samui in southern Thailand and is the al Qaeda leader in charge of all of their Southeast Asian operations.

"Back when President Clinton was in office, prior to him starting to lift some of the trade regulations on the Socialist Republic of Vietnam, Americans and American companies were not allowed to do any trade, bartering, or even negotiations with Hanoi. Senator Weatherford started his secret meetings with Nguyen Van Tran then. The main corporation he owned, Fair Weather Enterprises, Corporation, International, bought out a small company in the Philippines and simply made it an offshore subsidiary. Then, he made several major real estate deals with Hanoi through his brother, who was CEO of FWECI. Because Weatherford was a wealthy senator to begin with, his finances were put into a blind trust."

"And I will bet a thousand to one, sir," Bo interjected, "that his brother was the administrator for his blind trust."

"Exactly, Bo," the senior officer said. "And he still is, so Weatherford's blind trust has made him hundreds of millions since he has been a senator. You look at something like Martha Stewart going to prison for supposedly knowing insider information and manipulating a stock sale. Look what this guy has been doing for years, and do you know what kind of pension and fringes he will get the rest of his life as a U.S. senator? We should have 'sucker' tattooed on our foreheads. As a general officer, I never let anybody know my political affiliation. This has zero to do with that. It has to do with treason, in my opinion."

"I totally agree, sir," Bobby said. "This man has got to be taken down, let alone his commie and al Qaeda buddies. We owe them big-time, General Perry."

"I am going to be very involved with this operation myself, Bobby," Perry added. "I considered Boom not only a great American soldier and patriot but a close friend, as well. He was an original. I want to tell you two a story I haven't told too many people."

He poured another cup of coffee and took a sip, then continued, "I was assigned to Eighteenth Airborne Corps headquarters at Fort Bragg, North Carolina, years ago. It was one of my staff jobs, which I hated but had to do well if I wanted stars. Boom Kittenger at the time was . . . Oh, hell, I'm getting old. He was either a master sergeant or a sergeant major at the time, and I do remember he was assigned to the Seventh Special Forces Group, Charlie Company, in fact."

He saw Bo making faces and said, "You two are wounded warriors. Sit on that couch over there. Do you need to get your legs propped up or anything?"

Bobby said, "Sir, if you don't mind. That would help both of us, to elevate our legs."

Bobby and the general brought two chairs over in front of the couch and Bo put her leg up, sighing. Bobby sat down next to her and moaned as he lifted his up. He also set his fractured arm on a cushion on the arm of the couch.

"Thank you very much, General Perry," Bobby said.

"Yes, sir, this really helps," Bo added.

Perry went on. "Okay, I'll make a long story short. I was a colonel then and left a restaurant one night on Yadkin Road in Fayetteville with my wife. A gang jumped us in the parking lot. I tried to fight them off, but there were too many, and they had a knife and clubs. I got a fractured jaw, broken nose, and ended up having both eyes swell shut the next day. Anyhow, this one tall, kind of slender, good-looking guy saw us when he left the restaurant and walked right up into the middle of the melee."

Bobby said, "Boom Kittenger?"

The general smiled. "Of course. He held his hands up and was chuckling, like he was in the middle of a Saturday night poker party. In a humorous way, he told those sorry buggers that he would give them an opportunity to go home safe and healthy if they left immediately. My wife had made it to the car and locked it like I told her, while I was fighting, but now I was helpless. He stood between them and me. He was a really good black belt, you know?"

Bo said, "Oh yes, sir. We know that."

"Anyway, the idiots laughed at him, and while they laughed, he went on the attack," Perry continued. "He kicked the legs out from the closest guy and the guy broke his elbow on the parking lot blacktop. Then he swung around and the guy with the knife moved toward him, and he had palmed all the change in his pocket and blasted him in the face with a fastball throw that was like a shotgun blast. Then he kicked the guy in the balls so hard the air left him. Sorry, Captain."

With tears in her eyes, Bo raised her hand and smiled. "I am army, sir. No problem."

"Then Boom knocked that guy out with a hook punch I think, it was so damned fast," the general said. "Then he spun several times, throwing kicks and punches and dusted the whole damned gang. Do you know what he did after that? He rode in the ambulance to the hospital with my wife and me, visited me regularly, testified against the gang—they all went to prison, by the way—and later on,

I found out he contacted my sergeant major and asked him if he needed any admin help until I recuperated. That was Boom Kittenger. My wife and I named our youngest son, Brandon, after him. He is now a West Pointer."

General Perry briefed them some more and then summoned his driver, instructing him personally to take them to their places to pack and get their clothes and then drive them to Bolling Air Force Base in Washington, where a military jet would be waiting to take them to Nellis.

Two hours later, they boarded a C21A U.S. Air Force version of a commercial Learjet. The forty-eight-foot-long, eight-passenger jet was powered by two Garrett TFE-731-2-2B turbofan engines and cruised at around 500 miles per hour, which meant they would make Las Vegas in less than five hours.

For most of the trip, Bo rested her head on Bobby's chest and cried, then fell asleep. After she was asleep, he cried, too.

When they arrived, they were greeted by two FBI agents who had a black sedan waiting for them to ride in. They explained that the FBI would be totally out of sight the whole time they were in Las Vegas, but were there just in case they needed the cavalry. Bobby and Bo thanked them.

They were taken immediately to the Rio, where the lead agent explained that a suite was reserved for them and the bill was taken care of as a wedding present by Gen. and Mrs. Jonathan Perry. They checked in and then headed downstairs to catch a cab.

First, Bobby grabbed Bo by the hand and said, "We need to make a side trip, honey."

He led her to a large gift shop near some of the main crap tables and blackjack tables. Inside, there were racks of fancy designer dresses, as well as the items you might expect to see in a convenience store. There were also two glass cases, one featuring expensive men's jewelry and the other women's.

Bobby said, "Pick out an engagement and wedding ring you like."

Bo looked and saw a beautiful set, but it was very expensive with a large, near-perfect diamond in the engagement ring.

Bo said, "Bobby, they are nice but I don't see any I want. The only set that looks attractive is the most expensive jewelry in the case."

Bobby said, "You mean the swirly yellow gold rings and the one that has the big diamond, right there?"

She replied, "Yes, but you are an army major, not a mafia don. It is okay, honey. I don't need a ring, really."

Bobby said, "If you're going to be my wife, you'd better learn now. We are wealthy."

"What?" she exclaimed.

Bobby laughed, saying, "I had a very large inheritance. I am rich, and in about an hour, so will you be."

She laughed and shook her head.

He looked at the clerk and said, "She wants that ring set. How quickly can they be sized?"

The woman unlocked and opened the back of the case and got the rings out, saying, "Quickly, sir, but maybe they will fit. Let's see."

They fit perfectly and, wearing the engagement ring, Bo walked out, admiring it all the way to the casino entrance.

Bo stopped and said, "Wait, honey, I forgot something. It's important. I have to go back to our suite."

Bobby said, "I'll go for you."

"No, you wait here and play the slots," she said. "I'll be right back."

Seven minutes later, Bo tapped Bobby on the shoulder after he had lost twelve dollars.

He looked up at her and smiled. In the crook of her left arm was the blue teddy bear. He stood, moaning, and kissed her on the tip of her nose.

"Of course," he said.

They went out and hailed a taxi.

Bobby and Bo found a hokey marriage chapel, insisting that there would have to be an Elvis impersonator there. They found one in the minister who married them who said he was a pastor of a Southern Baptist church in the Green Valley section of Las Vegas, heading toward Henderson. In true Vegas fashion, the pastor said when people exited his church they could see one of the rock walls around Wayne Newton's estate.

Bo and Bobby had discussed it on the plane, and the wedding had to be a memory and the hokier it was, the more memorable. What was truly important to them was the complete sanctity of their marriage, not the wedding ceremony.

The ceremony, other than the outrageous circumstances, was pretty fast and uneventful, and the ride back to the Rio was spent with both moaning and groaning as they hit bumps in the street or went around curves.

Just beyond the gift shop was a hallway leading to a restaurant. Bobby took Bo there and ordered two coffees to go, and two pieces of pie, coconut cream for him and pecan pie a la mode for her, their favorites. They limped to their suite.

Inside, Bobby filled the large Jacuzzi with water, and soon the newlyweds were in the soothing hot water, finishing up their pies. They got out and after short trips to the two bathrooms, they went to the big bed.

Bobby rolled Bo over on her stomach and gave her a complete body massage for over an hour. She was ecstatic.

Bo asked, "What can I do for you, darling?"

Bobby smiled and softly said, "Just be you."

Their lips came together, slowly, softly, then more passionately. The wounds did not matter when they made love. The pain was not a priority. The new husband and wife finally fell asleep in each other's arms as the sun was coming up in the eastern sky.

Two days later, they flew into Peterson Air Force Base at Colorado Springs and were picked up by two CID agents from Fort Carson. They were immediately transported to Tenth Special Forces Group headquarters.

The group commander, a tall, distinguished-looking colonel, greeted them in his office and told them that the

CID agents had secret clearances, but orders were sent down that they were to be escorted by personnel with top secret clearances only. He said that he had an Operational Detachment-A or A-Team who would be their escorts, drivers, bodyguards, and silent sentries while they were in Colorado. Four of the men on the A-Team had previously served in CAG, better known to civilians as Delta Force. The whole team had taken a defensive-driving, bodyguard-type course in Florida, and the whole team had several tours in Iraq, and half had served in Afghanistan and several in Bosnia, Kosovo, and other hot spots.

Except for Bobby and Bo's chauffeurs, they would for the most part be out of sight. The men all had permission from the group commander to dress like civilians and not shave, if they chose. He would be attending the ceremony. He also said he did not know how they pulled it off being able to continue working together, but he understood congratulations were in order that they were brand-new newlyweds.

Bobby and Bo wore dress blues and everybody at the funeral stared at Bobby's Distinguished Service Cross and Silver Star with Oak Leaf cluster, Bo's Silver Star and Purple Heart, and their Soldier's Medals. Those who were new to Special Forces were immediately told who Bobby was and all knew the nationwide story about Bobby and Bo in the wilderness, and the story about Bobby escaping the al Qaeda in Baghdad before they could cut his head off.

When Boom's ex-wives saw Bobby, they immediately came over and hugged him, and he introduced them to Bo. Then Boom's sister and oldest daughter spotted him at the same time and ran over to him, throwing themselves against his massive chest sobbing. He ignored the pain in his broken forearm as he wrapped his arms protectively around each of them.

When he introduced Bo to Boom's sister, she told Bo that Boom told her that he could tell she and Bobby were in love and would end up getting married, when Bobby finally woke up and "got his head out of his ass."

Bo and Bobby kissed.

The funeral was an incredible testament to Boom Kittenger. The chaplain from the Rocky Mountain chapter of the Special Forces Association, or Chapter 4/24, read a short invocation and the Special Forces prayer. Bobby and Bo were asked to sit with the family. The SFA chapter president, a behemoth of a man, who in his late fifties could still bench-press over 500 pounds, told an anecdote about Boom that touched everyone present.

Taps were played, flags presented, bagpipes played, and Gen. Jonathan Perry gave the most moving, inspirational eulogy Bobby had ever heard. There was hardly a dry eye in the house.

The funeral was held in Canon City, Colorado, about one half hour south of Fort Carson. It was the closest city of any size, albeit small, to Boom's mountain ranch, near Westcliffe. There were so many people, the ceremony was actually held at a large historical landmark in southern Colorado called Holy Cross Abbey. The abbey had been a private Catholic school for boys for decades, but the church shut the school down in the late eighties, and the many buildings on the grounds were rented out for a variety of uses. After the turn of the century, a vineyard and winery was started, attracting more tourists to the area, already a major tourist area in southern Colorado to begin with. The cathedral itself had beautiful architecture and was large enough to hold the thousand-plus people who attended the funeral. The real highlight was when the general completed his eulogy and then read a very moving tribute letter about Boom from the president of the United States. Official copies were presented to each of Boom's five children and his sister.

Bo really let the tears roll when all the Special Forces men in the room, including Bobby, snapped to attention and sang along, as a fantastic singer sang Barry Sadler's "Ballad of the Green Berets."

For the first time, Bo really paid attention to the words, written by Robin Moore, who wrote the number one bestseller of the sixties, *The Green Berets*, which became a John Wayne hit movie.

Bo noticed how straight Boom's oldest son stood when he heard the song and how his chest puffed out and shoulders went back. She wondered if the young man was taking the words to heart. Little did she know, he had already been to the army recruiter at Fort Carson the day before and had dropped out of Colorado State University, with only one year to go. He knew he would pass the physical and mental tests to qualify, and he was going to enter the army as a PFC under their 18Xray program. He would have a guarantee for the SOPC (Special Operations Preparation Course), and after passing that, he would begin the Q-Course hoping to earn his own Green Beret.

Many Special Forces legends were there at the funeral, most coming from Fayetteville, North Carolina. Bo and Bobby stayed at Boom's ranch, and so did their Special Forces escorts, but they were relieved by two FBI agents. What all did not know was how serious Weatherford was now about getting rid of them. Nobody but the few knew the newlywed couple had been in Las Vegas, but through one of his sergeants, Weatherford passed it on to Muhammad and Tran that Bobby and Bo would be at Boom's funeral, along with information on his ranch and a MapQuest map showing how to get there.

The people at the small hotel in Westcliffe were very suspicious about the three Mideastern-looking men with the very thick Arabian accents, as they acted so arrogant and were so out of place in the town on the 7,900-foot-high valley floor of the Wet Mountain Valley. The 14,000-foot, 13,000-foot, and 12,000-foot peaks of the majestic Sangre de Cristo mountain range towered over the town to the west.

Abdul Haq, Abdul Hameed, and Ziyud Yoonus all served under Usama bin Laden and grew up in and around the Hindu Kush mountains in Afghanistan, and especially the area around the Sefid Koh Range. All three started out as drug smugglers through the Khyber Pass and later joined the Taliban, and finally, the al Qaeda. They knew maneuvering and moving through rugged high mountains, much higher than the "fourteeners" in the Sangre de Cristos, so it was with great joy they saw Bobby, Bo, and two undercover FBI agents saddling horses to hopefully head out from the ranch and up toward the big range. The three al Qaeda had been camped out since the day before the funeral on one of the lower ridges at about 10,000 feet and were watching with a powerful spotting scope.

The three were armed with one folding stock AK-47, and two SKS rifles, as well as bladed weapons, night vision devices, and pistols. They also had a number of HE (high explosive) hand grenades. All their ordnance had been smuggled into the United States across the Canadian border.

The three had been working on an attack plan to move down to the ranch house and kill Bobby and Bo there, but they could see with their powerful spotting scope that the four were loading full sleeping bags, bedrolls, and saddle-bags, so they assumed they were heading up into the mountains.

Bobby carefully placed the urn with Boom's ashes in his saddlebag. Boom's sister oddly enough did not want to accompany them into the "high lonesome," as cowboys used to call it, as she was scared to death of riding horses. She loved to pet, feed, water, and watch the horses Boom had at the ranch, but when she was a little girl on her first ride, the horse she was on spotted an open stable door and took off at full gallop. It frightened the wits out of her, and she never rode again.

They headed westward from the ranch house as the towering snowcapped peaks loomed before them. Bobby Samuels treasured his childhood days spent at Boom's ranch, mainly because of the untold wonder and beauty of these mighty mountains that stretched all the way down through New Mexico. Their Spanish name, meaning "blood of Christ" was not so named because they looked ugly at sunset or sunrise. It was because of the crimson hues on the snowcaps. Many considered this the most beautiful mountain range in the world.

Bobby intended to ride up to the timberline to some land-locked lakes he knew to spread the ashes over. Boom loved going up there to catch native cutthroat and rainbow trout out of the pristine glacial lakes.

Bobby held his wife gently under the arms, and she swung her leg over the saddle. He checked his own saddle-bag and immediately pulled out his loaded Glock 17 9 millimeter and belt holster. He climbed aboard, and they turned their horses toward the big range. The pair trotted toward the trees followed by the two agents. An hour and a half later found them in a large bowl right at the timberline. They had seen a red fox on the ride already as well as a flock of wild turkeys and several mule deer.

Bobby asked the FBI agents to wait while he and Bo rode up a ridge overlooking one of the crystal-clear ponds. The wind blew from the ridge toward the pond, and he and Bo prayed together and then tossed the ashes into the air, letting them blow all over the bowl down below. They spent some time up there reflecting on Boom, then saddled up and returned to the two agents. They had built a small fire already and had coffee brewing, having already drunk two cups.

Bobby said, "Guys, my wife and I want to spend a little alone time, if you do not mind. We will be on the other side of the lake in the forest just below the timberline. Do you mind?"

The two looked at each other and at Bo, and smiled at each other.

One said, "Go ahead, Major. Just do not mention this to our boss. We are supposed to shadow you two."

Bobby winked, saying, "We shouldn't be long. A couple hours. I want to show her a special place that Boom took me to up here."

"Take your time and relax," the agent said. "We aren't going anywhere."

Abdul Haq, Abdul Hameed, and Ziyud Yoonus were half jogging, half speed-walking as they followed the tracks of the four shod horses climbing up the rugged mountain trail. The snowcapped peaks, out of sight previously, were now in view through the trees.

Bobby and Bo took off with a steep ridge covered with tall pines to their right and the lake to their left. Bo was amazed looking out at all the little streaks of red or gold or silver, as trout twisted their bodies in the sunlight and could be seen so easily all the way across the lake. She looked around at the snowcapped peaks above her on three sides and the clouds brushing across the tops of some. She was so much in awe of the mountains and the majestic views.

They reached the end of the lake, and Bobby led her into a large grove of aspens, and they rode for ten minutes deeper into the trees.

Finally, she had to ask, "Bobby, where are we going?"

He said, "Right here."

Bobby dismounted and tied his horse's lead line around an aspen tree. He helped her down and tied her horse, too. All she saw was trees in every direction with white bark and long straight trunks. The tiny leaves fluttered above them like nature's whispering wind chimes.

Bobby removed his saddlebags and hers, then removed the bridles from both horses, hanging them on nearby branches. He hoisted the saddlebags over his shoulders, and the curious beauty followed as he headed toward a large group of cabin-sized boulders. Inside the rocks, it seemed a little warmer, with the mountain breeze blocked off. Right in front of them was a small dome-shaped hut. Or, at least, that was how it looked to her. Now her curiosity was really piqued. A few steps beyond was a small pond, crystal clear with a small brook bubbling into it, coming down a low grass-and-flower-covered ridge. Bo could see the bottom and the tiny forms of cutthroat trout swimming in the pure water.

Bobby smiled, saying to his wife, "Take off your clothes," as he pulled off his boots, then unbuckled his belt and unzipped his fly.

She was amazed as she watched him crawl inside the hut, and soon she saw smoke coming from a small hole in the roof. There was a stack of cut firewood piled next to the hut.

"What is going on?" she asked when he emerged from the hut.

Bobby grinned, removing the rest of his clothes.

"Come on," he said, husky-voiced.

She removed her clothes and left them in a neat pile. Bobby went back into the hut and emerged with a small metal bucket. He got water from the pond and led her inside. Bo could not believe the warmth inside. He sat her down in front of a fire ringed with large stones, which he poured water on. Steam filled the little dome, and sweat broke out everywhere on both of them.

Bobby said, "This was built by a friend of Boom's. He is a Jicarilla Apache. It is a sweat lodge."

She said, "An Apache. Does he live in these mountains? Is he . . ."

Bobby laughed. "No, honey, he lives in Marin County, California, in a mansion. He is one of the top web designers in the world and is a multimillionaire. He comes out here for vacation."

"You're kidding," she said. "Why did he build this?"

Bobby said, "For sweats. He is a modern-day success story, but he is also a traditionalist in many of the Apache ways."

She smiled and said, "Roots?"

Bobby Samuels grinned, saying, "That's a good way to put it. You know, many people in southern Colorado write and talk about the Southern Cheyenne, Utes, and Kiowas inhabiting this area, but many people are not aware that the Jicarilla Apache lived in this area, too, as well as in northern New Mexico."

"Wow," she said, leaning back and enjoying her steam bath. "I always pictured them in, you know, treeless mountains and hot desert, like in southern Arizona."

"I know, most people think that way, but the Apache nation itself covered millions of square miles," Bobby added.

"Oh, darling, this is wonderful!" she cooed. "I feel all the stress just draining out of my body."

Bobby grabbed her right foot and took it in both hands,

with the fingertips of both hands on the top of her foot and his thumb on the bottom. He gently but firmly massaged her foot, making tiny circles with his fingers and thumbs. She moaned in sheer pleasure. After fifteen minutes, he switched to the left foot, followed by her calves.

After making love, they emerged from the sweat lodge holding hands and dived into the pool. Bo followed Bobby, but was scared, as it did not seem the pond was deep enough to wade in, much less dive in. To her surprise, it was over six feet deep in most places. Bobby crawled out before her and found a survival blanket in each saddlebag, which he spread out for them to lie on. There was also a small towel, which they both shared.

They napped in the afternoon sun for a few minutes. Bobby awakened feeling refreshed like he had not felt in months, and it helped him with the very sad feelings he was having about Boom's passing.

Bobby had put food and utensils in his saddlebags, so he built a fire next to the pond while Bo slept.

Mrs. Bobby Samuels awakened to the smell of eggs and bacon frying and coffee perking. She sat up and smiled while looking at Bobby's broad back and wide shoulders. She really noticed all his scars and had a chill run down her spine, thinking about him receiving so many. He never looked back at her, but seemed to sense she was there, looking.

"Staring at my flabby old butt, aren't you?" he kidded.

She laughed. "You have to be kidding, Samuels. You have the ass of an Olympic athlete. I love watching."

He turned, grinning, and raised one eyebrow with a sly smile on his face.

"Hungry?"

She hummed, "Ooh, am I? But what about the FBI agents?"

Bobby said, "They told me they would be all right."

The three al Qaeda crept forward through the thick brush surrounding the low end of the lake. The two FBI agents sat by a fire drinking coffee and laughing. On a given

signal from the leader Abdul Haq, all three stood and began firing with their automatic weapons. Although their
bullets were 7.62 millimeter, they were far enough away
that the multiple hits on the Kevlar vests on the two agents
caused severe bruising but kept the bullet from penetrating.

Both men immediately returned fire and ran toward the
water, diving in. They swam as far as they could underwater while bullets tore into the crystal-clear liquid. Both kept
swimming out toward the center of the lake, and surfaced
treading water while the shooting stopped. The three terrorists were on the lakeshore and did not realize that the
water was very deep where the agents were now treading
water. They raised their weapons again and the two did
whale rolls and went straight down. They saw bullets streak
into the water high above, and they grabbed rocks on the
bottom and stayed there, holding their breath as long as
they could.

Both pulled out their own Glocks and nodded at each
other, kicking toward the surface and coming out of the
water firing toward the terrorists. The three jihadists
scrambled for cover, without thinking they probably would
not get hit. This gave the agents time to catch their breath
again.

One whispered to the other, "How the hell do we get out
of this? This water is cold. I don't want to die of hypother-
mia."

The other chuckled, saying, "Yeah, but I'm not fond of
bullets. In fact, I have one in my left calf muscle right now.
How about you? Hit?"

"Yeah, I have a broken rib," the other said. "It hurts like
hell. You know the background on Samuels and his wife.
Maybe he can pull off some Green Beret heroics."

The other said, "I hope so."

A bullet splashed off the water between them and their
eyes opened wide, as they whale rolled again. Bullets tore
into the water above them, and again they grabbed rocks at
the bottom, holding them with the insides of their feet.
Both men felt like their lungs were going to burst, and they

kicked off the bottom, guns in hand. They burst through the surface and aimed, but no terrorists. Bullets hit the water behind them and they dove down again.

This time, they had to get air, so they immediately kicked off the bottom and came out of the surface facing their right rear where the shots had come from.

They burst out of the water firing and the terrorists this time ducked behind shoreline rocks. They were now in front of a steep rock field that went straight up a thousand feet with two large avalanche chutes on it. Numerous boulders had rolled down here and dotted the shoreline. The weary federal officers would fire if any of the three started to rise from behind their rocks. This gave them more time to get their breath back.

One of them looked up and said, "Son of a bitch!"

One of the three men was behind a large boulder barely out in the water from the shoreline. He was also right at the bottom of one of the avalanche chutes.

Both agents looked up as Bobby Samuels, holding the reins to his horse, stood at the top of the ridgeline at the apex of the avalanche chute. Bobby raised a boulder high overhead, tossed it down the chute, and quickly ran toward the next chute. The boulder rolled down gathering more rocks in its path, knocking them loose, and a large slide was starting. In the other chute where there was more shade, there was still a large summer snowfield and Bo now appeared next to Bobby. They both emptied a magazine into the top of the snowpack from their own Glock 17s, and it was enough to wedge loose the avalanche that now started falling toward the second al Qaeda would-be killer.

The three jihadists looked up and the one on the right could not even think to move, as tons and tons of rocks and boulders crushed him several feet into the bed of the lake.

The middle one, Abdul Haq, smartly went out into the water, while Ziyud tried to scream but was choked by the falling snow, rocks, and debris that slammed into him. He had several broken bones, but panicked as the snow packed itself into his ears, nostrils, and mouth and he could not breathe. He felt himself immerse in water and was being crushed from all sides. He now realized he had just been buried under an avalanche and rock slide, and this would be his tomb. He wanted to scream but could not breathe.

He suddenly remembered the U.S. soldier he executed in Afghanistan who looked at him and spat in his face before he shot him and said, "We are going to bury you assholes."

Ziyud suddenly realized that the infidel soldier was correct, and then he died.

Abdul Haq looked up and saw that Bobby and Bo were gone from the ridge, but where were they? He was proud of himself. Once again, he had survived. Then, he heard a chuckle and spun in the water. The two FBI agents, pistols in hand, were swimming toward him.

He turned and splashed and dashed toward shore, trying to get his feet under him. Panicky, Abdul scrambled out of the lake and ran back toward the trail, then realized his AK-47 was behind the rock. He turned and ran back, and saw Bobby galloping through the water at the lake's edge toward him. He turned and ran toward the trail again, pulling out his pistol.

The FBI agents climbed out of the water. Bobby slid his horse to a stop along the shoreline.

"Are you guys okay?"

One said, "I got shot in the calf, and he has a busted rib. We'll take care of ourselves. Go get him."

Bobby turned in the saddle, "Bo!"

She was riding along the shoreline at a trot. Bobby pointed at the two FBI agents.

Bo waved him on. "Got it. Go!"

Abdul had stopped at the trailhead right at the edge of the forest and faced Bobby, who was now coming on at full gallop. Something was wrong. He should be running if all he had was a pistol. Bobby saw Abdul's hands come up and spotted the grenade. He waited for the arm to start forward with the throw and quickly reined the horse to the right and plowed into the thick scrub oak thicket, feeling branches whipping him on both sides. As he figured, the grenade exploded harmlessly to his rear.

Unfortunately, Bo was off her horse applying first aid to the leg of the wounded agent and was not watching. She heard the explosion and her heart leapt into her throat. All she saw was the giant cloud of smoke and dirt and Abdul Haq disappearing into the woods.

Bo ran to her horse and galloped off after Bobby. She did not see a dead horse, or even a live horse, so that gave her hope. She slid to a stop by the crater from the grenade and saw Bobby's horse tracks jumping off to the right and going into the scrub oaks. This relieved her so much, but she was also a cop. She rode into the thicket on Bobby's trail for about twenty feet and saw that he had gotten away clean. Bo turned her horse and went back out to the shoreline and headed at a gallop after the terrorist. She knew Bobby must have gone cross-country on a different route and did not want to ruin his plan. She turned down the trailhead and slowed to a fast walk, seeing the man's tracks running down the trail.

Abdul ran down the trail for one-quarter mile, then when he came to a series of boulders along the trail, he looked for a place to jump off the trail. He found a long log lying parallel to the pathway, and he walked to the end of it and jumped up sideways on the log, and ran back on top of it, jumping off into some mossy undergrowth. He made his way up among the boulders and perched atop one directly over the trail. From here, he could shoot straight down at anyone following.

Bo was coming fast as she saw by his tracks that he was still running. Her horse was trotting down the trail and soon came to the boulders. Bo was indeed a cop and immediately knew this was a potential ambush site. Bobby had warned her before that a simple and common tactic of many soldiers and trained guerilla fighters is to leave a trail on the ground, and at some point, to get off that trail and double back and set up an ambush.

She slowed her horse to a very slow walk and then only one step at a time. Bo held her Glock in her right hand. Abdul lay flat atop the big boulder lest he show a small part of his body to her. He simply listened, as her horse slowly, carefully approached. He held his own pistol in his hand, but was going to wait until she was safely past and then he would shoot her in the back.

Minutes passed, while Bo remembered what Bobby taught her about tracking someone or a predator. She looked at the tracks, but also let her eyes sweep outward in ten-meter arcs moving from side to side. She also looked up into all the trees to her front and sides. Every thirty seconds or minute, she would turn and look at her back trail, as well. Bo was also wondering where Bobby was, but knew he would be around somewhere.

Bo stopped as she looked ahead on the trail and saw the clearly obvious tracks of Abdul running stop at the end of the log running parallel to the trail. She instantly realized he had jumped sideways up onto the log and ran backward and must be up in the boulders on her left. She spun but it was too late. Abdul had been standing on the rock and was bringing the gun up slowly in a two-handed hold. He figured she and Bobby wore Kevlar, so he was going to take a headshot.

Something dropped over his shoulders, and he at first thought a branch had fallen by him, but he looked down at the loop of a lasso, which tightened quickly around his lower legs and jerked them together, and he heard the hooves of a horse taking off up the hill behind him and Bo's laugh. At the same time, he was jerked off his feet, his pistol flying, and he slammed facefirst on the boulder, breaking his nose and pulping his lips. Then he was dragged uphill by Bobby on his powerful quarter horse for twenty yards.

Bobby stopped, wheeled the buckskin, and ran back to the dirty, bloody, disheveled jihadist.

Abdul looked up and one of his eyes was already swelling shut, but he saw the barrel of Bobby's Glock pointed at him. Bobby was smiling behind that weapon. Abdul slowly started to move his hand for his tunic.

He said, "Go ahead, reach inside your clothes for that backup, and I will make you a martyr. Wanna go to paradise today, boy? Do you?"

Abdul, who understood English, stuck both arms straight out to his sides. Bo was right there and patted him down, finding a backup gun and a long knife as well as one other high-explosive grenade.

Bo looked up at Bobby and said, "I was going to say he is clean, but that's not true. He is unarmed."

Bobby got down and pulled a small coil of baling wire and a fencing tool from his saddlebags. Making multiple twisted wraps with the wire, he fashioned a crude but sturdy pair of handcuffs around the killer's wrists behind his back.

He and Bo then lifted Abdul to his feet and moved him to a desk-sized rock and bent him over, and now both searched him much more carefully. They removed all items from his clothing and moved him back down to the trail.

Bo said, "He could have shot me. Why didn't you shoot him?"

"We needed him alive for intel, honey. I was not going to let him get you in his sights," Bobby replied.

With Bo's help, Bobby lifted the defused terrorist up into the saddle of Bo's horse, facing backward. Bobby placed the man's crudely cuffed hands around the saddle horn.

He said, "Don't let go and whatever you do, Usama, or whatever your name is, don't fall off the horse."

Abdul finally spoke, asking, "Why?"

Bobby stuck the noose of the lasso over his head, tightened it around his neck, and walked over and climbed up into his own saddle, still holding the end of the rope.

He wrapped the lariat around his saddle horn, saying, "Because you'll choke."

He held his hand down to his wife, saying, "Come on up, ma'am."

Bo grabbed his hand and put one foot in his stirrup, as he pulled her up behind him, and they walked the horses back up the trail toward the FBI agents.

When they reached the lake, the agents were waiting for them.

One of the agents looked at Abdul and said, "Gitmo, huh?"

Bobby climbed down, saying, "I don't know."

He pulled Abdul out of the saddle, setting him on the ground, and said, "So can you say 'Sodium Pentathol'?"

Abdul kind of snarled because he did not get the joke, but all four cops were laughing.

Bobby said, "You know in all this, we have never even introduced ourselves. I apologize."

The one who now had a good bandage on his lower leg stuck out his hand, saying, "I am sorry. Chuck Baker."

"Bobby Samuels, and my wife, Bo."

They shook and the other offered his hand, saying, "Lee Spaulding."

He winced from the broken rib. Bo offered to bind it, but he refused.

Special Agent Baker said, "We got our cell phones working, and called it in. The cavalry is on its way."

Bobby said, "By the way, we were never out of your sight, when your bosses ask. When the shooting started Bo and I took off to try a flanking movement from the ridge."

Both agents gave each other relieved looks and stuck their hands out again. Bobby and Bo shook with them once more.

It was only minutes later that they heard the *wop-wop* of two Black Hawk helicopters approaching. While Bo moved the horses to the other side of the lake and held them, Bobby helped the FBI agents load Abdul on the helicopter; by now, Bobby had placed a blindfold over his eyes.

The choppers lifted off within minutes, and Bo rode over with Bobby's horse in tow. She then rounded up the agents' horses, which had been grazing in a nearby meadow, and each led a horse.

On the way down, he turned in the saddle, saying, "You know we are going to hit a circus when we get back down to Boom's ranch."

Bo smiled, saying, "Won't be the first time, honey, or the last."

Bobby said, "I just hope they get some good intel out of that jerk."

"How would you like to be the FBI agents that are assigned to go back up on the mountain and dig up the bodies of his two buddies?" Bo said.

Bobby laughed. "Yeah, I'm going to remember them every time I say I am buried in work from now on."

Bo chuckled, and then got serious. "Bobby, I want us to go to Laos."

"I know, honey," he replied. "You know they are going to try to kill us again?"

She grinned at his back, saying, "Yeah, well we'll just have to keep killing them one at a time, if need be. I know one thing about it though."

"Well, Mrs. Samuels, what is that?" Bobby responded.

Teeth clenched, she said, "The bastards better bring reinforcements."

8

JADE SECRETS

It was dark, but the moon was full and its streaking brilliance in the rippling waters of the Potomac made the river's polished surface look like a giant flag waving in the breeze and made of alternating strips of blue cloth and aluminum foil.

Behind the multicolumned Dwight D. Eisenhower Executive Office Building, right next to the White House and providing offices for many of the White House staff, at the end of the parking lot in the trees is the White House South Lawn security office. The White House was well lit and looked magnificent as it loomed to their left front as Bobby and Bo, wearing dress blues, followed General Perry, his aide, and others through the Secret Service security point. Bobby and Bo were pulled out of the line of the others by an agent, and they handed their guns to the agent, who promised they would not be scratched. They showed their badges and army IDs. They both were given badges to wear around their necks and were told to simply rub them across a scanner next to the sidewalk, which they did. They entered the grounds, escorted by the agent as well as General

Perry, his aide, and two new FBI agents who were escorting Bobby and Bo right now.

They walked down the wide driveway between the West Wing of the White House and the Eisenhower Office Building, which Mark Twain once labeled "the ugliest building in America," because of its numerous columns and almost overdone ornate architecture.

Bo felt a shiver as she walked by three black limousines, and the Secret Service agent pointed them out as the vice president's vehicles and pointed up at second-story windows, saying that was the vice president's office.

To their left was a big pair of double doors covering an archway going into the Executive Office (its actual name for many decades, until President Bill Clinton added the Eisenhower moniker to it in 1999).

To their immediate front-left, closer to Pennsylvania Avenue, were dozens of television cameras and video equipment covered with mainly green tarps and all asleep for the night. They turned to the right and went into a side door into the West Wing near the infamous press briefing room.

Another Secret Service agent behind a desk just inside the door politely greeted them and rescanned the badges hanging around their necks. In every hallway was another Secret Service agent and Bo noticed each one taking in Bobby's Distinguished Service Cross, Silver Star with Oak Leaf cluster meaning second award, let alone the Bronze Stars, Purple Hearts, Special Forces crest and metal tab, and so on. Bo was used to men staring at her breast area, as she could have easily modeled for a high-class magazine advertising bras. She did not realize the agents were also checking out her own Silver Star, Purple Heart, Soldiers Medal, and even jump wings.

Minutes later, they were in the Cabinet Room. Bo inquired about the brass-looking little plates on the back of each maroon-colored leather chair, with some having more than others, and the agent explained that each time someone serves in a presidential cabinet, they get the same chair and the little medallion is added to the back of the chair each time they serve. They were all seated in the room along with the secretary of defense and the secretary of homeland security, as well as the national intelligence director, the head of the CIA, and the FBI director and a surprisingly small number of staffers. Soon, the president was brought into the room, and Bobby noticed there was no press and no members of congress.

The president walked around shaking hands and acted like he had written Bobby and Bo's biography.

He nodded at an assistant and a large box was brought into the room gift wrapped with the presidential seal on the wrapping paper and a beautiful red, white, and blue bow. She handed it to Bo and everybody clapped.

Bo's face turned beet red when the president of the United States said, "It is for both of you, Major Samuels, please open it. We're all waiting."

Bo, being careful not to tear the priceless keepsake paper, opened it up and pulled out a beautiful silver bowl. She and Bobby wondered at it, and read together the engraving on the side. It had the presidential seal and was engraved personally to them, wishing them a long, prosperous, and happy marriage and was from the president and First Lady with their names on it.

Bo fought hard to hold back tears and Bobby had a lump in his throat as well. They both thanked the president and asked him to thank the First Lady.

He said, "Did you notice anything you thought was in error when I addressed you?"

Again, her face reddened, and she replied, "Honestly, sir?"

"Of course."

She said, "You addressed me as Major, Mr. President, and that is my husband, sir. An easy mistake to make."

The president stood, saying, "No, it is not. Stand up, you two."

They both jumped to attention. General Perry stood also and walked over to the president, carrying four shoulder boards for dress blues. One set had silver oak leaves and the other had gold oak leaves.

He handed them to the commander in chief, who handed one of each back to him, saying, "General Perry, these two have been your pet project from the get-go. You do the left shoulder on each, and I'll do the right. Major Bobby Samuels, effective today, you are promoted to the rank of lieutenant colonel of the United States Army. And Captain Bo Samuels, effective today, you are promoted to the rank of major in the United States Army. Congratulations."

Everybody stood and applauded and then they applauded more as Jonathan Perry presented two Legion of Merit medals, and they pinned those on.

The president said, "General, speaking of the army keeping it simple."

People chuckled.

Perry said, "Did you notice that your shoulder board background colors were green?"

Bobby said, "Yes, sir. I was wondering if I am going back to SF?"

General Perry said, "Yes, you are."

He looked at a piece of paper and said, "You two have no idea how much brainstorming was done here. You have your own little office of the army. First of all, the Married Army Couples Program was started in 1983 to try to keep married army couples from being separated by duty assignment, so I would venture to say you two will be working together the rest of your careers. We have also created a new MOS code for you two. You are 31/18AlphaSierras. What that means is you are military police slash Special Forces officers and Special Operations Support. Your 201 file will be changed to reflect that. You are no longer under the Provost Marshal's office, but are under the command of U.S. Special Operations Command out of MacDill Air Force Base in Tampa, Florida, but are working TDY attached to the staff of the U.S. Army chief of staff, that being me. Now, Major Samuels, Bo, you are now, because of

OJT classified as Special Forces qualified, however it does not mean that you are qualified to wear a Green Beret."

Bo said, "Sir, I am perfectly fine with that. I do not believe women should earn Green Berets. Some are capable, but I do not believe we should. That should remain male, and I am happy with my husband being qualified, sir. I cannot thank you enough, and you, Mr. President. I am in shock."

Bobby added, "Me, too, Mr. President, General Perry. I am deeply humbled and deeply honored, gentlemen. Thank you."

The president said, "Well, now that we have the pleasant part of this meeting out of the way, let's get to the very unpleasant part."

That got everybody's attention while he sat down.

He said, "Ladies and gentlemen, Colonel and Major Samuels most definitely proved themselves when Bobby Samuels was made head of our joint task force on those al Qaeda pukes smuggling nuclear devices into the United States across our southern border. Now Bobby is being put in charge of a new joint task force with his wife second in command. We have a traitor in our midst."

Everybody in the room looked around, and the president chuckled. "Sorry, I did not mean here. I meant in our U.S. Senate. This is very sensitive and cannot be whispered outside this room with anybody. Do not, and I mean do not decide on your own that your assistant, deputy, secretary, wife, or mistress has a need to know about this. All of you in this room are the only ones with a need to know for now, period. Are we all clear on that?"

Everybody said, "Yes, sir," or, "Yes, Mr. President."

Bobby and Bo were in even more of a state of shock.

The president went on, "We have proof positive, lots of it, that Senator James Weatherford of a state that was one of our original colonies, no less, is in collusion and has been meeting in secrecy with a high official of the al Qaeda terrorist organization as well as a high official of the Communist Party and a deputy prime minister of the Socialist Republic of Vietnam."

There was a lot of murmuring and head shaking in the Cabinet Room.

The vice president smacked his hand down hard on the table, and everybody stared. His face was red.

"I apologize, Mr. President," the VP said. "That son of a bitch came to my only daughter's wedding, and even danced with my daughter."

The president smiled softly. "It is much worse. He betrayed his fellow countrymen, not just you. We cannot prove it yet, but we are positive he was behind the killing of CIA Agent Boom Kittenger, which you all know about, and we are positive he is directly tied into the attempted assassination of Colonel and Major Samuels. Everybody take five and we will talk some more."

He stood and everybody jumped. The president shook a couple of hands on his way out of the room, careful to clasp each person's shoulder as he did, and smiled while listening to them. He then quickly went through the door into the Oval Office and dashed into his bathroom. He had a horrible case of diarrhea with cramping all through the first part of the meeting. Sitting on his commode, he looked at a beige towel on a rack in front of him with the presidential seal, and he chuckled, saying out loud, "They never realize the president gets the runs, too. Glad my opponents can't see me now. Ooh! Ow!"

Eight minutes later, the meeting began again.

The president said, "I appreciate you all leaving your families to join me for this important meeting tonight." He glanced at Bo and Bobby and added, "Or in one case, bringing your family here with you."

Everybody chuckled, and he went on, "We know that Senator Weatherford has considerable financial interests in the SRV and offshore as well. We also know there is some kind of al Qaeda plot to attack our west coast, a big attack. It is the job of this task force to find out what the plot is and stop it and to start dismantling the growing al Qaeda threat."

Bobby raised his hand, and the president smiled at him. "Yes, Colonel."

Bobby thought that sure sounded good.

He said, "Mr. President, what about Senator Weatherford?"

The president got a cold, steely look in his eyes and said, "That son of a bitch is mine. I have been playing this politics game for some time, and I personally will see to it that he is most definitely paid back for his contributions to this great nation."

He seemed to fume for a minute and then added, "Rest assured, ladies and gentlemen, that James Weatherford is going to rue the day that he betrayed the citizenry of the United States. Such an unscrupulous action shall not go unpunished." Borrowing from the Bible, the chief executive went on, "He will learn he would have been better off to tie a millstone around his neck and toss himself into a lake, when I get done with him. You all have my word on that."

To everybody's surprise, he stood suddenly and said, "Let's take another break. I have to deal with a world leader and we have some great coffee and pastries for everybody. Meet me back here in five minutes or so."

The president was always very prompt, so saying "five minutes or so" surprised everybody.

He went into the Oval Office restroom, quickly pulled down his pants, and said out loud, "Mr. President of Iran. I have a present for you from all the grateful citizens of the United States of America."

His diarrhea hit again full force. Afterward, he walked over to his desk and buzzed his personal secretary. Seconds later, she walked in the door carrying antidiarrhea medicine and immediately gave him the maximum dose.

The president said, "How in the world did you know I needed this? No wonder you are the president's secretary!"

She walked to a cabinet in the corner and produced a bottle of spring water, handing it to the commander in chief.

She said, "Mr. President, all I had to do was come in here after your last break. Now, sir, diarrhea dehydrates you, so you drink this bottle of water, and I will bring you more, as you need it."

Everybody in the room wondered if there might be a world crisis when it took a full ten minutes before the president returned. Two of the president's cabinet members, in fact, discussed it and started speculating on what might be happening and who he might be speaking to.

They finished the meeting after another half hour, and then the president had the White House official photographer come in to take posed photos of Bobby and Bo getting their promotions, silver bowl, and Legions of Merit.

When they left, they went out between the two buildings and back to the parking lot.

General Perry said, "You two must be hungry," and looking at the FBI agents escorting them, he added, "and you two have to be hungry, too. Come on. Let's go to Old Ebbitt Grill and get some oysters. Dinner is on me tonight. I know my amigos here are starved." He looked at his aide and entourage.

At the restaurant, they discussed what they could safely, making more plans.

Bobby said, "Will we have new offices, sir?"

"Yes," the old man replied, "a few doors down the hall from mine."

The next morning, Bobby and Bo were shown their new office and introduced to the new staff they had, two E5s and a staff sergeant E6. Bobby and Bo had their own little conference room, which had extensive communications gear set up in it. They could frequently hold meetings with other members of the task force, and the J-2 (intelligence) section had it swept for bugs (electronic) daily.

They were summoned to the chief of staff's office, and the general asked what their immediate plans were.

Afterward, the general's aide told them he heard General Perry bellow, "You want to do what?" all the way in the outer office.

It was a dark, dark night in Laos, and the B-1B stealth bomber, as expected, had soared over the countryside undetected. The bomb-bay doors opened and the stealth slowed to as close to stall speed as possible, and six black figures dropped below the craft in full flail for a few seconds, as they plummeted head down at 180 miles per hour. The six, breathing oxygen, were wearing high-altitude suits to prevent them from freezing to death.

Military skydiving or HALO (high altitude, low opening) rigs are known as HAPPS (high altitude precision parachute system), or "stealth parachutes" because they cannot easily be seen from the ground. All the handles are in the same places as you would find on sports skydiving rigs, but there are a number of attachment points for additional equipment and a harness for the O_2 equipment. The typical canopy size is 360 square feet on both the main and reserve. These six were also equipped with SSE, Inc Altimaster II and each included a nightlight (powered with two AA cells).

The space-age suits they wore were also scuba "dry suits," and they had fins strapped to their thighs and masks attached to spec ops rebreather apparatuses, which would extract the oxygen from blown breaths and incorporate a gill-like system that would take oxygen from the water passing through and convert it into breathable air. In this regard, they would be able to breathe underwater without wearing cumbersome aqua-type lungs.

The two leaders of the handpicked group, Lt. Col. Bobby Samuels and his beautiful wife, Bo Devore, were now stabilizing in a crab position and the others soon stabilized as well, slowing their descent to 120 miles per hour. The other four were volunteers who had served with or were trained in engineer demolitions by Command Sgt. Maj. Boom Kittenger. Bobby had called CAG (Combat Applications Group) headquarters at Fort Bragg, North Carolina, to seek the four volunteers to accompany him and Bo to destroy the al Qaeda training camp in Laos, and its inhabitants, where Boom lost his life. CAG was the correct military term for the unit better known by most everybody as Delta Force. The military description generally used to best describe the unit was First Special Forces Operational Detachment-Delta (SFOD-D) Combat Applications Group (CAG), Delta Force.

The U.S. Army's First Special Forces Operational Detachment-Delta is one of two of the U.S. government's principle units tasked with counterterrorist operations outside the United States (the other being Naval Special Warfare Development Group). Delta Force was created by U.S. Army Col. Charles Beckwith in 1977 in direct response to numerous, well-publicized terrorist incidents that occurred in the 1970s. From its beginnings, Delta was heavily influenced by the British SAS, a philosophical result of Colonel Beckwith's yearlong (1962–1963) exchange tour with that unit. Accordingly, it is today organized into three operating squadrons, all of which (A, B, and C) are subdivided into small groups known as troops. It is rumored that each troop, as the case with the SAS, specializes in HALO, scuba, or other skill groups. These troops can each be further divided into smaller units as needed to fit mission requirements. Delta also maintains support units that handle selection and training, logistics, finance, and the unit's medical requirements. Within this grouping is a little-known but vital technical unit that is responsible for covert eavesdropping equipment for use in hostage rescues and similar situations.

The unit is headquartered in a remote section of the U.S. Army's sprawling Fort Bragg, North Carolina. As units such as Delta do not get to choose when and where they will be needed, they must train for any eventuality. These skills are enhanced by the unit's participation in an ongoing exchange and training program with foreign counterterrorist units, such as Britain's 22 SAS, France's GIGN, Germany's GSG-9, Israel's Sayeret Matkal/Unit 269, and Australia's own Special Air Service Regiment. Such close cooperation with other groups provides innumerable benefits, including exchanges of new tactics and equipment as well as enhancing relations that might prove useful in later real-world operations.

Delta troopers are also equipped with the most advanced

weaponry and equipment available in the U.S. special operations arsenal. A significant portion of their gear is highly customized and cannot be found anywhere but in Delta's lockers. An early example of this was a specially constructed HAHO parachute rig that was adapted to permit jumpers to keep their hands at their sides during the descent rather than above their heads. This alteration prevents the loss of functioning that can occur as a result of prolonged flight time in such an unnatural position.

The vast majority of the unit operatives come from the United States' elite Ranger battalions and Special Forces groups; however, candidates are drawn from all branches of the army, including the Army Reserve and National Guard. Real-world examples of some missions with which Delta is tasked are represented below:

1979—Worked with the FBI at the Pan American Games in Puerto Rico as part of an antiterrorist team set up to anticipate possible terrorist activity at the event.

1983—Participated in Operation Urgent Fury in Grenada, including the air assault of Richmond Hill prison to free as well as assist in the seizure of a key airfield.

1984—Deployed to the Middle East in response to the hijacking of a Kuwaiti Airlines airliner, during which two Americans were killed.

1985—Again deployed in response to a hijacking, this time to Cyprus in anticipation of an assault on a seized TWA airliner.

1987—Sent to Greece to secure U.S. Army Col. James "Nick" Rowe in response to reports that Vietnamese communist agents were planning an action against him.

1989—Successfully rescued an imprisoned U.S. citizen during the opening minutes of Operation Just Cause in Panama and participated in the widespread search for Gen. Manuel Noriega and his advisors.

1991—Deployed to the Gulf in 1991, both to serve as bodyguards for senior U.S. officers and, later, as part of a massive effort to locate and destroy mobile SCUD launchers in Iraq's northern deserts.

1993—As part of Task Force Ranger, took part in numerous operations to apprehend warlord Mohamed Farrah Aidid in Mogadishu, Somalia.

1997—Small advance team sent to Lima, Peru, immediately following the takeover of the Japanese Ambassador's residence in January along with six members of the British SAS.

In Afghanistan and Iraq, some of the missions carried out by SFOD-D were some of the very most important of the global War on Terrorism.

The six, wearing night vision devices, were dropping through the night skies over Laos with a muddy drop zone below called the Mekong River. The waterway, which started miles north of there, ran all the way down into the delta region of Vietnam where its thousands of tributaries spread out like the roots of a grapevine gone wild, slicing and dicing wet furrows through the flatlands there, turning it into a giant brown sponge.

This type of parachuting technique, HALO, can be very dangerous. At higher altitudes, above 22,000 feet, the oxygen required for human respiration become thin, and a definite lack of oxygen at high altitudes can cause hypoxia, also called anoxia.

The six jumpers, before the stealth arrived, performed a pre-breathing period forty-five minutes prior to jump, where they each breathed 100 percent oxygen in order to flush all the nitrogen from their bloodstream. During the jump they all breathed from an O_2 bottle. One of the real dangers in HALO comes from medical circumstances affecting the jumper. For example, cigarette smoking, alcohol or drug use, anemia, carbon monoxide, or even fatigue might all lead to a HALO jumper being more susceptible to hypoxia. In addition, problems with the oxygen bottle and during the changeover from the pre-breather to the oxygen bottle can result in the return of nitrogen to the parachuter's bloodstream and, therefore, an increased likelihood of being affected by hypoxia. Even one breath of regular air will bring the jumper's blood nitrogen levels close to normal. The real danger is that a HALO jumper with hypoxia may lose consciousness and therefore be unable to open their parachute.

Another risk is from the low ambient temperatures prevalent at higher altitudes. The jumper can face subzero temperatures and can also experience frostbite. However, these six HALO jumpers were wearing scuba dry suits, and underneath they each wore polypropylene knit undergarments and other warm clothing to prevent this. Their dry suits were worth a lot of money in themselves, in that they are made to keep a diver dry in water temperatures between twenty-eight to sixty degrees, but were even warmer with them also wearing the polypropylene suits underneath. The ones they wore were a high-end neoprene hybrid and featured a telescoping torso with crotch strap and suspenders, warm neck collar, rock boot system and Kevlar kneepads, elbow pads, and butt pads, swivel inlet and adjustable, automatic exhaust valves, latex neck and wrist seals, and a number of utility pockets.

Once all six hit terminal in crab positions or a belly-down fall, they fell for well over three minutes before opening their chutes. The parachutes they used would sink after they hit the deep, wide river and the six would switch to their regulators and rebreathers, putting their fins on underwater. Their waterproof packs would hang below them on fifteen-foot tethers and hit the water first. The six would wait until they were close to the water and would then reach up across their chest with one hand, grabbing the riser on one side, then with the other hand, they would pull the safety clamp and turn the quick release. Shortly before hitting the water, they would smack the quick-release plate with the heel of their hand and grab the other riser while the harness would break free. Just before entry, they would then raise their arms over their heads and would slide into the water.

They all prepared for entry, and Bobby's IR LED indicator in front of him did not indicate any people along the river bank on either side, so they should be entering without detection, he hoped. They went into the water, quickly got away from their parachutes, and put their fins and rebreathers on. They swam downriver for two and a half miles and went out of the river on the eastern bank. Here, they switched to their tactical boots and shed the neoprene dry suits. They took the dry suits, fins, rebreathers, and placed them all together in nylon mesh bags and put several rocks in each bag, then tossed them far out into the river.

After getting their gear together, checking weapons and ammunition, the sergeant in charge looked up their location on his computer screen, and they headed off south paralleling the river. A UAV (unmanned aerial vehicle) high overhead flew and scouted their route for them with FLIR (forward-looking infrared), so they were able to move fast and cover a good distance. The UAV was being controlled by someone halfway around the world in Virginia sitting at a computer screen.

After forty minutes, they sat down in a circle for a rest break. The one common thread running through this six-person group was that each had experiences with Boom Kittenger and all loved the man.

M. Sgt. Dave Collingsworth took demolition classes from Boom and worked out with him in Tae Kwon Do after classes several times. He talked about how funny Boom could be, but how he also always had words to grow on.

He mentioned how much Boom loved Colorado and its mountains and wondered if anybody ever heard Boom's story about so many Californians and Texans moving to Colorado, and nobody had so he told it.

In fact, Dave loved to tell the story himself now.

He said, "There was in Colorado a rowdy drinking establishment and a man in a white Stetson was drinking a long-necked Lone Star beer. When he was halfway done, he suddenly tossed the beer up into the air, drew a walnut-handled Colt .45 Peacemaker, and fired, shattering the bottle and covering the screaming crowd with pieces of bottle and amber liquid.

"Laughing, the Texan declared, 'I'm from Dallas! And that's how we drink in Texas!'

"Miffed and his ego slightly bruised, a gentleman from Marin County, California, finished a half a stem of Silver Oak Cellars' Cabernet Sauvignon and tossed the crystal goblet into the air, pulling a nickel-plated .380 from his pocket, and firing a couple rounds, he nicked the stem and angered the crowd with another shower of sticky liquid.

"'Ya know, Buffy and I are from California," he declared, "upper Marin County actually, and in California, we enjoy fine liqueurs and drink in this manner.'

"There was a man there from Boulder, Colorado, who witnessed the two incidents, so he chained and padlocked his mountain bike to a beam in the corner, tightened his ponytail, adjusted his Birkenstockings. Then he drank half his Mad Dog beer, tossed the bottle high into the air, and drew from a hidden shoulder holster a Glock model 19 9 millimeter. He took careful aim and shot both the Texan and the Californian between the eyes, then expertly caught the falling bottle of beer.

"He then loudly stated, 'You know in Colorado, we have way too many Texans, and now we are being overrun by Californians.' Then, holding up the bottle, he continued, 'But in Colorado, we always recycle.'"

Everybody laughed in a whisper, but very heartily.

Bobby said, "Well, that is definitely a Boom Kittenger story, and a great one. I appreciate you men volunteering for this and risking your lives, but my wife tells me she will walk all of you into the ground tonight, because you are SF-wannabe sissy boys. We better get going."

Bo slapped his arm laughing and the others chuckled softly in the darkness. They moved on through the light jungle, keeping to clearings and mainly a large pathway that skirted the river.

After another hour, they stopped again, drank water, and removed leeches, which seemed to be everywhere. It started pouring rain.

A very large, tall black sergeant first class named Moses Trudy, but called Big Mose by everyone, said, "I have another Boom story."

Bobby said, "We have time and nobody is damned sure going to hear us in this rain."

Big Mose said, "I about died when I heard it from Boom at the NCO club one time, but, Major, the language is salty."

Bo said, "Thank you, Sergeant, but I am an army officer. You are not going to bother me with any language, and I will not be offended, but I appreciate you asking. Please?"

"All right, ma'am," the sergeant said, "but I am going to clean it up a bit."

He continued, "This man in a suit stood against this building in a busy downtown, and he would watch all the beautiful secretaries and businesswomen going by him in their minidresses and such, and as soon as they would walk by, he would say, 'I'd like to tickle your ass with a feather,' and when the woman would stop and say, 'What did you say to me?' he would say, 'I said it is particularly nice weather.'"

Big Mose took a bite of an energy bar and chewed it up while everybody waited to hear the rest.

Dave said, "Hey, Big Mose, don't eat again until you're done. Man."

Big Mose laughed and said, "Okay, sorry, you guys, ma'am, so anyhow, this guy staggers up who is really drunk and watches for a few minutes. Then he staggers over to this guy and says, 'Shay, man, I was jist watchinyu, and hic, that was beeyootiful. What d'jew say again to the women?'

"The man said, 'I simply wait until a nice-looking woman in a short skirt walks by, and I say, I'd like to tickles your ass with a feather, and when she turns and asks me what I said, I say, it is particularly nice weather, and smile at her.'

"On the second try the drunk clapped his hands and said, 'Man, that ish awshome, dude, jish aweshome. I'm gonna go do it myshelf.' So the drunk staggered across the street and leaned against the building."

"In a few minutes, this gorgeous woman walks by in a cute little miniskirt, and when she gets right next to him, the drunk blurts out, 'I wanna shove a feather up yer ass.'

"Shocked and angry, the woman turned around and said, 'What did you just say to me, mister?'

"The drunk laughed and clapped his hands, saying, 'Pretty frigging cold, ain't it?' "

Everybody in the patrol, despite the exhaustion and drenching rain, laughed their heads off for several minutes.

Every time they stopped, after that, several Boom stories or anecdotes would be told. Several men were glad that it was raining on them, so the tears would not be noticed, as each thought about the beloved Special Forces legend.

It was close to dawn when they arrived one kilometer outside the guerilla base camp of Y-Ting Tran and his men. They waited there and Bobby called Y-Ting on a sat phone. Within twenty minutes, they saw the man and two other Montagnard followers approaching.

They quickly introduced themselves and led the patrol back to their hidden guerilla base camp. The Americans were all surprised when they were led to a stilted longhouse with a matted rattan floor and a thatched roof that kept the whole place dry. Exhausted, they both fell fast asleep.

Bobby and Bo awakened simultaneously in the corner of the longhouse. Y-Ting squatted in front of them in the fashion of both Montagnards and Vietnamese, with the knees deeply bent, buttocks resting on the back of the legs. He was smiling.

"I am Y-Ting," he said, extending his hand.

In the manner Boom and his father taught him, Bobby grabbed his right forearm with his left hand and shook hands with his right.

"I am Lieutenant Colonel Bobby Samuels and this is my wife, Major Bo Samuels," Bobby said.

Y-Ting said, "Vietnamese call you Trung-Ta Samuels and call her Thieu-Ta Samuels, but we call you Chung-Ta and call her Thieu-Ta. Boom speak of you many, many times. He sound like a father."

Bobby got choked up.

Then Y-Ting looked at Bo and said, "Boom speak of you. He say you are a mighty, mighty warrior woman, but very, very beautiful."

Now it was Bo's turn to get choked up.

The four Delta Force sergeants, all wearing long hair and two with beards, were now sitting up from their sleeping places.

Big Mose said, "This is nothing like Afghanistan, Iraq, or Pakistan. Man, what sauna did we wake up in?"

Y-Ting looked at him with his eyes opened wide and said something in Rade to his compatriots outside the stilted longhouse, and they murmured excitedly among themselves. They had a fire going and were cooking food. Bobby reached into his pack and pulled out several MREs and tossed them to the Montagnard and Hmong warriors. The men got excited and tore the packs open and immediately started heating water to pour into the plastic bags of dehydrated foods.

Y-Ting said to Big Mose, "You are a very big man, like the elephant."

Moses stuck his hand out and said, "Nice to meet you. Call me Big Mose. This guy you can call Dave, and Trinity, and Speedy."

The other three sergeants shook hands with Y-Ting.

Y-Ting said, "You have long hair, are you men in army or out of army like Boom?"

Bobby interrupted and winked at Y-Ting. "They are tourists from a foreign country. Nothing we carry says Made in USA, even those MREs." He handed Y-Ting an MRE.

Y-Ting laughed, saying, "Oh, all of you must be in

Delta Force. Very best warriors in world. Good. We kill many bad guys."

The four looked at Bobby and each other then started chuckling.

Bo stared at the jungle-covered mountains in the near distance and felt the stifling heat, as if their longhouse was suspended over a giant boiling pot of water. She slapped a large mosquito and thought back to the incredible scenic drive she and Bobby made to Westcliffe from Boom's ranch and then to Canon City for dinner. She saw on that one-hour drive mule deer, elk, some buffalo on a ranch near Westcliffe, herds of pronghorn antelope, two coyotes, a bald eagle, and the most scenic vistas in the world. Drenched with sweat, she fantasized about living there and visualized that drive.

The towering peaks of the Sangre de Cristos were like a giant wall on their immediate right with giant caps of pure white, vicious winds blowing clouds of snow here and there on the tops and swirling the white powder into various curls that looked beautiful and harmless from thousands of feet below. The dark green carpeting of evergreens and hardwoods, which covered the mountains like a giant afghan, went all the way up to the timberline, somewhere around 11,000 or 12,000 feet high. Many of the peaks were over 14,000 feet in elevation and most all were at least 12,000 feet up into the clear blue sky. The Wet Mountain Valley floor went from the right side of Highway 69 and spread out for a mile or two to the base of each mountain, like a carpeted inclined walkway ramp to the big range.

Numerous thickets of scrub oak near the base of each, from the distance, looked like small groups of low bushes. In fact, some hid herds of mule deer or harems of elk bedded down for the afternoon. Distance was so deceiving in the wide-open spaces.

They arrived in Westcliffe and Bobby asked Bo if she was hungry. She said she was, and he headed east to Silver Cliff. Which meant an additional minute of driving. Then he turned left on Oak Creek Grade, an old stagecoach road that wound its way through San Isabel National Forest to Canon City a half hour distant and almost 3,000 feet lower. Bo thoroughly enjoyed the scenic drive on the hard-packed dirt road, which wound its way between towering rock walls and evergreen-covered ridges. This was after passing through several miles of mountain homes, which housed everyone from retired professionals with a desire to get away from it all, lawyers, laborers, illegal woodcutters hiding out from child-support enforcement warrants, to wannabe modern-day mountain men and women. Such little communities dotted the mountain ranges all over Colorado and each had similar personality traits, which almost always included such diverse attitudes as a mini–Peyton Place mind-set to one of nobody ever passing someone whose car was broken down on the road. A car breakdown on the way to town and an unexpected mountain storm could mean death, so most people living in such communities are totally different than those in cities and towns all over the rest of America who avoid ever stopping for fear of a mugging or carjacking. Bo was also amazed at the fact that virtually everyone, except obvious tourists approaching from the other direction on that mountain road, waved at you.

Then Bo thought about Boom's self-sufficiency. He did not have to depend on the government or anybody to take care of him. Then she thought about the similar self-sufficiency of so many who were Special Forces like her husband, and the intelligence of Boom and these four men he trained or worked with. Still daydreaming, she remembered the amazing experience she had the morning of that day Bobby took her on that drive.

She was so impressed with the beauty of Boom's ranch, but was also a little intimidated by the enormity of the looming snowcapped peaks, it almost frightened, yet fascinated her.

She said to Boom, "What if there is one of those mountain

blizzards I heard about and power lines go down here. Wouldn't you be stuck?"

Boom chuckled and pointed down his mile-long driveway, saying, "Do you see any power lines?"

"No," she said, "I don't."

Bobby held the back door for Bo, saying, "Come on, baby sister, I want to show you something out back."

She spoke with Boom as they walked to a small building behind and attached to the main house. They walked into the building and Bo was amazed. It looked to her like they were in the engineering room of the starship *Enterprise*. Attached to the outside of the building was a large propane tank with copper tubing running into the outside building.

"What is this?" Bo asked, looking about the room full of modern-looking contraptions.

Boom said, "See the copper tubing coming through the wall."

She nodded.

He went on, "It goes into this fuel cell, which in turn is connected electrically to that geo-exchange pump over there. Now, it automatically converts the central air-conditioning unit there into a furnace system in the winter, and there is a photon cell, which you saw earlier, up on the roof that is also incorporated into the system. Now, see that computer-looking device over there?"

She said, "Yes, what is it?"

He replied, "A computer device."

She chuckled, and he continued, "My computer is tied into this whole system through there, and it automatically turns my appliances on energy-saving mode whenever they are not in use."

She pointed at the floor and asked, "What is that?"

There was a latched, locked trap door on the clean tiled floor, and Boom opened it to reveal a very clean-looking large tank of pure water. A large pipe came out of the floor and through an electrical pump and was connected to a large fiberglass-looking tank with another pipe running out of that, with two plastic bottles that looked to Bo like blender canisters, and then the pipe ran into the house.

Boom said, "You know how you go into the store to buy a bottle of Rocky Mountain clear, pure spring water?"

She said, "Yep."

He said, "That's what you've been drinking. I have a large spring up above and behind the house a few hundred yards. Remember where you commented on all the flowers and greenery?"

She nodded.

He went on, "I have a collection tank buried underground there, with pipes that carry the water to this cistern. There is an aerator in the cistern that keeps it bubbling and full of oxygen, and prevents it from becoming stagnant. Then it is pumped out of the cistern and into that pressure tank, then when you get a drink of water or take a shower in the house, the water goes from there, through those two canisters, which are filters, and then into the house, and you end up drinking about the purest water in the world."

"Wow!" she said. "Fascinating!"

"That's not all," he went on, excited. "There is an overflow pipe outside that runs underground from the top of the cistern and it carries excess water to our gardens, lawn, and watering troughs. Even the watering troughs overflow all the time."

She said, "I noticed that. It seems so muddy around them."

"We do that on purpose," Boom explained. "When the horses water, they stand in the mud and moisture, which helps keep their hooves from getting dried out and unhealthy."

Bo came out of her daydream and said, "Bobby, when we retire I want a ranch like Boom's."

Bobby looked at her and suddenly started laughing, saying, "Where did that come from?"

She said, "My heart."

Bobby said, "Then that is where we will make our home, honey."

They took care of their morning needs, although it was now early afternoon.

Y-Ting explained, "In Vietnam and here, nobody moves when sun is on top of the sky. Too hot. Most sleep. Besides you say to me on phone, we work tonight."

Now Y-Ting stopped smiling, saying, "You know Boom was our friend, too. We all love him very much. We want to pay back the Cong-An and the al Qaeda for what they do to Boom. It is bullshit."

"I know," Bobby said. "We will. I promise you."

The rest of the day was spent in preparations for the evening patrol. They took off at 1600 hours, or 4 p.m., headed toward the objective, which was the al Qaeda training compound. After the killing of Boom Kittenger, because of the shallow thinking of the SRV, the compound was simply moved to the other side of the mountain ridge next to it. The spy in the sky flying high overhead recorded every bit of the movement, and Y-Ting had men watching from distant ridgelines as well.

Back in Washington, D.C., in the meantime, the president called in some senators and representatives for a top secret meeting while Bobby, Bo, and the SFOD-Delta personnel were on board the stealth jet. He made sure that Sen. James Weatherford was invited.

After those present were advised that the briefing was classified top secret and was only to be discussed on a need-to-know basis, would be automatically downgraded at three-year intervals, and automatically declassified at the end of twelve years unless otherwise specified, and all the other warnings, each present was given a classified briefing folder.

The president had discussed it with his advisors and a few who were present for the evening closed meeting in the Cabinet Room, and they had concluded that they would tell all these congressmen a complete fabrication for the sake of protecting, Bobby, Bo, and the others; later he would explain all to them and include all of them in credit for busting the traitor Weatherford.

The secretary of defense spoke briefly, then the director

of national intelligence, and finally the briefing was turned over to Gen. Jonathan Perry.

He said, "Ladies and gentlemen, this briefing is of the highest sensitive nature and what is told here must not leave this room, not to aides, assistants, nobody. The commander in chief insisted that each of you, because of bipartisan involvement in various crucial congressional committees, such as the House and Senate Intelligence Committees, appropriations committees, and so on, be totally informed of this operation from the outset. We have received a number of substantial humintel report of recent sightings of the top al Qaeda leadership, several key figures operating out of safe houses in two different towns not far from the Khyber Pass in Pakistan.

"You are all familiar with the tremendous success at preventing another 9/11 by special ops CID agents Major Bobby Samuels and Captain Bo Devore, when they spearheaded a multioffice task force that interdicted and prevented the detonation of two Soviet backpack nuclear devices that were to be detonated simultaneously in New York City and Miami, Florida. Well, I am pleased to announce that both have been promoted to lieutenant colonel and major and recently got married, so it is now Lieutenant Colonel and Major Samuels."

Several in the room who were in the president's party applauded, and the others politely joined in.

General Perry continued, "We have confirmed the sightings with UAVs and satellite digital imagery, so we have the Samuelses and four members of Combat Applications Group from Fort Bragg, North Carolina, who are currently wearing sterilized uniforms and carrying sterilized equipment and are on board a B1B Stealth for a HALO insertion hopefully undetected into the area of Pakistan south of the Khyber Pass."

One of the senators said, "General, excuse me, but how can Mrs., I mean, Major Samuels make a HALO insertion when she has never attended U.S. military schools for such, or special forces training?"

The general replied, "Major Samuels did a considerable amount of civilian skydiving, even competitively, which well prepared her for such an undertaking. She has also, on her own, Senator, undertaken many classes and courses, which only strengthens her for the job she is performing, such as Ironwoman competitions, scuba diving, and she has taken many refresher courses frequently. Just in case there might be a concern, sir, that we are trying to re-create *G.I. Jane*, we absolutely are not. Major Samuels has a specops MOS but is not allowed to wear a Green Beret, can never be assigned to a Special Forces unit, or Combat Applications Group, or anything of the sort. Major Samuels would be the first to tell you she does not want that. She believes strongly that there are some women who could qualify, but their presence in those prestige units would complicate and not enhance the mission and would be a detraction instead of an asset. As far as forced road marches of twenty or thirty miles carrying weapons and eighty-pound rucksacks through harsh conditions such as is done in the Q-Course, Major Samuels says she physically would not be able to carry that out and has no desire to. However, she is very much mission-ready for this particular, or similar assignments, as she has already certainly proven under fire. Mr. Senator, when you asked that, I wanted to address it clearly, so I could also alleviate any concerns some of you may have. I hope I have answered your question, sir. Have I?"

The senator smiled and said, "Very well, General. Thank you."

The briefing continued for some time and afterward the president invited the general and several others for lunch in the West Wing dining room, which is just down the hallway from the Oval Office and on the other side.

Over some gourmet sandwiches, the president smiled at Jonathan Perry and said, "General, you just lied through your teeth to those people. How does that make you feel?"

Perry chuckled, saying, "Like a politician, Mr. President."

Everybody in the room laughed and the chief executive simply said, "Touché."

Bobby called a halt to the patrol, and they moved slowly through the undergrowth down the side of the ridgeline they approached on. All wore night vision devices and could see the entire compound before them set up the same as before. Bobby pointed out various bunkers and buildings, assigning them to each man in the patrol. Each man would be accompanied by one Hmong or Montagnard, who would sneak in with them. Two guards had been assigned to each of the two towers, but in both towers the guards were lying fast asleep, and Bobby saw thankfully the rest of the security in the camp seemed lax to nonexistent.

Green Berets, especially engineer/demolition specialists have used materials found in the field such as junkyard scrap, glass champagne bottle bottoms, and steel plates, and then molded the explosive to them in an attempt to increase the efficiency of the charges for specialized missions. Their training for years has been expedience: How can they make do with what is available? However, since the advent of munitions incorporating explosively formed penetrators as warheads, the Special Operations Forces have learned to build demolition charges using this technology. Oftentimes, through trial and error, they succeed in building EFP (explosively formed projectile, but also meaning explosively formed penetrator) demolition charges that will destroy the intended targets. These are actually the bastard stepchildren of the old army shape charges. The spec ops operator's improvised demolition EFPs are rarely optimized nor do they have consistent and reliable performance because of the variability in materials and building techniques they employed.

Besides fabricating the charges, the soldiers needed to improvise methods to attach the charges to a wide, wide variety of targets, often for extended periods of time, in virtually all types of environmental conditions. The attachment methods also required the operator's direct presence at the target. It could be a bridge's support columns, an electrical power substation, a dam, an enemy headquarters building, or munitions bunker, etc. Many of these missions did not permit a safe standoff distance from the target during emplacement of the demolition charges. This exposed the soldiers to detection and eradication by the enemy forces, especially in the commonplace spec ops direct-action missions of infiltration undetected, target destruction, and exfiltration undetected. This is what Bobby and his men were facing. Unless one employed a timing device, usually an expedient one as simple as attaching a positive wire to a metal screw and negative wire to another, and then separating them by a variety of methods, such as one screw attached to the metal lid inside a jar of rice or beans with water poured in. The water causing the rice or beans to swell would make the lid with the screw and positive wire attached slowly rise toward the contact with the screw attached to the negative wire. Once the two touched, the circuit would be complete from the battery used, and the detonator would ignite. The opposite methodology could be achieved by having the lid with the positive contact drop down to the bottom of a container, a drum or can, while the water within slowly leaked out through a prepared hole at whatever rate of leakage desired. Even a lit cigarette stuck between the matches in a matchbook has been used as a timing device for an explosive by Special Forces operators. There are many more expedient means, but all of these are simply guesses on how long it will take for a detonation, and there is no control over the timing on the blast.

To overcome these deficiencies, the US Army TACOM-ARDEC (Tank-Automotive and Armaments Command-Armament Research, Development and Engineering Center) developed the M303 Special Operations Forces Demolition Kit to provide the spec ops soldiers with state-of-the-art components and methods needed to accomplish their missions more safely, efficiently, and effectively while improving their survivability. The official line about the M303 states:

> The SOFDK allows soldiers to remotely acquire their targets at extended standoff distances using munitions that defeat targets using less explosives than conventional demolition operations. The SOFDK provides components and methods that greatly improve the soldiers' fighting ability by lightening the soldiers' load and reducing time-on-target.
>
> The Kit is a collection of inert metal and plastic parts and commercially available items that give the SOF soldiers a wide selection of warheads and attachment devices which he can tailor to defeat a specific mission target. The various warheads include three sizes of conical-shaped charges, four sizes of linear-shaped charges, and a new capability with two sizes of explosively formed penetrators with more sizes to follow. The warheads are provided in a set configuration that contains all materials, less explosives, needed to pack the warheads with explosive, set them up and attach them on or near the target. It also gives the user a new capability in the form of an inert kit containing the components to tailor-make various explosive charges and securely employ or attach these charges to targets, which is critical for mission success and user survivability.
>
> The centerpieces of the M303 Kit are the new EFP warheads that provide a standoff capability, previously not available to the SOF soldier, to defeat hard targets. All materials in the kit are inert and thus can be carried to the mission area using any available means of transport from military to commercial, air, sea or ground. In the last friendly area near the mission jump-off site, called the Isolation Facility, the user will study his target folder and select the proper warheads and hand pack the

warheads with Composition C-4 moldable explosive. The warheads are then carried in the soldiers' rucksacks to the target site. The EFP warheads are set up on standard camera tripods included in the kit and aimed with a built-in Omega sight or with one sight from the soldiers' standard set of four interchangeable carbine sights. Use of these sights provides the maximum accuracy at the greatest standoff distances attainable for numerous types of targets and mission scenarios. The warheads are primed with standard blasting caps or detonation cord and when initiated, from the EFP or "Cannon Ball" that is explosively projected at high velocity to impact the target with devastating results. All warheads can be used in environments ranging from tropic to arctic under limited visibility conditions. The EFP warheads can even be used in total darkness, when using the soldiers' standard visible laser or infrared (night vision goggle–compatible) laser sight. The EFP warheads are effective in defeating a wide variety of targets ranging from eight-inch-thick reinforced concrete block walls to three-inch-thick armor plate.

The M303 was developed for and will be issued exclusively to the Army proponent within the Special Operations Command. Due to the strong user support from the Navy Seals for the EFP warheads and the medium and large linear-shaped charges these items will also be procured for Navy use.

To carry it a step further, these men would emplace directional firing-shape charges with EFP warheads, and in some circumstances on tripods, around the al Qaeda training compound, and they would also emplace a digital video camera far enough away from the potential blast site that it could capture the images of the blast. It would be projected to a computer screen on a laptop with the patrol and simulcast to the spy sat overhead back to Langley and D.C. Bobby could watch in real time to insure that everything would be okay to set off the explosion.

Fadl Ulaah was the al Qaeda camp commander. Like so many of the al Qaeda cadre, he had previously had homosexual relationships with both Usama bin Laden and his second in command Ayman al-Zawahiri and was personally trained by both, not only in the art of fellatio but in terrorist activities.

He had journeyed to Koh Samui in southernmost Thailand to meet with his boss Muhammad Yahyaa and was now returning, very weary from the travel. He had taken a train to Bangkok, a boring four-hour ride, and then vehicles, and between two northern Thai villages, even an elephant, and then more vehicles. Now, because he could not compromise his facility's location, he had driven by all-terrain vehicle to a spot where the camp's inhabitants hid their vehicles, five clicks away from the camp, and he was now approaching the camp on a hike through the jungled terrain accompanied by the squad sent out to meet him and escort him back to camp. The men, not wanting to step on banded kraits, bamboo vipers, or poisonous centipedes in the dark, would have preferred waiting until dawn to move, but the leader had night vision goggles and so did the squad leader, and Fadl was anxious to get back to his hooch. He did not like the jungle at all, and at his hooch he could at least have electricity and some of the comforts of home, as well as young trainees to prey on sexually.

The men of the patrol with their southeast Asian counterparts slowly moved through the jungle growth like the spitting cobra, taking the route of least resistance under the giant elephant's ear plants and around and through the tangle-foot and wait-a-minute vines.

For this operation, Bobby, Bo, and each of the Delta Force members carried a SOPMOD (Special Operations Peculiar Modification) kit on the M4A1 carbine, with thirty-round magazines and automatic firing that would fire rapid-fire auto in three-round bursts. The modification kits for each man's weapon was suited to their particular taste but included all or part of the following modifications to the M4, which is a CAR-15 carbine with an A-203 grenade launcher mounted underneath the barrel: Knight's Armament Company (KAC) Rail Interface System (RIS) forearm, KAC's vertical fore grip, KAC's backup iron sight (BUIS), Trijicon's model TA01NSN 4x32-millimeter Advanced Combat Optical Gunsight (ACOG), improved combat sling, which allows for secure cross body/patrol carry, Insight Technology's AN/PEQ-2 Infrared Target Pointer/Illuminator/Aiming Laser (ITPIAL), Insight Technology's Visible Light Illuminator (VLI), Trijicon's ACOG Model RX01M4A1 reflex sight, KAC's quick-detach sound suppressor (QDSS), KAC's quick-attach M203 grenade launcher mount, quick-attach sight for use with the M203 with a nine-inch barrel, and Insight Technology's AN/PEQ-5 visible laser.

For a personal sidearm, like Bobby and Bo, several carried a Glock model 17 9 millimeter, and the rest carried customized army Colt .45 1911s. One of the men, Trinity, having served in the Pacific Rim under the First Special Forces Group out of Fort Lewis, Washington, did not want to carry the M4 because of bullets not penetrating the thick jungle foliage, but instead carried a Mini-14 with a space-age polymer plastic stock and firing the standard 7.62 Remington copper-jacketed, soft-nosed, hollow-point ammunition. He had his next-door neighbor, a Special Forces 18Bravo or weapons sergeant, convert his rifle to full automatic, and he just had to remember to fire in bursts and keep his barrel and receiver cooled down. Two of the men carried the spec ops popular SR-25.

The men in the group easily emplaced each of the special munitions, and knew that they would also get secondary explosions when the two ammunition bunkers and the fuel storage blew. With as much stealth as they used to climb into the compound perimeter area undetected, they now egressed without incident and met at the rendezvous point at the eastern end of the valley.

Following Bobby, who walked point, they made their

way up the jungle-choked ridgeline. They set up a quick perimeter and set up the laptop. They could also see the explosions from the ridgeline. Dawn was just now lifting up the corners of the horizon and sending little shards of light onto the countryside.

Just as they were ready to detonate, Bobby got a call and the UAV high overhead reported a squad-sized unit closing in on them. Bobby requested and was able to see on the computer screen IR images of the patrol from the FLIR apparati in the nose of the UAV. He left Bo and half the patrol, U.S. and foreign, on the ridgeline and scurried down the ridge to the valley floor to set up a hasty ambush, as he did not want to allow them the opportunity to get to the compound, spot the explosive devices, and sound the alert.

He set up a quick L-shaped ambush and had told the patrol above to blow the camp when he sprang the ambush. In the L-shaped ambush, which was a very common hasty ambush tactic, the patrol would be allowed to walk into the killing zone of the main ambush line, and the second line would lay down withering fire all along the front of the patrol, without exposing themselves to the overlapping fire of the main line of the ambush along the trail.

The ambush came into sight, and Bobby had already told them to wait for his fire. He could tell by his demeanor and body language that Fadl Ulaah was a Mideasterner and a leader of some sort. He whispered to the man next to him that he wanted the man alive. This was passed on, and Bobby held his own holographic sights with the illuminated red center dot right on the man's right hip. He made a mental note to hit the man on a front quartering angle so he might shatter the hip and anchor him, but not hit the femoral artery running down the inside of the leg through the groin area. This man might give them intelligence on the operations of Muhammad Yahyaa and al Qaeda Pacific Rim operations.

He squeezed off his shot and saw it hit the hip, exiting

the right buttocks, and the man went down immediately. The rest of the ambush went off without a hitch, and the gray, dark, misty morning erupted into loud booming explosions to their side and rear, and stabbing flames of fire erupted from their deadly weapons. Copper-jacketed harbingers of death spun forth in a cacophony of hate, a symphony of horror. One of the al Qaeda patrol tried to raise a Chicom-made 7.62-millimeter light machine gun. Then Big Mose aimed at his center mass an fired an HE round from his M203 grenade launcher. The round caught the man perfectly in the center of his chest, and went off, and his torso and machine gun simply exploded. Bobby heard secondary explosions going off from the compound and grinned.

As directed by Bobby, everybody opened on automatic, then switched to semiautomatic and aimed at targets of opportunity. The firing ended, and Bobby jumped up and led the others forward and arrived at the moaning body of Fadl Ulaah.

He yelled, "Big Mose!"

And the big man hollered back, "Got him, sir. Go ahead."

Bobby approached the moaning man and was soon angry at himself for his carelessness. He pulled Flex-Cufs out of his cargo pocket and grabbed the wounded man's wrist. From underneath, as Bobby pulled on his left wrist to cuff him, a khanjar, a long, curved-blade Arabic dagger, suddenly appeared in a sweeping arc in his right hand that cut across Bobby's bicep and immediately drenched his arm in blood.

Bobby heard a gun cocking to his right rear and said, "Don't shoot. He's mine."

The killer swept back across the other way, ripping a large slash through the front of Bobby's uniform, but wearing Kevlar, Bobby ignored it and grabbed the man's right arm after it passed by, slowed by the scalpel-sharp blade dragging across the Kevlar.

Fadl Ulaah grinned at Bobby, who held the man's arm

steady in a viselike grip, and the al Qaeda leader said, "Ha, this blade cut off the head of the last infidel who came here."

Bobby clenched his teeth, and his right foot came up and the outside blade of his foot came down viciously on the back of Fadl Ulaah's kneecap on his right leg, and his left hand punched the man with a straight left, as he was dropping, screaming in pain. Because Fadl Ulaah's mouth was open while he screamed, the punch fractured the right side of his jaw and cracked his cheekbone as well.

Bobby cuffed the unconscious man's wrists, and Trinity appeared and pulled him away, immediately cutting away Bobby's sleeve with a razor-sharp Cutco.

Bobby started to protest, but Big Mose was already cutting away Fadl Ulaah's clothes and he pointed at Trinity, saying, "He is in charge right now, Major. SF medic."

Bobby smiled. He knew better than to argue right now. Special Forces medics, 18Deltas, go through the most intense 322-day paramedic-type training course one could go through.

The U.S. Army JFK Special Warfare Center says this about 18Delta training:

> Company D, 4th Bn, is responsible for all medical training at the USAJFKSWCS. The Special Forces Medical Sergeants Course consists of the 24-week Special Operations Combat Medic (SOCM) Course and an additional 22-week training cycle that completes the 18Ds medical training.
>
> The 24-week Special Operations Combat Medic (SOCM) course is also taught to enlisted Army personnel from the Ranger Regiment, Special Operations Aviation Regiment (SOAR) and Special Operations Support Battalion (SOSB). USN SEALs and USN personnel supporting USMC Recon units as well as Air Force Special Operations Command (AFSOC) ParaRescue personnel also attend the SOCM course.
>
> Although 19 of the 24 weeks of SOCM training is

focused on anatomy and physiology and paramedic training, the remaining five weeks cover such military unique subjects as sickcall medicine environmental medicine. A four-day field training exercise in a simulated combat environment culminates the SOCM course. During the SOCM course students receive American Heart Association certification in Basic and Advanced Cardiac Life Support (ACLS) as well as certification by the National Registry of Emergency Medical Technicians at the EMT-Basic and Paramedic levels. Upon graduation a SOCM is capable of providing basic primary care for his Special Operations team for up to seven days and is capable of sustaining a combat casualty for up to 72 hours after injury as required.

Special Operations Combat Medic students receive clinical training in both emergency pre-hospital and hospital settings. This training is conducted during a four-week deployment to one of two major metropolitan areas: New York City or Tampa, Fl.

U.S. Army Special Forces students attend the 46-week Special Forces Medical Sergeants (SFMS) course. Students in this course must successfully complete the 24-week SOCM curriculum before continuing on for an additional 22 weeks of specialized training in medical, surgical, dental, veterinary, laboratory, pharmaceutical and preventive medicine subjects. Upon completion of this course students are trained to function as independent health care providers. In addition to the four weeks of clinical training provided during the SOCM portion of their training, SFMS students receive another four weeks of clinical experience at selected health care facilities throughout the United States. The focus of this training is on honing student skills as independent, general practice, health care providers.

Before Bobby knew it, Trinity had treated him with cleansing wipes and asked, "You want a local anesthetic, sir? I have to suture you."

Bobby said, "No, thanks, Trinity," looking at the now clean, deep, wide gash. "Go for it."

Trinity had on rubber gloves and pulled a completely sterile hermetically sealed suture kit from one of his cargo pockets. He put on a new pair of gloves. The Montagnards gathered around totally fascinated and watched as he first used his little curved needle and sutured Bobby's torn muscle tissue together with eight stitches. Then he changed needles and sutured the skin together. He finished by covering the straight, clean line with a brown-tinted antiseptic, and covered the wound with a clean dressing.

Bobby thanked him, got off the log he had been sitting on, and turned around. Big Mose stood there chuckling and pointed at the terrorist, almost naked except for the suicide belt he wore around his midsection.

Big Mose said, "Sir, the next time you want to go toe to toe with one of these al Qaeda pukes, you might want to make sure he's not a walking bomb."

Bobby laughed and said, "So much for his seventy-two virgins."

Big Mose removed the belt, having already defused it.

He tossed it on the ground next to Y-Ting and yelled, "Boom!" when it landed, and Y-Ting jumped out of his skin, even giving a little yell. All the indigenous patrol members started laughing and teasing him, as he held his heart, laughing. Big Mose came over and grabbed him in a big bear hug, and they laughed together.

In the meantime, Trinity was now performing first aid on the now-coming-around terrorist leader.

While he was working, Bobby stood by and asked, "So how did you get the nickname Trinity?"

The medical sergeant looked at him, smiling, "Because of the Holy Trinity. I am a very devout born-again Christian, Colonel. Are you saved, sir?"

Bobby replied, "Yes, I am, Trinity. How soon can we move him? We need to saddle up."

"Five minutes, sir," he replied. "We're gonna have to carry him on a litter or something."

Big Mose said, "I got him, sir. We'll toss him over my shoulder and hope you don't see me accidentally dropping him over any cliffs."

Bobby laughed.

The group on the ridgeline came down to them, immediately set up a perimeter, and set the laptop up again. Bo was torn between being a wife and a partner, as she saw the sleeves missing and bandage on Bobby's sutured arm. The split team had been communicating back and forth, so she was prepared.

Waiting several minutes until they were alone, she quietly said, "Bobby, how bad is it?"

He did not lie. "It went through the muscle, but I don't think it cut the tendons or ligaments. Trinity is an 18Delta, and he stitched me, inside and out, and I could tell he did a good job of it. I can still use my arm, honey."

During the ambush, Trinity took a crease right along his left rib cage and it barely bled. He was not going to mention it, but Big Mose told Bobby about it.

Bobby looked at the wound area, but Trinity had already cleaned, dressed, and bandaged it.

Bobby said, "Looks like you got yourself a Purple Heart, Trinity."

"You, too, Colonel," he replied.

Bobby replied, "I should get busted endangering my patrol fighting him."

Trinity said, "With all due respect, sir. The guy is a jihadist, America-hating jerk, and killed Boom. You are a human, and nobody on this patrol saw you do anything unprofessional."

From behind Bobby, he heard Big Mose's deep voice saying, "Amen to that, my brother."

Bo said, "Colonel, we have good guys on the way for pickup in two Pave Lows. We are to move west two clicks to a trail and road junction. We have the coordinates. They want us to take these guys, too."

"Thanks, Major," Bobby replied.

Dave started chuckling as they walked along.

Bobby said, "Okay, Dave, I give up. What's so funny?"

The big, bearded sergeant said, "I bet you two call each other Colonel and Major at home, sir."

This really struck Bo as funny, and she chuckled heartily. The other Delta Team members would not allow Big Mose to carry the prisoner the whole way, taking turns carrying him over their shoulders, too. They patrol made good time arriving at the rendezvous in two hours. They took a rest break and were just getting rested and rehydrated when they heard the sounds of big tactical helicopters coming from Thailand, but they were shocked to see two Apache attack helicopters accompanying the two big choppers. Trinity went out and gave hand signals for the two to set down, as smoke from a green smoke grenade was swirled up by the rotor wash. The Apaches circled around and remained airborne.

Several Special Forces personnel and a civilian, presumably CIA, were on board each helicopter and the patrol was treated warmly. The civilian started speaking to Y-Ting in very fluent Rade, and Y-Ting translated.

The man came over to Bobby and Bo and explained, "We are taking them for some well-deserved R and R, Colonel. Then we are reoutfitting them and sending them back home with lots of money and groceries, and seeds, and such for their families and villages."

"Cool!" Bobby said.

When Y-Ting turned his head toward their direction, Bobby and Bo both saw tears of happiness.

The man said, "They do not want to relocate to America. They want to stay and fight."

Bobby asked why they had two Apaches flying escort.

The Special Forces major on board said, "Because, sir, it came down from DA. I heard from the Charley Oscar Sierra that we were to fly you back directly over Vientiane and engage anybody that wanted to bitch about us invading airspace."

He chuckled and said, "I believe, Colonel. Somebody at higher really wants to send a strong message to all our commie buddies over here."

They flew right over downtown Vientiane, the capital of Laos, without incident. It was never reported in the press either.

Bobby was soon being checked out by an air force flight surgeon at the fifty-bed modular hospital at Udorn Air Force Base in Thailand. The surgeon complimented Trinity on his fine work and pronounced Bobby good to go. They were headed back to Washington and the Delta Force members to Pope Air Force Base and Fort Bragg, North Carolina.

Good-byes and thank-yous were passed out all around, and Bobby and the other soldiers flooded the Montagnard fighters with gifts.

They boarded jets to head home.

9

BACK TO THE OFFICE

Bobby and Bo reported to the Pentagon after returning home and were immediately called in to the chief of staff's office. He asked about Bobby's arm and laughed about how many Purple Hearts the two of them were collecting and suggested postage stamps was an easier thing to collect. He told Bobby and Bo they were both getting another Silver Star when Bobby put his hand up.

He said, "Sir, by your leave." The general nodded and Bobby went on, "General, thank you very much, sir. Based on my observations on the ground, I felt the men on my patrol each deserved a Bronze Star with V device, and I was planning on submitting them for that today, as well as a Purple Heart for one of them, called Trinity, who was slightly wounded. Sir, I did not feel our mission merited a Silver Star for anybody, but if anybody gets a Silver Star, I would prefer it would be them."

Bo added, "I concur totally, General Perry, and not because he is my husband."

"Very well," Perry said. "All, including you two, will get the Bronze Star with V device. I'll send someone up from awards and decorations, with a clearance, and let them write it up for you. You two are too busy. After debriefing, we are going to have a briefing from the First Group command sergeant major and some of my staff. We have got some heavy-duty things to discuss. Great job on the prisoner snatch. This guy is already at Gitmo with orders to light his ass up. He was the camp commander, and we know he had just met with Muhammad Yahyaa, Weatherford's buddy and the al Qaeda honcho for the Far East."

Bobby and Bo went for debriefing with J-2, the CIA, the DIA, and others. The digital video was like a front-row seat to the complete destruction of an enemy target and a BDA (bomb damage assessment) patrol all rolled into one. The DVD of the target acquisition was replayed over and over in slow motion, and much of the debriefing was Bobby, and even Bo, answering questions.

After lunch, all assembled in the COS's conference room, and placards were placed outside the door stating the briefing classification, with two white-gloved, armed MPs standing at guard on each side of the double doors. Several VIPs came up to shake hands and congratulate Bobby and Bo on their success in Laos. Some in the room had no clue what went on, but could tell they had just had some kind of success, and everybody knew what they had done previously in New York City and Miami.

A number of Special Forces personnel were in the briefing room and all of them flooded around Bobby. Bo was proud seeing the level of respect her husband received from these very special men.

Everybody got coffee, water, and soft drinks and sat down.

The assembled were given the obligatory classification lecture and then General Perry was introduced.

He said, "Ladies and gentlemen, we have a unique situation here that we are going to address today. A lot of our focus is having to be shifted from our theater of operations, primarily in Iraq and Afghanistan, to the Pacific Rim area in the Far East. As most of you know, but the American public does not know, the very largest al Qaeda training camps in the world are not in Afghanistan, Pakistan, Somalia, Iran, or some of the places you may think, but the southern Philippines.

"The operation is classified top secret, but Lieutenant Colonel Bobby Samuels just led a patrol along with his wife, Major Samuels, and four men from Fort Bragg, North Carolina, where they executed a nighttime HALO-scuba infiltration deep in the country of Laos. They rendezvoused with a small indigenous force on the ground and completely destroyed a newly constructed al Qaeda training complex, as well as captured the camp commander who is a senior al Qaeda official and now being interrogated by our personnel. During the course of the operation, Lieutenant Colonel Samuels got involved in a hand-to-hand situation and suffered a deep knife cut on his upper arm, requiring numerous internal and external stitches. Additionally, one of the operators from Fort Bragg suffered a minor bullet wound to his chest. The enemy forces, with the exception of the one POW were wiped out to a man."

Everybody in the room applauded and the general pointed at Bobby and Bo, and they all stood and applauded. Bobby and Bo acted "army" and simply sat there with blank expressions on their faces.

General Perry continued, "Our First Special Forces Group headquartered at Fort Lewis, Washington, with one battalion permanently deployed to Okinawa, has primary responsibility for the Far East theater of operations. They have been working for years in the Philippines, not only with a counterinsurgency training mission but with a great deal of effective civil affairs and psychological operations as well. To that end, and to our delight, the First Special Forces Group has excelled beyond reasonable expectations in recent years. The Philippines still has kidnappings, beheadings, ambushes, and skirmishes, but it is a far cry from what it was just a few years ago, thanks to the diligent efforts of our First Group operators. We are going to put up on the screen for you a recent article by the First Group command sergeant major and it will brief you on what has occurred specifically, but first I want to tell you all this. My daddy taught me a saying and that was 'Never go backward,' meaning we have accomplished a lot in the Philippines, and I do not want it to become an al Qaeda stronghold again. We are now working on Indonesia, but they are making inroads in Thailand. Ladies and Gentlemen, the *Special Warfare* magazine is an official bimonthly publication of the U.S. Army John F. Kennedy Special Warfare Center and School at Fort Bragg, North Carolina. In the October/November 2006 issue, the cover story was written by Command Sgt. Maj. William Eckert of the First Group. He really hit the nail on the head, and I feel it important that you all read this article, so we are putting it up on the screen up here and the fine young Major John Trudel is going to come up here and read aloud, while you all read along. Afterward, we will talk. Major Trudel."

A balding, stocky major came to the podium and had a PowerPoint presentation to accompany his words, which gave hope on the global War on Terrorism to everyone in the room, and he began reading the text:

"Is the U.S. winning a war?" The headline wasn't referring to Iraq or Afghanistan but rather to another front in the Global War on Terrorism—the Philippines. Unlike the other two conflicts, where American soldiers are daily engaged in armed conflict, the war in the Philippines is one for peace and prosperity. The battle in the Philippines is a battle against an idea, and it is being waged by the Joint Special Operations Task Force—Philippines, or JSOTF-P.

The work by JSOTF-P has gained the attention of senior military leaders who believe its work may change the way the United States operates around the world. During the Pacific Area Special Operations Conference in Honolulu, Hawaii, in May, Maj. Gen. David Fridovich, commander of U.S. Special Operations Forces-Pacific, noted, "We think there is a model here that's worth showcasing.

There's another way of doing business. We've been doing it for four years with some decent results—not grand results, not flashy results, but some decent results. We think it's worthwhile."

The most telling result is the decline in terrorist activity in and around the islands where JSOTF-P is operating. In 2001, Basilan Island, a remote island in the southern Philippines, was home to hundreds of members of the violent Abu Sayyaf Group, or ASG, and Jemaah Islamiyah, or JI, two terrorist elements with links to al Qaeda. Prior to 9/11, terrorist training camps operated unchecked in the region, with up to 40 percent of the 9/11 operatives having links to the region. As is the case in the Middle East, kidnappings for ransom and beheadings were commonplace.

For example, in May 2001, the ASG assaulted the Dos Palmas Resort and took guests there hostage. The hostages included Americans Martin and Gracia Burnham, U.S. missionaries in the Philippines, and U.S. businessman Guillermo Sobero. The kidnapping ordeal lasted more than a year, during which Sobero was beheaded, Martin was killed during the rescue, and Gracia was injured.

The predominantly Muslim population in the area had, over time, become disenfranchised, disgruntled and dissatisfied with the government and the abject poverty of the region. Together, these conditions created an environment in which extremists could operate freely. The Armed Forces of the Philippines, or AFP, and Philippine police elements were unable to control the violence or address the conditions that gave rise to the lawlessness.

Though the challenges in Basilan called for military action, the response did not warrant the deployment and use of U.S. conventional military forces. Because of the political climate in the Philippines, U.S. troops cannot involve themselves in combat operations there.

This battlefield in the southern Philippines necessitated the use of many different unconventional capabilities—increasing the capacity of our allies through foreign internal defense, or FID; civil-military operations, or CMO; and information operations, or IO. These three mission areas, for which SOF are well-suited and well-trained, have become the cornerstone of JSOTF-P's operations.

The mission in the Philippines required two things to happen concurrently. The AFP had to increase its ability to establish a secure environment for the people, and the economic and political environment that allowed extremists to recruit, seek sanctuary and prosper on the islands had to be changed.

To be effective, JSOTF-P needed to devise a plan for meeting both requirements simultaneously. During the ongoing capacity-building and humanitarian missions, the JSOTF also engaged in an information-operations campaign—using all aspects of the information mission, including public affairs, information operations and psychological operations, to inform and positively influence the islanders.

The battle in the Philippines is a battle against an idea: the idea of intolerance and subjugation to totalitarian rule. In the southern Philippines, that idea is endorsed by the ASG and JI, whose goal it is to eliminate a way of life for freedom-loving people. For 15 years, SOF leadership has implemented a vision and capability for this unconventional warfare battlefield through a steady buildup of capabilities. These capabilities have enabled Special Operations Forces of the JSOTF-P to reach out to the populace while providing positive influences across the military, demographic, government and economic spectrums. SOF leadership also made the investment of resources for the development of professional military training and doctrine specific to the Philippines. As a result of the foresight of the U.S. Special Operations Command in establishing these disciplines in the special operations community, the men and women of Joint Task Force 510, and its follow-on, JSOTF-P, have accomplished what few others could.

Throughout the year, U.S. SOF personnel from JSOTF-P work jointly with the AFP to assist and support the AFP's ability to sustain its counterterrorism capability in the region, while addressing, at their root, the conditions that foment the enemy "idea." Success in Basilan is measured by prosperity; by reduced AFP presence—from 15 battalions in 2002 to only two today; by new development, and by a nonviolent method of problem resolution. That success, known as the Basilan Model, has resonated throughout the region and is being duplicated with great success on nearby Jolo Island.

Capacity Building

The cornerstone of this operation is the successful training of the AFP and the Philippine National Police. Prior to 2002, lawlessness was the rule, rather than the exception, on Basilan. Kidnapping for ransom was commonplace, and villagers lived in fear. In order for the island to prosper, the rule of law had to be enforced, and that could happen only through expanding and developing the capacity and capability of the country's security forces.

Additionally, to ensure the greatest return, getting the best possible information on the threat faced in the region is vital. Working in close coordination with the U.S. Embassy, JSOTF-P uses Special Forces, Civil Affairs and Psychological Operations forces to conduct deliberate intelligence, surveillance and reconnaissance in very focused areas, and based on collection plans, to perform tasks to prepare the environment and obtain critical information requirements. The information is used to determine the capabilities, intentions and activities of threat groups that exist within the local *population and to focus U.S. forces—and the AFP—on providing security to the local populace. It is truly a joint operation, in which Navy SEALs and SOF aviators work with their AFP counterparts to enhance the AFP's capacities.*

Recently, intelligence collection on the island of Jolo has been used to track two JI leaders, Umar Patek and Dulmatin, and the Abu Sayyaf chief Khadaffy Janjalani. The two JI members have been tied to the bombings of nightclubs in Bali, as well as to a bombing of the JW Marriott Hotel in Indonesia.

The information gathered early on, combined with the overall plans of the AFP leadership, allowed the JSOTF-P to prepare focused subject matter expert exchanges through which the AFP units acquire the skills needed to gain and maintain security within the joint operations area. During the time the JSOTF-P has focused on Sulu, the subject matter expert exchanges have been conducted with the AFP on an almost daily basis, including topics such as the combat lifesaver course, small-unit tactics, marksmanship, maritime interdiction operations, radio communications, night-vision goggle use, close air support and leadership development.

This increased capability for providing security is critical in contributing to the ability of the host-nation government to govern more effectively, and the improved security and effective governance also provides greater legitimacy to the host-nation government—a critical reason the AFP presence on Basilan has dropped so dramatically since 2002.

Civil-Military Operations

With support from U.S. SOF, the AFP didn't just show up on Basilan or Sulu with guns, rather it brought the resources to rebuild schools and hospitals, and the engineers to dig wells to provide fresh water. But the CMO line of operation is more than social and infrastructure

*projects. In JSOTF-P, it encompasses the full range of
support to the AFP and local civil authorities to increase their ability to address needs while managing the
expectations of the local population. Further, the operations address the root causes that allow the idea of
subjugation and intolerance to flourish.*

*While the JSOTF-P presence was initially regarded
with suspicion by the local population, the humanitarian and development-oriented approach of Philippine
and U.S. forces in the southern Philippines has proven
to be even more effective than a direct military approach. As a result, U.S. and AFP forces have gained
access to areas where they had previously been unwel-
come. The people now see the government and the U.S.
forces as a force for change and a way to better their
lives.*

*For example, in November 2005, the AFP was not
seen on Sulu as a trustworthy advocate. Access into
barangays, or villages, and communities was met with
suspicion by the local populace. One year later, after
the AFP has engaged in extensive CMO and capacity-
building work on schools, roads, wells, community centers and more, the civilian population is responding
positively to the presence of the AFP—no longer a bully
but rather a "big brother." As a result, the people are re-
fusing to harbor the terrorists and are instead turning
to the AFP for protection from those "lawless" elements.*

*The people in the region need development, and the
AFP has given them hope for development. Without exception, when given the choice, the population chooses
development, peace and prosperity. That changing view-
point has garnered the support of the local population
and is now denying the terrorists the sanctuary and
physical support they need to thrive.*

*Because resources are limited, JSOTF-P has formed
a strong link to nongovernmental organizations such as
3P-USA, Knightsbridge International and the Mabuhay*

Deseret Foundation. The support of these organiza-
tions, as well as of the government of the Philippines,
has greatly increased the scope and nature of the hu-
manitarian projects on the islands. Projects like school
construction; infrastructure development in the form of
water lines and wells; and medical care are the lifeblood
of the JSOTF-P's mission in the southern Philippines.

There was an elderly woman in Jolo City who had
been blind for 14 years as a result of cataracts. Her
mistrust of the AFP was topped only by her suspicion
of U.S. forces in her town and on the island. In June,
her desire to see overcame her mistrust, and she al-
lowed herself to try out the promises of the U.S. forces
and to visit the USNS Mercy, *a naval hospital ship, dur-*
ing its week-long stop off the shores of Jolo City. While
there, she allowed AFP doctors and clinicians to oper-
ate on her cataracts.

The operation restored clear sight to her for the first
time in 14 years. After her eyes adjusted and she recov-
ered from the surgery, she wanted to personally meet
and thank those U.S. and AFP personnel who gave her
back the gift of sight. She graciously offered them her
gratitude, and as a result of actions making her life bet-
ter, this one-time opponent of the AFP and U.S. forces
now supports them.

In many instances, CMO projects are undertaken
with strong buy-in by the local population. The JSOTF's
goal is to ensure that the projects are not only needed
but are also sustainable by the local population. Once
complete, every project is turned over to the local
barangay for maintenance. This buy-in and responsibil-
ity for the project by the local populace ensures that the
project will continue beyond the stay of JSOTF-P.

During 2006, the AFP and JSOTF-P have built 19
school-construction/renovation projects, dug 10 wells,
begun five road projects, started work on five commu-
nity centers and built five water distribution centers on
Jolo Island. Additionally, more than 13,000 people have

benefited from the medical, dental and veterinarian civic action projects. These projects have positively affected more than 25 communities on Jolo Island and provided the critical access into areas that were previously sanctuaries for terrorist groups.

At one medical civic action program, or MEDCAP, in particular, in the Indanan area of Jolo Island—a stronghold of the ASG at the time—an ASG operative was ordered to set off an improvised explosive device during the MEDCAP. The operative refused the assignment because his wife and children would be attending the program and receiving needed medical care.

Influencing Others

Everything that we do in the security, capacity-building and CMO arenas can go awry if we fail to communicate our plans and objectives to the local populace. Many Filipinos still view the U.S. with a wary eye from their days as a protectorate. They see the presence of the U.S. military in their country as a threat to their independence. JSOTF-P has to ensure that U.S. presence is seen as beneficial to the community by working with the media and other key communicators within the local communities. Throughout its tenure on the island, JSOTF-P has engaged in a powerful information campaign to ensure that the populace is informed. That campaign has created a positive atmosphere.

Rather than using the doctrinal definition of IO as "information operations," the personnel of JSOTF-P define IO as "influencing others" in a positive and effective manner. Through public affairs efforts, the task force is constantly telling people what it is going to be doing, how it is going to do it and how it will benefit them. The goal is to ensure that people are not surprised or caught off guard by anything the teams are accomplishing.

An example of this acceptance occurred in the small town of Tiptipon on Jolo Island. An AFP commander and his U.S. counterpart entered a town to assess the work needed for a school and for a hospital improvement project. The Muslim town leader, a self-acknowledged former ASG member, speaking to the team in his native Tausug, assured the team of its safety in his town, stating, "We want your development, and we want you to help repair our school and hospital and help us improve the lives of our people. We know what you did in Basilan, and we want that, too."

The mission of positively influencing others in the joint operations area is more than scheduling media and community relations events. Those are important, but the planned, focused use of PSYOP teams is just as critical.

The Soldiers assigned to the JSOTF-P PSYOP teams conduct assessments at each location and propose projects for each location by analyzing the various cultures and subcultures. With more than 7,100 islands making up the Philippines, the cultures of regions, provinces and neighboring communities can vary substantially. By reviewing the culture and history of the specific islands, clans and provinces, the team is better able to positively communicate its intentions and activities.

The teams assigned to the JSOTF-P have produced a multi-dimensional influencing operation on Jolo Island and throughout the joint operations area. Some of their activities have publicized the Department of Defense's and Department of State's Rewards for Justice Program that supports the war on terrorism. Other activities have focused the thoughts of the local populace on the choices they can make to take control of their lives by no longer tolerating terrorists who operate in the midst of their communities. Each PSYOP campaign utilizes the media that will best get its message across.

One example of a product line that the JSOTF-P's PSYOP team has worked hard to produce, aimed at giving *hope and bringing awareness of the evil that terrorism brings to families and communities, is a unique, first-of-its-kind graphic novel series. The 10-part series, which is still in production, contains local culture and real-world correlations. The title, names, attire, scenery, dialect and historical subtleties are all designed to appeal to the targeted community.*

Each book in the series is reviewed at multiple levels, including a focus group of local professionals, to ensure that any culturally offensive dialogue, gestures or activities are avoided. The reviews help to ensure that the product and others resonate with the island people.

Conclusion

There is no question that while the environment in the southern Philippines is improving, the Sulu Archipelago is still a volatile area. Bomb threats, kidnappings for ransom and detonations of improvised explosive devices are a daily occurrence. Only through the skill and professionalism of the Special Operations Forces and the support of the local population have JSOTF-P casualties been avoided so far.

For this unconventional mission, the U.S. Pacific Command and the U.S. Special Operations Command have the right force with the right skill sets in place for success. SOF will continue to develop and refine the mission as they achieve positive effects in the southern Philippines now and in other troubled spots in the future.

As the SOF role diminishes in the southern Philippines, the key for Philippine success over the long term will lie in sustaining the improvements thus far achieved. Perpetuating the peace will require continued involvement of the U.S. government; interagency efforts with other agencies such as the U.S. Agency for International Development; and most important, the collaboration and commitment of the Philippine government, non-governmental organizations and private investors to work and prosper.

The SOF indirect role is proving itself in the southern Philippines, and with patience and persistence, the unconventional warfare tools used here, along with proven SOF methodologies, will continue to succeed and to provide a powerful new tool for our nation in fighting the global War on Terrorism.

After Major Trudel finished reading the entire article, everybody was given a ten-minute rest break, then reconvened to discuss the article and the Philippine operations. At the conclusion of this, General Perry dismissed everybody except those who were involved with the task force headed by Bobby. While cabinet members and other VIPs arrived, Bobby and Bo sat with the general talking.

He said, "We have got to determine what is going down as far as the rumored al Qaeda attack on the West Coast. We have learned nothing yet from the camp commander, but we have learned from other prisoners that the al Qaeda is planning some kind of event or attack, and it is called 'Akrahuka, Amerikka!' "

"What does that mean, sir?" Bo asked.

Bobby immediately answered, "I hate you, America!"

"We have been watching Senator Weatherford for some time now and have photographs and video of him meeting several times with Muhammad Yahyaa and with Nguyen Van Tran of the SRV," the general continued. "But we do not have much audio."

"Sir, could we look at the tapes and photos we have?" Bo asked.

"Absolutely," Perry replied. "This is your task force. The president wants you to do the same thing you two did in Miami and the Big Apple. Stop the al Qaeda."

Bobby said, "Sir, we haven't figured out where we will live. If one of us is moving into the other's place. If it would be okay, could we check out some of the evidence and take it home with us, let our batteries recharge, and see what we can sort out?"

"As soon as we finish here, check out the evidence you want, but I want your place swept for bugs and anything visual by the FBI," General Perry said.

"Thank you, sir," Bo replied.

Bobby and Bo went out in the hallway and started talking while others were showing up.

"You know," she said, "we haven't figured out if we are going to stay in one place or the other. It does not matter to me at all, honey."

Bobby said, "Do you own your condo?"

She said, "Yes."

He said, "I own mine, too. It is paid for. How about yours?"

"Mine is, too," she replied. "Yours seems to have more room and more storage. Why don't we move into yours and rent out mine?"

Bobby said, "That was easy enough. Are you certain?"

"Yes."

"I have to go to AA meetings," he said. "You understand that, don't you?"

"Why wouldn't I?" she answered. "I have been going to Al-Anon meetings for months."

"You have?" he said. "Even before I admitted I was an alcoholic, and we weren't married then. Why did you start going to meetings?"

Bo said, "I knew you were an alcoholic, after I got out of my own denial about you. I started going because I was madly in love with you and wanted to understand."

He smiled at her, saying, "I love you."

Bo said, "I love you, too. You don't know how long I have been wanting to say that all the time."

Bobby said, "I wish the MPs would go away. I want to tear off all your clothes, throw you against that wall, and make mad, passionate love to you, right here, right now in the Pentagon."

Smiling brightly, Bo walked past him and slapped him in the lower stomach, saying, "Male!"

He bent over, grabbing his stomach, and reached out, pinching her butt right before she got close to the MPs. She turned, grinning, and slapped his hand.

They went back into the briefing and assignments were made to various individuals. Bobby said he and Bo were going to the Philippines to see what they could learn about Weatherford's ties there and poke around to learn what they could about Akrahuka, Amerikka.

Riding in the crazy speeding taxi was quite a thrill for Bobby and Bo and driving around Manila seemed to be quite a challenge. The seemingly millions of motorists did not respect the rules of the road, read the road signs, or even look at them, and their own taxi driver seemed like he was aiming at tourists. There was way too much congestion, smoke pollution, and very bad road conditions to suit the two investigators. They at least saw a wide variety of life and even vehicles, very colorful jeepneys, fancy cars, junky cars, assembled cars that are put together out of many items, large tricycles, bicycles, motorcycles, and putt-putt motor scooters.

Bobby and Bo were depressed driving through the long stretch of squatters' shacks along the pier area all the way to Roxas Boulevard. They had been everywhere but had trouble imagining how people could live and survive, and some thrive, in such misery.

However, they saw a completely different look to Manila by the time they reached the financial district of Makati, and it was like any other advanced country metropolis. Skyscrapers and high-rises were everywhere and the roads were much cleaner and wider.

In that long drive to the corporate headquarters, Bobby and Bo basically saw what Manila was about, two worlds, the haves and the have-nots. When they got out of the taxi, Bobby pointed out to the driver that he had taken a nice scenic route through some of the city's slums, but had he simply driven east on the road they started out on, they would have ended up in the same place, without five extra miles being added to the meter. There was a little arguing, but the driver had no leg to stand on, and ended up without the generous tip he might have had.

They walked toward the towering skyscraper and stopped briefly. Bobby gave Bo's hand a little squeeze, and they entered.

He whispered, "Keep your beautiful eyes wide open, sweetheart."

The place was impressive. The skyscraper was a very impressive thirty-story office tower situated in the heart of Makati, in metro Manila, where a great number of institutional and corporate headquarters are located. The tower had obviously been carefully designed to provide clients with a first-class corporate environment. Inside there were a number of modern-looking facilities including an international business center, broadband internet connectivity, function rooms, a health and fitness center, banks, restaurants, and even a large corporate dining room, where lunch bags could be carried in or meals from the restaurant served.

The interior of the building was equipped with a double-glazed curtain wall system for additional energy and efficient cooling that was complimented by a combination of a polished tan granite exterior wall.

There were two lobbies finished in two shades of imported granite from Spain, and one lobby contained a bank of eight high-speed elevators.

The building also featured a very advanced communication wiring system, and six levels of basement parking, plus there was a functional helipad on the roof. The computer-controlled building management system monitored and controlled the building's air-conditioning, ventilation, lighting, power distribution, and security, alarm, and fire management systems.

Bo said, "Somebody's making money here."

There was a big brass plate approximately ten feet tall

and thirty feet wide with what looked like engraved large letters reading PEARLS 2 BAMBOO, LTD. CORPORATE HEAD-QUARTERS. This was the latest corporate name for the international distribution company that was the shill for the various real estate and stock deals with Hanoi. The company was actually purchased back in 1992 when the senator's brother could not deal directly with Hanoi.

A beefy uniformed American security guard came up to Bobby and Bo, who were carrying briefcases and dressed in business attire.

He said, "May I direct you to a specific office, sir, or give you directions?"

Bobby smiled and said, "No, sir, thank you. We have thought about doing business with Pearls 2 Bamboo and thought we might come in and investigate first." He grinned. "You know, snoop around a bit and get a feel for the place. How do you like working here?"

The man straightened up. "Oh, I really like it. It pays good, and they have great fringes. I miss being a cop, but, hey, it's a job."

Bo said, "You were a cop?"

"Yes, ma'am. By the way, there is a bunch of corporate information over there on that table. Help yourself and snoop all you want," he said. "You need anything, just ask."

Bobby said, "Thank you, sir."

The man went on, as Bobby and Bo both sensed he would. "Yeah, I was a cop in Chicago, eighteen years. Well, actually, it was Naperville, kind of southwest. Anyhow, I loved it. I was a good cop."

Bobby and Bo were now sitting in a large, leather stuffed couch and picking up brochures from the fancy teak table for visitors.

He went on, "I had some problems with my ex-wife and decided on a change of scenery."

Bo said, "I'm sorry. How did you end up here all the way from Illinois?"

He shrugged his shoulders and said, "Well, it was kind of one of those mail-order-bride-type deals, but that didn't work out. I decided to get a job and see if I could find me a good woman here to take back. There's plenty who want to go."

Bo walked over to him and kept talking. Bobby looked at their business brochure and read the words carefully while Bo won over the heart and mind of the guard. The brochure read:

As a major international business firm, with many partners and subsidiaries, we manage a broad range of international corporate, commercial, investment, financial, import/export, trade, regulatory, real estate, and other business matters for our clients throughout the world. Some of the types of business transactions we have handled for our clients include: cross-border mergers and acquisitions; foreign corporate direct-investment and joint-stock ventures; complete corporate project development and finance; commercial (and some high-end personal) real estate investment, development, finance, and management; cross-border equipment leasing; manufacturing, licensing, distribution, and business technical assistance; international trade and business disputes, negotiations, and buyouts. We also represent a diverse and extensive list of American and non-U.S. multinational entities, public and private companies, multilateral institutions, governmental organizations, and individuals. Our clients are engaged in many different businesses and industries, including banking and financial services, venture capital, manufacturing, real estate, pharmaceuticals, health care, and others.

On top of that, some of our closest contacts hold senior positions within the U.S. government, other international businesses, and major nonprofits, as well as high government positions in the Oriental marketplace. Our extensive experience in handling complex international transactions and matters in countries throughout the world and juxtapositioning sensitive foreign entities with trade-hungry corporate America enables us to provide effective expertise in the diverse business cultures throughout the world, and most especially the countries of the Orient. We can fulfill your corporate need in the Pacific. Just speak with our management personnel, and let's get the pearl rolling for you.

And just below that in small letters it read: "Pearls 2 Bamboo, Ltd., an international corporation, a subsidiary of FWECI."

Bobby stood up with the brochure, after having put two more in his briefcase.

He walked over to Bo and said, "Honey, I looked at their business brochure, and I am impressed. I have noticed since we have been here, there is a steady stream of people walking in and out. I like what the brochure says, and they are a subsidiary of FWECI, and I know I have heard good things about them, but for the life of me, I do not know what that stands for."

The guard said, "No problem."

He walked over to his desk and console of TV monitors and picked up the phone.

He pushed a button and in seconds said, "Hi, Rose. It's Rufus. Right. I am. Hey, I have a question."

Bobby handed him the brochure and pointed at the script at the bottom of that page, and Rufus said, "At the bottom of the company's brochure. Yeah, the fancy tan-and-blue one, it says, 'Pearls 2 Bamboo, Ltd., an international corporation, a subsidiary of FWECI.' What the heck does FWECI stand for? Yeah, wait, let me get my pen out. Okay."

He wrote on his tablet and repeated, "Fair Weather Enterprises Corporation comma International. Okay, Thanks, babe, Talk to you later."

He tore off the paper, handed it to Bobby, and said, "There ya go, sir."

Bobby took it and said, "I knew I heard of them. They have a good rep for solid business affairs."

Rufus said, "Oh, heck, yes, they have to. I heard it was owned by the brother or family of Senator James Weatherford. Fair Weather, get it? You know he plans to run for president. I may be working for the president someday soon. I figured if I stick it out here, maybe I can get a good in to the Secret Service."

Bo immediately said, "Good thinking. Maybe you'll get to meet him someday."

"Are you kidding?" Rufus said. "He knows me by name. He comes here a couple times a year, sometimes more. I think it is to visit his brother, and you know . . ."

Bobby grinned and whispered, "What?"

Rufus said, "I could get fired for telling you this," and hesitated.

Bo said, "Only if someone tells."

He leaned forward, chuckling, and said, "Well, the senator likes to get away from Washington for more than the weather. I work late hours a lot and make lots of overtime, you know. Well, there have been several times late at night, when the senator has come or gone from here with some pretty nice-looking Philippine babes. Sometimes two of them at a time."

He chuckled for a minute and said, "Must be nice to be a senator, huh?"

Bobby smiled broadly, clasped Rufus's shoulder, winked, saying, "Rufus, this is my wife here. I am not answering that one. By the way, my name is Barry Greenfield and this is my wife."

Rufus said, "I know, Cookie. How can I forget a name like that?"

Bobby said, "So if we want to speak with a corporate executive or set up an appointment, where do we go?"

"Oh, third floor," he said. "Here're two visitor's passes. There is a big reception desk, and they will take care of you."

"Great!" Bobby said. "You've really been helpful. So, all the corporate offices are on the third floor?"

"Oh, no," Rufus said, "that is just reception and marketing. The big shots are on the tenth floor."

They walked toward the elevator and Bo said, "Thanks, Rufus. Good luck on getting Miss Right."

He smiled broadly and waved, as they entered the second elevator.

As Bobby surmised, Rufus never looked at the numbers above their elevator, or he would have seen it stop on "10." Bobby and Bo never observed Rufus looking at any of the TV monitors the entire time they were in the lobby.

On the tenth floor, they walked off the elevator and saw a very fancy boardroom with a massive hand-carved table with dragons and elephants on it, as well as many gold and ivory inlays. The boardroom was apparently left open to show off the corporate wealth. The furnishings were very expensive and extravagant. While Bo watched, Bobby immediately opened his briefcase, lifted out his Day Runner, notebook, and laptop, and tapped twice on the bottom right corner. The bottom of the briefcase opened up to reveal a fake bottom and compartment underneath. Bobby pulled out a small camera/microphone attached to a recorder/transmitter. He stepped up on the table and could not reach the ceiling, so he quickly grabbed a heavy chair and set it on the table.

A door opened down the hallway and a large man in a suit walked out and headed down the hallway toward them. Bo was standing in the doorway, so he could see her, and she smiled, saying, "Bobby, man coming."

Bobby had lifted a ceiling tile and had turned on and placed the recorder/transmitter on top of the next tile and was now positioning the tiny microphone and fisheye digital video camera down along the seam of the tile. He worked quickly.

Bo smiled at the approaching man and whispered through clenched teeth, "Five seconds! Five seconds!"

She turned her back to Bobby and looked at the man,

making sure she pulled her arms back, so he would get the full outline of her well-proportioned breasts, which men had ogled her whole life since puberty, and which she wished often that she could cut off. He was no exception.

"Hello," Bo said.

"Hello, ma'am," the man said almost to her, now. "May I help you?"

Bo started to speak but Bobby stepped out of the boardroom from behind her and stuck out his hand, smiling. "Hi, we seemed to have gotten lost, and I was just in wonderment looking at your conference room. It is beautiful."

"Yes, it is. We spent a lot of money on it," the man said. "Lost?"

Bobby said, "Yes, we asked the guard downstairs where we could schedule a sit-down with one of your marketing executives, and I could have sworn he said the tenth floor."

Bo clenched her teeth, saying sarcastically, "I tried to tell you, honey. He told us the third floor. He said the corporate board offices were on the tenth floor, but you never want to listen to me, honey. I'm just a woman."

The man started laughing and Bobby held his breath, so his face would turn red. He pretended to give Bo an angry sidelong glance.

The man laughed and said, "I hate to tell you this, sir, but the little lady was right. Third floor. As soon as you get off the elevator, you will see the big reception area."

Bo looked at him flirtingly and said, "Thank you, sir. You have been most helpful."

Bobby was already at the elevator and the man grinned and winked, saying, "Anytime."

Bo winked back and walked over to the elevator.

Inside, she and Bobby started laughing as soon as the door closed. They got off on the third floor and went to the receptionist's desk.

Bobby said, "Can I have a business card for one of your

marketing managers or consultants, please, so I can set up an appointment?"

The woman gave him a card, and they got back on the elevator and went down to the lobby. They handed their passes to Rufus and bade him farewell, promising they would return.

10

PRESIDENTIAL POWER

Back in Washington, D.C., the president told his secretary to have General Perry come in.

Then he said, "Wait a minute. Get me whoever is head of my Secret Service detail this morning."

A tall agent in a blue suit and maroon tie came in the door.

The president said, "Hi, Tom. How is your wife doing?"

"She is doing well, sir. They used dissolving sutures," the agent answered. "She wanted me to thank you very much for the flowers and card, sir."

The president said, "No problem. Now, hysterectomies can lead to serious depression, so you be very understanding with her."

"Yes, sir."

"Now, I have our little celebrity waiting to come in with General Perry," the president said. "I need to know for certain you guys swept her."

Tom grinned and responded, "Mr. President, we sweep everybody who meets with you, and they never know it. She is not wearing a bug or video camera."

The president winked and nodded and Tom left the room.

Again, he pushed the button and said, "Sandra, please have General Perry and his guest come in."

General Perry held the door open and a ravishingly beautiful woman walked in. She had perfect body parts everywhere, a face that would make men immediately think secret thoughts, and make many women want to take their husband elsewhere. Her hair was long, shiny, and jet black. She walked right up to the president, gave him a firm handshake, and looked him straight in the eye.

General Perry shook hands with the president, and he invited them to come over in front of the fireplace and be seated.

National network news special reporter and occasional anchor Veronica Caruso had been a former love of Bobby Samuels, solely to use him and get information. A bisexual, she had an affair with Bobby and Bo's assistant and got her to divulge many of their secrets, information she was feeding to an al Qaeda operative who had infiltrated the U.S. Army as a military reporter and was killing American soldiers in Iraq by committing acts of sabotage.

Bobby and Bo caught her and her lover on video and audiotape, and she was confronted along with General Perry in his Pentagon briefing room. General Perry booted the secretary out of the army, not for her sexual behavior, but for divulging military secrets. He essentially blackmailed Veronica Caruso and let her know she may be called upon in the future again. She was worried that she was being called upon now.

"Mr. President," she said, "I have spoken to you in press conferences and a couple reception lines, but I have always wanted the honor of meeting you face-to-face in this hallowed room, sir."

He chuckled and said, "Ms. Caruso, were you actually thinking that a couple years ago when you did that hatchet job on me about illegal immigration with your buddy Senator James Weatherford?"

Her face reddened, and she said, "I am sorry, sir. I am a reporter, and it's my job to report the news."

He laughed and said, "Yeah, yeah, I know. I am only teasing you anyway. How would you like to do a one-on-one interview with me, in this hallowed room for let's say one half hour uninterrupted?"

"Whoa!" she said. "Are you serious, Mr. President?"

"Do you think I would joke about that?"

She laughed, and showing she was a longtime hardcore crusty news reporter, said, "No, I don't. Gee, who do I have to screw?"

Without hesitating, the president said, "James Weatherford, along with one of your girlfriends."

Perry chuckled out loud.

Ronnie Caruso laughed and her face reddened again, but she felt light-headed.

She said, "Seriously, Mr. President, to what do I owe this honor?"

He laughed and leaned forward with his elbows on his knees.

"The honor of serving your country by helping to rid it of a traitor who has been consorting with our enemy," the president said very seriously and quietly. "I have been made well aware of certain talents you have, Ms. Caruso, besides looking damned good on a TV screen. I want you and one of your beautiful girlfriends to seduce and have a sexual threesome with Senator Weatherford, and I want it all on videotape. I believe given his own habits and your capabilities, it should be an easy task for you. It will be our secret, along with the good general here."

"No, I absolutely will not!" she said. "No way!"

General Perry cut in, "Fine, there is no statute of limitations on treason. Can we have her neck stretched like Saddam Hussein, Mr. President, or will it have to be lethal injection?"

"Okay, okay." She sobbed into her hands.

The president went to his intercom and said, "Sandra, coffee and tea for the three of us, please."

"Yes, sir."

Less than a minute later, there was a knock on the door. A Secret Service agent opened it and a white-gloved orderly pushed a cart in with two large silver coffeepots. There were small cookies, and china cups and saucers, along with various types of tea. He took everybody's request and poured coffee for the president and general and hot tea for Veronica. He left the cart at the president's request.

The chief executive said, "Ms. Caruso, I did not become president of the United States without knowing how to be as ruthless and cunning as you and Senator Weatherford, except I save that power to use in benefit of our nation, not for my own career or well-being. I will do whatever is necessary to protect the United States. I hope you understand and appreciate that commitment."

"Yes, sir," she said resignedly, then becoming Veronica the survivor, she brightened up, adding, "Were you serious about the interview, Mr. President?"

"Yes, I was," he said. "That is your benefit in this. I have already seen you naked on video, and so has the general, and I happen to be very happily married, and unlike your friend the senator, I do not use my position to bed other women. We will be the only people who see this, unless you act stupidly at some point."

"I understand, Mr. President," she said. "But don't you feel any guilt about ruining his career?"

He laughed out loud. "Lady, if I had my way, we would decriminalize dueling and I would shoot the son of a bitch. I was not joking about him committing treason. We have plenty of proof positive."

She asked, "Then why use me?"

The president said, "Ms. Caruso, look around you. Do you know how many important decisions affecting the world have been made in this room? Decisions by great Democrats and great Republicans? Decisions to go to war, many wars, and to sign peace treaties, to form alliances and to end them, to abolish slavery, to provide for women's rights, to initiate certain taxes, and to eliminate certain taxes. So very many world-altering decisions have been made in this very room. I do not even allow visitors to enter the White House wearing blue jeans, because of the storied history and tradition in these halls. Yet, we had a president who got blow jobs in this room by a twenty-one-year-old wide-eyed intern no less, and afterward there were people who laughed about it, minimized it, and still lionized the man as some kind of hero. That will not happen to Weatherford. I will bury him politically so deep, he will have to use a two-story ladder just to see daylight."

"You have made yourself very clear, Mr. President," Ronnie responded. "But how do you know you can trust me? What if I did go to bed with him and told him everything?"

He looked her straight in the eye and said, "I am the most powerful man in the world. I will have you assassinated, simple as that. As I said, I will do whatever it takes to protect this nation. Any more questions?"

She started to cry again. Veronica had proven she definitely feared death.

The president gave her the plans that had been made. A senator from his party would take Weatherford out to dinner at 1789 Restaurant on Thirty-sixth Street in Georgetown.

In its own words,

The 1789 Restaurant is the quintessential Washington, D.C., dining experience. Chosen by readers of *Gourmet* magazine as one of America's Top Tables, its inspired creativity is delivered in a relaxed country-inn elegance. Decorated with American antiques, period equestrian and historical prints and Limoges china, its five dining rooms offer comfortable surroundings in a renovated Federal house.

Regionally acclaimed chef Nathan Beauchamp joins the masterful wine pairings of William Watts to create a premier dining experience unique to the nation's capital.

General Perry and the president both got hungry just speaking about the very classy and popular restaurant. Because of its popularity, and its dining elegance, the president felt it was a sure bet that Weatherford would agree to a free dinner there. The senator, who was a friend of the chief executive, would only know he was to get Senator Weatherford there, and he would assume the president was up to some clever political scheme, but would also know enough and be politically astute enough not to ask any questions.

Veronica was to show up at the restaurant for dinner with a beautiful girlfriend and then seduce the senator and videotape the event.

After she left the Oval Office, General Perry looked at the president grinning, and said, "May I ask a question, sir?"

The president laughed, saying, "Would I actually have her killed?"

The general said, "Yes, sir."

The commander in chief responded, "Of course not. I'm not a murderer, Jon, but I damned sure will lie if I need to do so to protect this nation. I was just being a bully, because I read her demeanor and felt it would work. Obviously, it did."

It was three days later when Sen. James Weatherford and Sen. Thomas Atha met outside the 1789 Restaurant and went inside where they were seated and offered tasty wines.

Both men selected Lobster Cioppino with braised fennel, roasted tomatoes, clams, and sourdough croutons.

They both started with a first course of Yukon Gold potato soup with lobster and pickled chanterelles, and then for the second course, Weatherford ordered Foie Gras Torchón, hazelnut biscotti, huckleberry jam and cardamom caramel, and Atha ordered Cavatelli wild mushrooms, poached farm egg and mascarpone.

During the main course, two ravishing women in low-cut evening gowns appeared at their table, and both men jumped up, recognizing Veronica, a national television celebrity. Veronica introduced her "close friend" Suzette to both men and laughed to herself watching both men drool.

She leaned forward toward James Weatherford and caught him looking down at her ample cleavage twice.

The second time, she grinned at him and winked, whispering, "Watch it, Senator. I am a mind reader."

Standing, Ronnie said, "Gentlemen, I am sorry to bother you, but you are both famous lawmakers, and Suzette has always had a secret crush on you, Senator Weatherford, and just had to meet you."

At another table, a man in a gray pin-striped suit dialed his cell phone. He was wearing an earpiece.

Thomas Atha's cell phone rang, and he said, "Hello."

The man said quietly, "Senator Atha, the president would like you to say this is an emergency phone call and excuse yourself."

Without missing a beat, the senator said in a distressed voice, "Oh, my gosh. How bad was he hurt?"

The man said, "Great job, sir. No wonder the president speaks so highly of you."

"Thank you. Thank you so much," he said. "I'll head right to the hospital. I'm just glad he's going to be okay. Good-bye."

He stood and said, "Ladies, Senator. I am so sorry. One of my kid's best friends was in an accident. I need to get to the hospital. The kid's going to be okay but is like a part of our family. Rain check, Senator?"

"Absolutely, Thomas. I am sorry. You go right ahead and call if I can be of any help," Weatherford said, secretly relieved.

He shook hands with the senator and said, "Don't worry. I have the bill."

Atha headed toward the door, saying, "Ladies, nice to meet you, Suzette. Always great to see you, Veronica."

They bid him adieu and Weatherford, still standing, said, "I have nobody to accompany me for dinner. Why don't you both sit with me, please?"

Ronnie whispered in his ear, "I don't know if that is such a good idea, Senator. Suzette is such a fan of yours, I am afraid she won't be able to contain herself."

"Holy hell." He laughed. "All the more reason for you two to join me. Please, dinner is on me."

After moving from their other table, both women ordered, and Veronica, with touches, hair strokes, and flirty pouts, made it clear to him that she and Suzette were much more than simply bosom buddies. By the end of dinner, the normally smooth senator was the one who could hardly contain himself.

Ronnie had previously told Suzette that she wanted her to help her seduce Weatherford, so she could get news stories from him. Suzette thought it would be great fun and was more than game.

The entire dinner was one big game for Suzette and Ronnie, making the senator go crazy, so at the end of the dinner, when he suggested an after-dinner drink, Veronica leaned over and whispered in his ear, "Why don't we go to my condo and have a drink?"

The senator was beyond ecstatic. Veronica had a condo in Washington, which was supplied by her network, and she also had her own penthouse apartment, overlooking Central Park in Manhattan. He followed Veronica to her place, and they all went in together, both women hanging on his arms. On the way there, the two women made sure he could see their overly friendly antics in the car.

Suzette had no clue about the two cameras hidden in Veronica's bedroom. Ronnie excused herself while Suzette poured drinks. The news woman changed into a flimsy nightie, a very flimsy nightie, and turned both digital video cameras on.

When she came out into the living room, she said slowly in a very husky voice, "I hope you don't mind, Senator, but I just had to slip into something more comfortable. Wouldn't you like to slip into something more comfortable?"

"Oh my, oh my!" he said. "Would I ever!"

Suzette snuggled up next to him, unhooked his belt and pulled it from his trousers.

That night, Veronica got the president over an hour of digital video, which was more than he ever could have asked for.

BANGKOK RENDEZVOUS   185

Bobby dangled his feet over the edge, thinking that this would make for some...

Then the beautiful Bo, refreshed, reappeared, this time in another fine outfit fit for a royal honeymoon.

· 11 ·

THAILAND

Bobby and Bo actually got to spend two days honeymooning at the four-star Rama Gardens Resort Hotel in downtown Bangkok.

Bobby said, "Honey, you wanted to stay in an authentic Bangkok resort hotel, and not just an American chain hotel. This is the real deal."

The U.S. Navy says of its Bravo Model Seahawk:

SH-60B Seahawk (Bravo):
The SH-60B Light Airborne Multi-Purpose System (LAMPS Mk III) deploys primarily aboard frigates, destroyers and cruisers, and, prior to the fleet introduction of the MH-60R "Romeo," was considered the Navy's most advanced helicopter. The primary missions of the Bravo are surface warfare and antisubmarine warfare, which it accomplishes through a complex system of sensors carried aboard the helicopter including a towed Magnetic Anomaly Detector (MAD) and air-launched

*sonobuoys. Other sensors include the APS-124 search
radar, ALQ-142 ESM system and optional nose-mounted
forward looking infrared (FLIR) turret. It fires the Mk-46
or Mk-50 torpedo, AGM-114 Hellfire missile, and single
cabin-door-mounted M60D or GAU-16 machine gun for
defense. A standard crew for a Bravo is one pilot, one
ATO/Co-Pilot (Airborne Tactical Officer) and an enlisted
aviation systems warfare operator (sensor operator). Operating Bravo squadrons are designated Helicopter Anti-
submarine Light (HSL). HSL-47, an SH-60B squadron
based at Naval Air Station North Island in Coronado,
California, participated in the Navy's humanitarian relief operations during the Indonesian Tsunami and Hurricane Katrina.*

Because Bobby and Bo were carrying various weapons
and surveillance devices, they could not fly down to Koh
Samui on one of the colorfully decorated Bangkok Airways
charters that flew several times per day. Instead, they were
picked up in Bangkok and transported by a Seahawk crew
flying off a big Nimitz-type carrier off the coast. The crew
of the big bird could not have been more helpful, and the
ship's commander told them over the radio that he would
have a chopper standing by twenty-four/seven in case they
needed it. Apparently, word had come down through the
chain that Bobby and Bo were "the man" and "the woman."

They were dropped off at Koh Samui airport and an
American civilian greeted them with a shiny red Jeep
Wrangler and handed them the keys, telling them it was
their rental car while on the island, and said to just drop it
anywhere when they were done and leave the keys under
the back of the front seat.

They got a place on one of the very white, beautiful,
gently sloping sandy beaches. Koh Samui is an island fifty
miles off the coast of southern Thailand, and its primary
industries used to be coconut farming and fishing, but
tourism buried both industries a long time ago. The island

is about ninety square miles, covered with white-sand beaches, with a rugged, jungle-covered mountainous interior with magnificent rock formations, even on some of the beaches. There are rocky, beautiful waterfalls and gorgeous jungle flowers everywhere, and the island is covered by palms and coconut palms. The ocean waves are hardly the breakers one would see in California or New England, but more like the gentlest beaches in the Gulf of Mexico, because they are so gradual in their slant. Out away from the shore, however, is some very appealing scuba and snorkeling territory. There is a population of maybe 42,000 to 48,000 residents, with many being foreigners from all nations, but since 2000, many Muslims have moved in and opened businesses. And after the global War on Terrorism began, many members of al Qaeda moved into southern Thailand, including Koh Samui.

The most notable of these was Muhammad Yahyaa, and Bobby and Bo were going to seek him out.

Muhammad had a large but private apartment above a tailor shop on Chaweng Road. The tailor was an al Qaeda operative and people could either go up the back stairs to the apartment or go in and out the front door of the tailor shop without arousing suspicion. Muhammad always had at least five bodyguards in his apartment, heavily armed.

Niran Vanida was one of Muhammad's Bangkok-born recruits who had been in training for over a year. He ran up the stairs and one of the bodyguards let him approach Muhammad.

He stopped and bowed in the Thai custom, with his hands up, palms together, and the hands raised up face level while bowing; the higher they were, the higher the authority he faced.

He said, "*Sawadee kup,* Muhammad."

"*Asalakalakum,*" Muhammad replied.

Speaking English, the one language they both understood, Niran said, "Muhammad, my men have been watching at all the hotels and the American man and woman you want us to find have arrived. They stay at the beach at a hotel. They drive red American car, a Jeep. My men watch now."

Muhammad pulled 10,000 baht out of a drawer, which is about $248, and handed it to Niran.

He said, "You did good. You give half of this to your men, and save the other. Tell them to kill this man and woman and give them the rest. I must leave, but I will return when they are gone."

Thanking Muhammad, Niran put his palms together again bowing and said, *"Kahm koo cup."*

He headed toward the stairway, saying, "We kill them. No problem."

Meanwhile, Bobby and Bo put on bathing suits and wore tropical shirts unbuttoned over the suits. This hid the crisscross leather shoulder harnesses with holsters holding their Glock 17s tucked safely away under their left arms. They started jogging side by side along the beach, really enjoying the run, even though it was late afternoon and very hot.

"Darling," Bo said, "isn't this just beautiful? It's a shame we are on assignment here."

Bobby said, "I know. It is beautiful. We will have to vacation here, when we can, without working."

They only planned to run a short distance and start to get acclimatized and check things out along the beach anyway.

"What is that smell?" Bo said.

"Burning coconuts," Bobby responded.

"Really?" she said. "That's a different fragrance."

"Bo," Bobby said, "keep running, but we are being watched."

"From where?" she said. "I don't have any visuals yet."

"I don't know," he replied. "It's that sense of knowing or feeling I have talked to you about. I feel it strongly."

"I'm a believer, sweetheart," Bo said. "You have proven yourself enough. What do we do?"

Bobby said, "First, we find out who's watching us, following us, or whatever."

He had noticed earlier two men on mopeds pass them far off to their right on the road paralleling the beach. They were under the line of trees, and he remembered seeing their brake lights come on. If they were ambushers, that would put them ahead of him just around the bend to the right. He stopped and Bo followed suit.

Bobby said, "We have to move fast. I think there is an ambush of two men right around that bend. It would put us out of sight of the resort and other buildings. They could shoot us from the trees and get out of there quickly. I saw two men on mopeds riding up a road there that parallels the beach. After getting that feeling, I remembered noticing their brake lights come on, which meant they had to be stopping up ahead. Both were wearing big backpacks, so they could have automatic weapons or anything in them."

Bo asked, "How do you want to play it?"

Bobby said, "Turn you into bait."

"Gee, darling. Thank you," she said sarcastically, then said, "What do you want me to do?"

Bobby said, "Take off your shirt and holster."

She did, and he threw the shirt on the beach, grabbed her Glock and stuck her two extra magazines in the back of his trunks.

Bobby said, "You go out in the water and keep jogging, but make sure you are far enough from shore that you are out of effective range of any rifles like AKs. They are men and you are jogging in a bikini. They will be panicked looking for me, but still won't take their eyes off you long. I will come up behind them through the trees."

"What if they have a scoped sniper rifle?" she asked.

He said, "Then you'll be dead, honey, but so will I right after you. We can jog back if you want."

"Hell no!" she said.

He laughed. "My partner! They will get out of position to look for me. That will give me a chance. The second you hear firing, go in the water and get away from shore. Count to fifty, go straight out, then start jogging in the water. Questions?"

"Yeah, can I have a kiss?"

He kissed her and then kissed the tip of her nose for good measure, saying, "I love you. Don't worry."

She said, "I'm not, but don't miss."

He ran up into the line of palm trees and wove his way toward the direction of the moped drivers.

Bo counted then jogged out into the water, then turned right and paralleled the water. In a string bikini, she was going to provide a sight to the would-be killers straight out of the movie *10*.

A minute later, Bobby's theory proved correct, as two Thai Muslim men looked from behind palm trees as they saw Bo jogging along in the water. Both made comments to each other about her appearance and beauty as she bounced along. The larger of the two cursed their luck that she was so far out. They would have to come out of the trees to kill her. They both were standing now, one holding a folding-stock SKS rifle, and the other an American-made Ruger Mini-14 using a twenty-round magazine and standard NATO ammunition. Both weapons were converted to fire full automatic.

Suddenly, they heard a noise behind them and turned to see Bobby rapidly bearing down on them through the trees with a Glock 17 in each hand. Then they realized he was coming very quickly, as he was driving one of their mopeds. He had let go of the handlebars, and let out a primal scream as both men tried to raise their weapons. Before they could get their weapons up, Bobby was putting double taps, two shots fired in quick succession, into their torsos. Both, to their credit, remained on their feet and kept trying to raise their weapons, and Bobby kept yelling. He tossed one Glock aside and steered the vehicle toward the wavering man to his right front. Bobby jumped off at the last second toward the man on the left and did a flying side-kick, catching the rather large man right in the windpipe with the blade of Bobby's foot.

The kick went in perfectly under the chin, and one bone cracked in his neck as the kick struck hard right on the point of the Adam's apple. Already shot in the torso, the man panicked, trying to breathe or even swallow. He looked down and saw frothy red bubbles coming out of one of the holes in his chest, then he looked at Bobby. Then he thought back to his childhood and how much he wanted to grow up in a Muay Thai camp and become a national hero, retiring before he hit thirty.

Bobby felt his pulse, while pointing his gun back at the other, but it was obvious that was not needed as the moped sent him back into a palm tree in a sitting position. Bo appeared from the beach, her hair and body totally wet from following directions. Seeing he cleared the bodies, she threw her arms around his neck and kissed him.

"Thank God, you're safe," she said.

Bobby gave her a quick kiss and said, "Let's check their pockets and get out of here. Cops in Koh Samui do not care about foreigners and won't get involved, but these two are not foreigners.

Three minutes later, carrying the IDs of the two men, Bobby and Bo rode back toward the resort on the mopeds, picking up Bo's blouse and shoulder holster first. They dumped the motor scooters in a side alley near the beach. The two cops held hands and walked to the hotel like two tourists enjoying the sights.

Bobby said, "Hand me your gun carefully."

He started coughing and stopped and bent over, and she handed him her gun as he bent over and patted his back with her other hand. Quickly, he ejected her almost-empty magazine, slipped in another, and closed the receiver. Acting like his coughing spasm ended he slipped it back into her holster, as if they were hugging.

Bobby said, "I used up most of your rounds in that mag, and I feel like we better be ready every second. Obviously someone knows we are here."

Muhammad Yahyaa was boarding Bangkok Airways flight 503 to Singapore at about 4:20 p.m. when he got the news sent to him that two men had failed and were found dead along the beach. It sent a chill down his spine. From

Singapore, he would catch the next flight to Manila. Safe there, he would rendezvous as planned with the others and finalize plans for Akrahuka, Amerikka! Three of his closest bodyguards, all Arabs, flew with him. They would be met in Manila, and the three would be given weapons right away.

Bobby and Bo took turns showering in their room. Then he opened the false bottom on their suitcases and got out the rest of their weaponry. They got dressed up and Bo wore a long flowery sarong with a slit up one leg. Her Glock 19, a smaller version of the 17, was in a holster on the inside of her thigh. She also wore a long silky matching jacket and had a pair of Glock 17s in twin shoulder holsters under the jacket.

Bobby wore a cream-colored silky pullover shirt and tan slacks, and under the shirt, under his left arm, in a specially made leather quick-slip holster, Bobby carried a Heckler and Koch MP5 machine pistol.

Officially, the spec ops popular H&K MP5 is described historically:

> The MP5 was first introduced by Heckler & Koch in 1966, under the name HK54. This name comes from HK's old numbering system: The "5" designates the model as a submachine gun, while the "4" identifies it as being chambered for 9 × 19 mm ammunition. The current name dates from when it was officially adopted by the West German government for use by its police and border guard as the Maschinenpistole 5 ("Machine pistol 5," or MP5), in mid-1966. The GSG 9 (the counterterrorist unit of the German Federal Police) then introduced the MP5 to other Western counter-terrorist units.
>
> With the increased use of body armor, the future of the MP5 is uncertain. Several new trends in firearms design have begun to eclipse the submachine gun; small caliber personal defense weapons (PDW) like the new Heckler & Koch MP7 and compact carbines such as the

M4, AKS-74U, the G36C variant of HK's G36. The only major criticism of the MP5 has been its high cost—approximately US $900 for an MP5N (the United States Navy variant). Heckler & Koch has started to complement the MP5 series with the cheaper UMP, which is available in .45 ACP, .40 S&W and 9 mm Parabellum calibers. However, since the UMP uses a simple blowback action as opposed to the MP5's roller-delayed blowback, the two weapons may not necessarily be competitors among the most discriminating users. In addition, the lighter weight of the UMP makes it more difficult to control during fully automatic fire than the MP5.

One famous counter-terrorist operation involving the MP5 was Operation Nimrod. It took place on April 30, 1980, in the United Kingdom, when the Special Air Service (SAS), armed with MP5s, was deployed to assault the terrorists who had taken over the Iranian embassy in London.

The MP5's accuracy, reliability, and wide range of accessories and variations have made it the submachine gun of choice for military and law enforcement agencies worldwide for over thirty years. Users include counter-terrorist groups, special operations forces and police forces.

The weapon is one that has been used in modified versions officially by the FBI and U.S. Navy SEALs and is a very popular weapon among the United States military elite spec ops units such as Special Forces, Combat Applications Group, and so on. Bobby could also hide it well under his shirt.

For backup, he also carried his Glock 17 tucked into the small of his back in his belt line. Bobby also had magazines for both the MP5 and Glock 17 tucked into the small of his back and into his hip pockets.

In Thailand, including Koh Samui, organized crime is very much a part of society, and most especially centering around Muay Thai. Thai kickboxing is the national sport in

Thailand and is the individually toughest sport in the world. Millions of dollars are gambled each day in Thailand over matches.

The Thai "mafia" as Americans sometimes call it deals almost exclusively with the matches going on all the time. They are very careful about things like "hits," which are usually related to cheating at gambling or welching on gambling debts. If a man is going to be hit, he is shot almost always at close range, and they are extremely careful not to involve family members or innocent bystanders. In such cases, it is not only not investigated but many times the police are deeply or even directly involved as well. Most hits occur in streets, alleys, or when a person is seated in their car, but seldom are they carried out in public places like restaurants, because of the care taken not to kill innocent bystanders.

For this reason, Bobby, while ordering dinner, told Bo, they should not be concerned about being shot while eating dinner or dancing or any similar activity. Their biggest concerns would be going to and from their Jeep and getting isolated anywhere on the island.

An attempt had been made on their lives when they had barely been on the island for any time at all, so Bobby knew more was coming, and they would have to work fast.

He discussed all these things with Bo while they ate, and she said, "But these guys are Alpha-Quebecs not Thai mafia, so why does that affect us?" Alpha-Quebec was code for al Qaeda.

"Good question, honey," Bobby replied. "Because the Thai mafia being businessmen and greedy above all else may put up with certain things for the sake of not making waves and just making money, but if the al Qaeda comes in and tries some of their terrorism tactics in the towns big enough for Muay Thai stadiums, they may be opening a can of 'whup-ass' on themselves. You know, when in Rome."

Bo said, "That makes sense. So what are we going to do after we eat?"

The lieutenant colonel chuckled, saying, "First, try to make it to our car without being assassinated."

Bo started laughing.

"What then?" she asked.

Bobby smiled and said, "Have you ever seen a Muay Thai match?"

"No," she responded.

After dinner, the two carefully went to the vehicle and left there without incident.

Although Thai boxing is regarded as the world's most dangerous martial art it is surprisingly aesthetic and graceful to watch. Chaweng Stadium near the Reggae Pub is the biggest on Samui Island and is also the only commercial stadium on the island. It hosts all the major fights on the island twice a week on Tuesday and Friday nights—although when the real season hits, they also hold fights on Sundays as well. Fights begin usually about 9 p.m. and there are usually about eight matches, but sometimes even as many as ten smaller matches, before the main fight.

Some serious Muay Thai aficionados just show up for the main event around 10 p.m. The atmosphere in Chaweng Stadium is outstanding. There is a live commentator. Traditional Thai music is constantly playing and the stadium, like all Muay Thai stadiums, becomes quite boisterous, with gamblers everywhere making wagers while fights are going on, after, and in between. Both Thai fighters and foreign fighters compete in the ring, and almost all of them are professionals.

Bobby and Bo parked and entered Chaweng Stadium thinking they might be followed. Bobby paid for a ringside table. Bo knew better than to ask why they were there. Bobby never did something for no reason. She had been in very few bars, or other places, that had ever been as loud and electrically charged with excitement.

It really is not very surprising that a boy as young as seven or eight would start training and actually living at primitive Muay Thai stables all across the country.

Muay Thai is fought in five three-minute rounds with

two-minute breaks in between. The fight is preceded by a Wai Khru dance, in which each contestant pays homage to his teachers. Besides the symbolic meaning, the dance is a good warm-up exercise. Bo noticed that each boxer wore a headband and armbands. The headband, called mongkhol, is believed to bring luck to the wearer since it has been blessed by a monk or the boxer's own teacher. The headband is both a lucky charm and a Buddhist spiritual object. It will be removed after the Wai Khru dance, but it can only be removed by that boxer's trainer. Bo noticed fighters waiting in the wings and saw the colorful armbands tightly tied over each bicep muscle. Those armbands, meanwhile, are believed to offer protection, are also religious in nature, and are only removed when the fight has ended.

The Wai Khru, which is also known as Ram Muay, or the boxing dance, is a very important part of any evening watching Muay Thai and most foreigners like Bo did not really understand the import to the whole match. These are ceremonies that are performed before each Muay Thai bout. Sometimes the Wai Khru are brief and basic, but other times they may be very eloquent performances that draw praise and kudos from the crowd. Muay Thai instructors are very highly respected in Thai society, and many other artistic disciplines also perform Wai Khru or "respects to the teacher."

Bo watched the fighters in the first match and was fascinated with the almost kung-fu-looking fluidic movements of the Wai Khru, where they kind of danced with slow, rhythmic techniques, ranging from ones where one leg is up and the other is behind it, knee on the ring floor, but the foot behind it is raised off the ring floor and goes up and down in sync with the music, while the arms are spread out almost in a breaststroke or flying motion. It was fascinating to her.

A match is decided by a knockout or by points. Three judges decide who carries the round and the one who wins the most rounds, wins the fight. The referee plays a very important role, since boxers' safety depends on his decision.

As brutal as the sport is, Muay Thai referees—the good ones—will often catch a fighter's head before it hits the canvas when there is a knockout.

To one side of the ring is the band section, with a clarinet, some drums, and cymbals. They accompany the fight from the Wai Khru dance to the end of the match. The tempo of the music goes up every time the action inside the ring intensifies, and Bo finally noticed that the influence of the sound of the music would make her get even more excited.

Muay Thai is what the Thai people call "their own martial art." It has been Thailand's most popular spectator sport for centuries and is very unique among other kinds of fighting disciplines in its approach. Fighters are able to more effectively use their elbows, knees, feet, and fists than in other martial arts. They also are not broken up when clinching, as they do what is called neck wrestling, hoping to maneuver their arms into a better controlling position, so they can deliver knee strikes to the sides of the ribs or maybe straight up to the face. Sometimes, when completing neck wrestling and breaking away, a fighter might sneak in a vicious elbow strike into the face. They also will use neck wrestling leverage to try to twist and throw the opponent to the floor of the ring. This adds points and can cause aches and pains.

Much of Muay Thai is kicking to the upper and lower legs. Instead of the feet, the shins are generally the weapons used to strike with and are thrown with the velocity intended to fracture an opponent's leg bone or rib.

Boxing gloves are worn on the hands and standard boxing techniques and combinations are usually employed, interspersed with the leg kicks and other Muay Thai techniques.

By the third match, Bo noticed that neither fighter in any match really came on strong in the first round. She did not know, but Muay Thai trainers teach their students to feel out the other fighter the first round, and really start attacking in the second. Foreign fighters with very good boxing skills have had success against native Thai boxers, because most training is on leg kicks, neck wrestling, elbows, and knees.

Kon Muay is the preliminary name for the movements by their use. For example, Kon Muay JuJom means an "attack," whereas a defense or counter is called Kon Muay-Kae. Kon Muay-Kae using fists is called Kon Muay-Kae Mad. Kon Muay-Kae Tao means to defend or counter using the feet. To use the knees is called Kon Muay-Kae Kao.

The Muay Thai boxing trunks were very colorful, and Bo was fascinated during a later match when an American fighter called Joshua the Avenger came out. His trunks were shiny blue with white lettering and had a pair of green eyes on the front. Besides "The Avenger," the trunks on the side said "Joshua 1:5," which was the Old Testament verse that reads: "No man shall be able to defeat you all the days of thy life: as I have been with Moses, so will I be with thee: I will not leave thee, nor forsake thee."

The young man had blond hair and very powdery blue eyes and was exceedingly handsome and all-American looking. He performed his Wai Khru dance like he had grown up in Thailand, but did not feel out his fighter in the first round. He went after the man with a quick shin kick to the back of the man's thigh and then a series of eight boxing techniques in machine-gun fashion; the Thai fighter tried to cover up, and Joshua hit him with a vicious elbow smash, breaking the man's nose and knocking him out cold in just over a half minute of round one.

An American sat down by Bobby and Bo, looking at his watch, and said above the crowd noise, "The kid is amazing. That makes seven knockouts within forty seconds of round one. Listen to the crowd here—they love him, but he's leaving."

Bobby asked, "Who are you?"

The big ruddy-faced man said, "Your guardian angel," and, looking at Bo, continued, "and yours, too, Major. Act like we are friends. We're being watched."

Bobby pointed at the Avenger, actually helping medical officials carry the man out of the ring and place him on a gurney.

He said, "The young man is amazing. Very well built, too. Why is he leaving?"

The man said, "He has trained and fought in Thailand for two years now, the past six months in Koh Samui, and Bangkok before that. His older brother lived in Bangkok and fought there, too, but the guy went home, joined the service, and earned his Green Beret. Now this kid, Joshua, is leaving kickboxing and is going to do the same thing."

Bobby smiled and said, "Wow!"

The man went on, "His dad was a Green Beret captain during the Vietnam War. Was in the top secret Phoenix Program and served on an A-Team in 1968–1969."

Bobby said, "A father and two sons earning their Green Berets. That is cool and very rare."

The man said, "You should know. I served with your dad in Forty-sixth Company up north of Bangkok."

Bobby nodded his head, saying to Bo, "A classified Special Forces unit that started here in Thailand during the Vietnam War. Welcome home, sir."

Bo said, "Thank you for your service to our nation."

"You two are the ones needing thanks," he said.

Bobby asked, "So you are in the military?"

The older man laughed. "Hell no! I'm a PFC."

Bobby laughed and Bo said, "A PFC?"

"He is a private," Bobby explained. "Well, a private civilian. Just let it go at that, honey."

The man laughed and said, "I got called right after you called the hostile incident report in to higher headquarters. I have been a civilian living around here for decades. I snoop around a bit, but I guess you could call me a consultant. The cops here will not help you at all. You are American. They will take the side of the Thais every time, by the way. My name is Boo."

Bo said, "Boo?"

He said, "Yes, ma'am, like Casper the Ghost, you know, Boo."

Bobby got sad for a minute, and said, "Speaking of Boo, did you know Boom Kittenger?"

Boo said, "I know all about Boom. I was there at the funeral in Colorado. I saw you both there in your dress blues. I know all about you."

Bobby said, "I don't remember seeing you there, and I am a cop. I usually notice people."

Boo laughed, saying, "Son, I am a consultant and my job is to not be noticed. But during the ceremony, you walked over and got a small box of Kleenexes for Boom's sister and oldest daughter, because they did not bring any, and those two sure did need them. Afterward, I thought it was kind how you went over and held her, Colonel."

"Geez," Bobby said, "I did not mean I questioned you being there, but more that I was mad for not seeing you. What were you wearing?"

Boo said, "A uniform."

Bobby asked, "What kind?"

He said, "Dress blues, too."

Bo asked, "What rank were you wearing?"

He said, "Brigadier general."

Bo said, "Holy cow, sir!"

Boo said, "Please, I am a civilian. Call me Boo. Do not say sir, and since I know you two are happily married newlyweds, if you don't mind, I will call you Bobby and Bo."

Bobby said, "Of course, sir. Sorry, I mean Boo. I remember you now."

Bobby looked at Bo and said, "Remember when I pointed out the general who was also wearing a DSC, a Legion of Merit with two Oak Leaf clusters, two Silver Stars, and seven Purple Hearts?"

Bo said, "Oh my gosh. That was you."

Bobby said, "I heard all about you from Boom, General Perry, my dad, and others. You were one of the most decorated men in Vietnam."

Boo chuckled, saying, "Christmas trees are decorated. I was just allowed to take credit for the actions of lots of great teammates and indigenous people."

Bo said, "Why did you act like you did not know him when he sat down, if you came here to meet with him?"

Bobby said, "I didn't come here to meet him."

Bo said, "Then who did you bring us here to meet?"

Bobby said, "I didn't know."

Boo chuckled. "He called the HIR in and knows you two are top priority in all intel and tactical circles. He knew that if there was any cavalry around, they would be here on a night there was a fight and would know what you two looked like. You know this is like going to the Super Bowl twice a week for these people. He figured, if not, someone would hook up with you two at the hotel. He also figured if there was no cavalry here, this would still be the safest place in town for you two to be tonight."

Bo smiled, saying, "Because the Thai mafia would not stand for anybody trying to attack us here, including the Alpha-Quebecs."

Bobby said, "Exactly."

Bo said to Boo, "How did you know he was thinking all of that?"

Bobby interrupted, "Because he spent thirty years in Special Forces and knows how to think outside the box. What are we facing, Boo?"

"Stay behinds."

"Stay behinds?" Bo said.

Boo went on, "Muhammad Yahyaa and three of his bodyguards got on a plane today at 1630 for Singapore. He'll get an adjoining flight to somewhere from there. We got word to people in Singapore who will hopefully get there and find out where he goes. He left behind two bodyguards who are hardcore Mideasterm-trained Alpha-Quebecs. The ones who attacked you were part of some disenfranchised locals who were training under Muhammad. He is a younger version of Ayman al-Zawahiri. He probably put a hit out on you two before he boogied. They all want his approval badly. Their mommies didn't suckle them enough, I guess."

For some reason this line really struck Bo as funny and started her giggling like crazy. Maybe it was just because she was feeling relief knowing they were not alone in this. Boo and Bobby both just watched her laugh and grinned.

Later, Bobby and Bo were both naked and lay on their bed looking out at the moonlight rippling off the expansive sea. Each had their weapons right by the bed, but Boo had reinforced what Bobby had said. Chances are they would not get attacked at their hotel, but somewhere on the street, in their car, or off away from the public eye.

Bo laid her head on Bobby's massive pectoral muscle. Even though they had enemies outside that room plotting ways to kill them, Bo felt like she could not have felt safer than she did when lying in the arms of her hero, her boss, her partner, her lover, her best friend, her husband . . . Bobby Samuels.

He looked at her looking out the window at the still ocean and saw a tear roll down and drop on her pillow. He kissed her forehead lightly and wiped a new tear away.

"What's wrong, darling?"

She said, "Nothing's wrong. They are happy tears."

"Happy tears," he said, surprised. "How can you be happy now, honey? We are in a hornet's nest."

"Because I'm with you."

He smiled and kissed her.

Then he said, "We are still in a lot of danger."

"Not when I am with you," she replied. "I never am in danger. You will always handle it."

His chest puffed a little, but he said, "Thanks, honey, but there is no S tattooed on my chest."

"That's funny," Bo said. "I have always seen one tattooed there, ever since I first met you."

He kissed her again. Bobby knew they would not be getting much sleep that night.

Boom had given them the address, description, and directions for Muhammad's place. While Bo slept after making love again, Bobby lay there thinking about how he could attack the two hardcore AQ fighters.

He climbed out of bed, gulped down a bottle of water, and started putting on black night tactical clothes, Kevlar, and his weapons.

Bobby turned to see Bo sitting up in bed. She hopped out and went to the suitcase.

Bobby said, "Why don't you sleep?"

Bo said, "Because I am going with you. You have their address. I was wondering when you would go after them."

The window to their room was on the first floor facing the ocean, so they simply opened it and climbed out. Both were wearing night vision devices.

Bobby whispered, "It is less than a half mile to their place. I suggest we go on foot and stay in the shadows."

They took off at a brisk pace, and were in an alley near the tailor shop building within ten minutes. Waiting for an opportunity, they crossed the street tactically, each covering for the other. They then made their way to the back of the building. Bo was ready to just sneak up the back stairway, but Bobby put his hand on her arm.

He whispered, "You ever see one of those movies where someone is sneaking up the stairs and suddenly steps on the one that creaks real loud?"

Bo said, "Yes."

Bobby said, "What happens to the guy who makes the step creak?"

Bo laughed, whispering, "He always gets killed. So what do we do?"

Bobby looked around the immediate area and saw there was a balcony on the building next door. It also had a closed business and no residence on the second floor.

Being careful to stay out of sight of Muhammad's windows, he pointed, saying, "Let's go up there, then cross over."

"Whatever you say, honey," Bo replied.

The steps to the balcony next door were made out of concrete blocks, some of which had been concreted, but some were loose. Bobby whispered to Bo, warning her about moving a block with her feet. They found a crude ladder lying behind that building and Bobby carried it up with him. Once on the balcony, they easily climbed up onto the flat roof from the balcony railing. Bobby went up first, and Bo handed him the ladder, which he pulled up, then grabbed her forearm when she stood up on the railing.

Bobby took the ladder and tested all the rungs with his hand, and then carefully lowered it to the roof of Muhammad's building. He told Bo to hold the end, and he walked across on his hands and knees, then held it for her. Once on the roof, they crawled slowly forward on hands and knees, with Bobby testing the structure of the roof with his hand each time.

They made it to the edge of the roof overlooking the back balcony, and peering over the edge, Bobby saw the front end of two weapons, looking to be SKSes or AK-47s.

He leaned back, and laid Bo on the roof, cupping his hands around her ear, ever so softly. "They are waiting for us on the balcony. I just saw the ends of their barrels. Automatic weapons."

Bo cupped her hands around his ear and said, "What will we do?"

Both of them had the advantage of wearing night vision goggles, so peering down at the ends of the barrels in the shadows was easy as long as they did not make noise.

He again cupped his hands carefully and whispered, "Crawl to the edge and watch until you see the ends of the barrels, then picture where they might be standing or sitting. Then crawl back."

She edged forward on her belly and saw the ends of both barrels. Being that close to an ambush that was meant for them almost took her breath away. Quietly, Bo backed away.

Bobby took her by the arm and eased her back several feet more, so they could talk.

He again cupped his hands around one ear and whispered, "You will empty your magazine with searching fire into the one on our right. I'll get the one on the left. Cover both ears. After the flash-bang, roll over on your tummy and open up, and only have your right hand exposed over the edge after the flash-bang goes off. Okay?"

"I'm ready," she said and pulled her Glock out ready to fire. "But why not just use an HE."

Bobby whispered, "In case they have women or even family inside the residence. An HE can blow out a wall and kill others, plus blow us off the roof."

The U.S. Army describes the M84 Stun Grenade like this:

> The XM84 Stun Grenade is a non-fragmentation, non-lethal "Flash and Bang" stun grenade that is intended to provide a reliable, effective non-lethal means of neutralizing & disorienting enemy personnel.
>
> The M84 non-lethal stun grenade is a non-lethal, low hazard, non-shrapnel producing explosive device intended to confuse, disorient or momentarily distract potential threat personnel. The device produces a temporary incapacitation to threat personnel or innocent bystanders. This device will be used by military personnel in hostage rescue situations and in the capture of criminals, terrorists or other adversaries. It provides commanders a non-lethal capability to increase the flexibility in the application of force during military operations.
>
> Detonating the M84 Stun Grenade in the presence of natural gas, gasoline, or other highly flammable fumes or materials may cause a serious secondary explosion or fire, resulting in death, or severe injury to friendly forces or unintended victims, as well as serious property damage. The operator must wear proper hearing protection when employing the M84. Injury to personnel could result if the grenade functions prior to being deployed.
>
> The M84 contains a minimal amount of explosives and, when initiated, produces illumination through

oxidation (burning) of the components of the charge. Some non-toxic smoke is produced in minimal amounts. In the event the grenade functions prematurely or bounces back when tossed, the user could feel the effects of the grenade. Approved eye protection should be worn when employing the M84 to preclude possible damage to the eyes. The grenade when initiated produces an intense "bang." The noise levels will be above 170 decibels within 5 feet of initiation. The user must wear approved single hearing protection when employing the grenade in the event of a premature functioning or bounce back when tossed. Activation of the M84 should not ignite paper or cloth. However, other hazards such as volatile fumes in the space where the grenade will detonate should be considered prior to tossing it into a closed structure.

The US Army Military Police Corps is involved in missions that require the use of a stun hand grenade (diversionary device) to confuse, disorient, or momentarily distract a potential threat. The device will be used to apply the minimum force necessary by tactical and non-tactical forces while performing missions of hostage rescue and capture of criminals, terrorists and other adversaries. The congressionally mandated Soldier Enhancement Program (SEP), of which one purpose is to enhance the survivability items used by the US Army soldier, is the initiative to provide this increased level of protection.

They crawled to the edge, then Bobby carefully looked over and made sure both men were still there. His man had switched hands but both were still there, waiting, watching, wanting to kill the two people who had been less than five feet away above their heads for the past ten minutes.

Bobby gave her the signal, and they rolled over on their backs, Glocks in their right hands, and she plugged her ears with her fingers.

Bobby plugged his left ear with his left hand and had already pulled the pin in the flash-bang, holding the spoon on the side with his fingers. He roled on his side and tossed it down on the balcony, as he quickly laid on his back and covered his right ear and closed his eyes.

They started to hear one word in Arabic and then boom!

Both rolled over on their stomachs and swung their right hands down over the edge of the roof pointing at where they thought the two ambushers were. They unloaded their clips almost simultaneously, and rolled back on their backs. They ejected magazines, slammed another into place, and released the slide, jacking the first hollow-point Corbon round into the chamber. And rolled back on their stomachs.

Bobby slid to the edge and swung his right arm, shoulder, and head over, while Bo, without needing to be told, grabbed his left arm and held him. Looking through his night vision goggles, he saw both men down, unmoving, and shot full of holes.

Bobby holstered his Glock, pulled his left arm free, and swung off the roof, dropping onto the balcony and landing on the balls of his feet. He pulled his weapon again and pointed at each man with a double-hand tactical grip on the pistol, shoulders forward to challenge recoil, high right-hand grip, and left hand cradling the right with the left leg forward in a boxer's stance.

He eased forward, checked the pulse on each, finding none, and yelled, "Clear. Come on, quickly."

Bobby holstered his gun, moved out on the balcony below the edge of the roof and caught Bo as she dropped from the roof. They both pulled their Glocks again, and she covered him while he checked the pockets on the two men. Dogs were barking all over, lights were coming on in houses, and they went in the door and went through the residence as quickly as they could.

They worked fast like two investigators could, and started grabbing papers that Bobby slammed into a backpack there. They ran through the place as fast as they could and soon heard sirens approaching.

Soon they saw Koh Samui police outside on the street, flashlights in hand, searching around for whoever caused the explosion and gun shots. They, so far, had not pinpointed the building. After searching the front of the building and the street for a good ten minutes, the three officers moved toward the back of the building. Bobby and Bo, having gone down through the tailor's shop, simply opened the door and went out into the street, Bobby wearing the backpack. They dashed across the street undetected, save for one old woman down a block who saw them from her window and thought they were probably police.

Still wearing their night vision devices, they fast walked and jogged toward their hotel.

Moving into the shadows of the line of palm trees around the parking lot, they noticed two men at their Jeep. One was underneath.

Bobby whispered, "Let us try to do this without noise, so we do not attract more local yokels and Barney Fifes."

They moved forward, weaving through the cars with stealth. Out over the ocean lightning flashed in the distance and thunder rumbled. Bobby and Bo made the last few steps in a dash. He rammed into the man standing with the power of an NFL linebacker on a blitz slamming into the Jeep. At the same time, Bo ran up and saw the man under the vehicle was on his back, apparently wiring a bomb under their car. She stomped down full power on his groin, and he raised up quickly bashing his face on the transfer case and knocking himself out cold.

Bo grabbed his shins and dragged him out from under the car. His body was a limp rag.

Bobby hit his suspect in the side of his head with an elbow smash and felt it strike home right under the man's ear. He went down like a sack of potatoes.

Both Bobby and Bo grabbed the pair and placed handcuffs on them. They were both Thai Muslims. Bo found their homemade bomb under the car and it was obvious it had to be hooked up to the car battery to detonate. The man had just started.

Bobby pulled out his cell phone and called Boo. Ten minutes later, Boo showed up in an older BMW. He jumped out and Bobby and Bo immediately tossed the two men, now gagged, in the back of the BMW, while Bobby briefed Boo on what they did.

The thunderstorm was much closer, and the normally mild surf was making a lot more noise. They could also hear the flapping of the edges of the large beach umbrellas right behind the resort on many tables.

Boo said, "Dawn is coming soon. We'll talk later. I need to get out of here. I'll take care of these two. Get back to your room and get some sleep. I'll call when we get a line on where Muhammad flew to. He must have used an alias, and he was not spotted by any of my fellow consultants."

They made it to the room undetected and slipped in through the window. Bobby and Bo hopped in a shower together, and then crawled into bed, falling asleep with their arms around each other, listening to the sounds of the storm outside.

They wondered what was going on with the rest of the suspects.

12

THE BODY POLITIC

Sen. James Weatherford wondered what major world event might be going on. He was summoned to the White House by the president. Secret Service agents were there to whisk him through security.

Marine One was warming up on the South Lawn of the White House, and he wondered if he was going on it with the president. With an escort of Secret Service agents around him, Sen. James Weatherford was too arrogant to think anything other than he had really arrived. There was some kind of international crisis going on, and he was being brought in, he figured. He was very excited.

The vice president came out to meet him just outside the Oval Office. A small crowd of VIP visitors stood at the base of the steps to the veranda at the back of the White House, behind a barrier. To their right front was the Oval Office, with several large windows facing them and a double-framed door, full of glass panes where the president could walk out onto the step overlooking the Rose Garden. When the president was inside, there were usually two or three Secret Service agents just outside the door keeping an eye on the crowd behind the White House.

On that side of the back of the White House toward the Rose Garden was another roped-off area which contained a dozen or so news media personnel and their cameras. These people assembled in the back of the White House were only there when the president was flying in or out on Marine One. These visitors now waved at Senator Weatherford and the vice president.

The vice president said, "Thank you so much for coming, Senator Weatherford. The president needs your immediate consultation and assistance. He is waiting for you with others at Camp David, if you would be so kind."

James asked, "What's going on?"

The vice president said, "I can only tell you this will be an historical meeting regarding our national security. The president appreciates your assistance."

Weatherford threw his shoulders back, saying, "Of course. It is my honor to join the president."

The vice president shook hands, saying, "Thank you so much. The helicopter is waiting for you."

Senator Weatherford ate up the attention as he headed toward the aircraft, but hardly waved at any of the well-wishers. He was feeling too self-important. Besides, he decided, it would be more dramatic to jog up the few steps to the front door and turn on the top step and wave. Unlike the president, he did not return the salute of the marine guard at the base of the steps. Instead, he brushed past him, a legend in his own mind.

Camp David serves the president, providing the First Family and their guests with a healthy, safe, and uniquely private place to work or relax. Established as "Shangri-la" by president Franklin Delano Roosevelt, it was subsequently renamed Camp David by Dwight Eisenhower after his grandson.

During times of conflict, war, strife, and acute stress ever since World War II up to more recent events, Camp David has offered the president solitude, peace, and tranquility.

A majority of presidents have used Camp David to host visiting foreign leaders, with Prime Minister Winston Churchill of Great Britain being the very first, during May 1943.

Catoctin Mountain Park was originally considered kind of useless land purchased by the U.S. government in 1936, to be developed into a recreational facility. The purpose of the land was to demonstrate how rough terrain and eroded soil could be turned into productive land.

But under the New Deal program of president Franklin D. Roosevelt, the WPA began the work in the brand-new Catoctin Recreational Demonstration Area. They were joined by the Civilian Conservation Corps, the CCC, in 1939.

Franklin Delano Roosevelt was accustomed to seeking relief from hot Washington summers and relaxing on weekends aboard the presidential yacht the *Potomac* or simply staying at his home in Hyde Park, New York. In 1942, the Secret Service became concerned about the president's use of the *Potomac*, because World War II had brought in the possibility of attack by German U-boats. The muggy climate of the Washington area was considered detrimental to FDR's health, significantly affecting his sinuses. A brandnew retreat within a 100-mile distance of the capital with cool mountain air was sought.

Several sites were considered but Camp Hi-Catoctin in the Catoctin Recreational Demonstration Area was selected after the president's first visit in 1942. So Camp David was already built on the site and the estimated conversion cost was under $20,000. It was also usually ten degrees cooler than Washington. Roosevelt quickly renamed the camp Shangri-la, after James Hilton's 1933 novel, *Lost Horizon*.

Camp David continues to serve as the primary presidential retreat today. It is a private, secluded place for a president's recreation, contemplation, rest, and relaxation, and has been used for many important meetings with many world and political leaders. In fact, very many historical events have occurred at the presidential retreat, including the planning of the Normandy invasion, the Eisenhower-Khrushchev meetings, the Carter Israeli-Palestine peace meetings and subsequent signing of the Camp David accords, discussions of the Bay of Pigs invasion, Vietnam War discussions, and many other meetings with foreign dignitaries and guests. Maintaining the continued privacy and the very secluded atmosphere of the 125-acre retreat is an important role for Catoctin Mountain Park. The presidential retreat still remains within park boundaries but is never open to the public. It is a place where presidents can relax, unwind, or entertain distinguished guests in a very informal setting. On top of that, Camp David has, on numerous accounts, acted as a means of safety and security for the president.

Today it would host a very historic meeting.

Landing in well less than an hour, the senator had an even bigger ego stroke, as he was escorted into the main lodge and was taken to the conference room. The president was seated there, jacket off, tie off, and sleeves rolled up, as well as Gen. Jonathan Perry, the U.S. Army chief of staff, the secretary of defense, the secretary of homeland security, the director of the Secret Service, the national intelligence advisor, and several more notables. All had removed their jackets and were drinking pop, iced tea, water, and a couple had beers.

He shook hands with all and was warmly greeted by the president, who bade him to take a seat right next to his.

The president turned to a large-screen laptop on the conference table.

He said, "Senator Weatherford, I am so damned computer illiterate. Can you show me how to start this video on here?"

Weatherford confidently said, "Sure, Mr. President, let me look at it."

He stuck his head over next to the president and looked at the computer screen. On it was a video box with the words "Classified Top Secret" on it. Only he and Perry, on the other side of the president, could see it, but all others in the room could hear it.

He used the finger mouse to move the cursor down on the play button on the left side of the video control below the video screen. He left-clicked and looked at the screen, expecting to see a covert tape of al Qaeda leaders being discovered.

The men in the room chuckled hearing the sounds of grunts and groans and orgasmic moans, as he looked at a video of him and Veronica and Suzette engaged in a sexual threesome. His jaw dropped and tears filled his eyes.

The president said, "You know, James, you really ought to get some tanning on that lily-white ass. Oh and when you roll over. Well, I don't think we can help you out there. Sometimes Mother Nature just plays mean tricks and short-changes us."

The men in the room all chuckled, except General Perry. He was grim-faced and angry.

James Weatherford, for the first time in his life, was at a total loss for words.

The president said, "That's nothing, James. Look at this video, but I am not going to play the audio because the room has not been cleared yet by the Secret Service."

Lying effectively to cover for the lack of audio they had from their surveillance, the president's bluff was perfect. To Weatherford, the pictures they had of him meeting in Paris with Muhammad Yahyaa and Nguyen Van Tran were top-quality video.

Then the president, still bluffing on the audio, said, "Hell, that's nothing, Jimbo, my man. Look at this video taken not long ago, here in Washington in a restaurant. Again, I have not had the room swept yet, so I'm keeping the audio off, but I can play it for you privately in my office. Do you need to hear it?"

Weatherford began sobbing like a baby and shook his head.

Speaking for the first time, he said, "I am ruined. I am ruined. I am ruined. How could you do this to me?"

The president, now no longer jovial, said, "You did it to yourself, you self-serving, treasonous, murderous son of a bitch, and I just happen to be a son of a bitch myself when it comes to hardcore national politics. Did you think I became president because I am stupid?"

Weatherford, tears dropping from his cheeks, looked around the room at all the cold stares.

He said, "I'm going to kill myself."

General Perry said, "I have a big gun collection, you traitorous bastard. You want to borrow one?"

The president looked at Perry and silently laughed, shaking his head in wonderment.

"By the way, you know Lieutenant Colonel Bobby and Major Bo Samuels?" the president asked. "You must know them, you have had hit men trying to kill them like the hit you put out on an outstanding patriot Command Sergeant Major-retired Boom Kittenger. Guess what? Your hit men all failed and ended up dead. And they had your two army contact flunkies arrested by CID agents, and both of them are singing like canaries."

The president went on, "We could give you your Miranda rights, and allow you to have your attorney present, but I assume you want to cooperate fully and not worry about all that silly stuff. Am I correct?"

Still bawling, between sobs, Weatherford said softly, "Yes, Mr. President."

The chief executive said, "Well, we will get into great detail later, but for the next hour, you will tell us what you know about the proposed attack on our west coast, where Muhammad Yahyaa went after he bugged out of Koh Samui, Thailand, the other day, and where we might expect to meet Nguyen Van Tran."

Sympathy did not work at all, so now Weatherford got angry, mainly at himself for acting like such a wimp.

He looked up, chin out defiantly, and demanded, "Mr. President, I am not saying anything else. I do want my attorney present."

The president looked at him and laughed.

Then he said, "Still think you are in the political game? Do you think we are in front of the news media you have played like a cheap fiddle for years?"

"No, I know my rights," Weatherford said with more courage now.

The president said, "Jon, do you still carry that nickel-plated Colt army model 1911 .45 automatic in your briefcase?"

General Perry said, "Yes, I do, Mr. President."

The chief executive went on, "Wasn't Boom Kittenger a very close friend of yours?"

Perry said, "Yes, sir."

The commander in chief said, "I want you to take that .45 out and unload the magazine into this traitor's body, starting with his joints. If you are charged with murder or any crimes, I will immediately give you a presidential pardon."

Perry said, "I will be glad to shoot this son of a bitch, sir," as he rose and walked to his briefcase.

Weatherford's eyes opened wide, and he put his hands up.

"Okay! Okay!" he said, voice quavering. "I will cooperate fully. Please?"

Perry looked at the president, who nodded, and Perry sat down.

The other men in the room gave the president winks, nods of approval, or shook their heads grinning.

13

BACK TO MANILA

Bobby and Bo got the call on their sat phone personally from General Perry. In the scrambled transmission, General Perry described the discussion the president had with Weatherford, and Bobby told Bo after hanging up. They high-fived and hugged each other.

Bobby grabbed his pants that were sitting on the chair and folded them, putting them in the suitcase.

"Saddle up, baby," he said. "We're going somewhere."

They packed quickly and Bobby called the commander of the aircraft carrier and asked for the helicopter to take them to where they could get a U.S. Air Force jet or U.S. Navy plane to wherever they had to go.

Bobby and Bo were in the big Seahawk naval helicopter on their way to the Nimitz-type supercarrier when he was called by the secretary of defense personally and told that Muhammad Yahyaa flew from Singapore to Manila, and the CIA who had been watching the Pearls 2 Bamboo headquarters building since Bobby and Bo had been there, reported that Yahyaa had been there most of the time for the past day. As soon as they arrived in the carrier, Bobby told the commander that they had to get to Manila as quickly as possible.

The navy captain who commanded the aircraft carrier smiled at Bobby and Bo, saying, "Colonel Samuels, how would you like it if I could get you to Manila, or actually to Manila in well under three hours?"

Bobby said, "Captain, if my wife wouldn't mind, I would give you a big, wet, sloppy kiss."

The captain laughed. "I knew you used to be a Green Beret and should have known better than to ask. I can't help you now."

Playing right along, Bo slapped Bobby on the arm, saying, "See, I told you, in the military it is don't ask, don't tell."

All three of them laughed heartily, then the captain said, "Seriously, our Lockheed S-3 Viking can do the job easily. It has a max speed of five hundred seventy-four miles per hour and a cruising speed over four hundred miles per hour. We have several variations, and it used to be used for submarine hunting, but the al Qaeda don't have too many of them. Most have been converted for other uses, and they used to take a crew of four, but now we have a crew of two, and can fit you both and your luggage."

Bobby said, "Sir, thank you very much for your help. We need to boogie ASAP."

The captain had already nodded at a chief petty officer when he started talking, and he said, "We already have them getting a fast mover and crew ready to go. God speed to both of you."

The U.S. Navy says this in part about the Lockheed S-3 Viking:

The Lockheed S-3 Viking is a jet aircraft originally used by the United States Navy to identify, track, and destroy enemy submarines. In the late 1990s, the S-3B's mission focus shifted to surface warfare and aerial refueling. After the retirement of the A-6 Intruder and A-7 Corsair II, the Viking was the only airborne refueling platform organic to the Carrier Air Wing(s) until the fielding of the F/A-18 E/F Super Hornet. It also provides electronic warfare and surface surveillance capabilities to the carrier battle group. A carrier-based, subsonic, all-weather, multi-mission aircraft with long range, it operates primarily with carrier battle groups in anti-submarine warfare roles. It carries automated weapon systems, and is capable of extended missions with in-flight refueling. Because of the engines' high-pitched sound, it is nicknamed the "Hoover" after the brand of vacuum cleaner.

The S-3 Viking was designed by Lockheed with the assistance from Ling-Temco-Vought and UNIVAC to fit the United States Navy VSX (Heavier-than-air, Anti-submarine, Experimental) requirement for a replacement for the piston-engined Grumman S-2 Tracker. Since Lockheed had no experience in building carrier-based aircraft, LTV was responsible for construction of the folding wings and tail, the engine nacelles, and the landing gear which was derived from A-7 Corsair II (nose) and F-8 Crusader (main). UNIVAC built the on-board computers which integrated input from sensors and sonobuoys. The first prototype flew on January 21, 1972, and the S-3 entered service in 1974. During the production run from 1974 to 1978, a total of 186 S-3As were built.

The S-3 is a conventional monoplane with a high-mounted cantilever wing, swept 15°. The two GE TF-34 high-bypass turbofan engines mounted in nacelles under the wings provide execptional criuse efficiency compared to turbojets or earlier turbofans. The aircraft can seat four crew members with the pilot and the copilot/tactical coordinator (COTAC) in the front of the cockpit and the tactical coordinator (TACCO) and sensor operator (SENSO) in the back. . . . All crew members sit on upward-firing Douglas Escapac zero-zero ejection seats. At the end of the 1990s the sonar operators were removed from the crew. In the tanking crew *configuration, the S-3B typically flies with only a crew of two (pilot and COTAC). The wing is fitted with leading edge and Fowler flaps. Spoilers are fitted to both the upper and the lower surfaces of the wings. All control surfaces are actuated by dual hydraulically boosted irreversible systems.*

The aircraft has two underwing hardpoints that can be used to carry fuel tanks, general purpose and cluster bombs, missiles, rockets, and storage pods. It also has four internal bomb bay stations that can be used to carry general purpose bombs, torpedoes, and special stores (B57 and B61). Fifty-nine sonobuoy chutes are fitted, as well as a dedicated Search and Rescue (SAR) chute. The S-3 is fitted with the ALE-39 countermeasure system and can carry up to ninety rounds of chaff, flares, and expendable jammers (or a combination of all) in three dispensers. A retractable magnetic anomaly detector (MAD) boom is fitted in the tail.

Bobby and Bo arrived at the Manila airport and immediately took a cab to a high-rise hotel that was just a stone's throw away from Pearls 2 Bamboo corporate headquarters. They asked for a room facing the main street, so they could set up surveillance on the building. Bobby called in their location and said they also needed to know where Nguyen Van Tran was.

An hour later, there was a knock on their door. Two men stood in front of Bobby, who held a towel in his hand and said, "Yes?"

Both men were black and wore light weight tropical shirts and slacks. Both were nice-looking men and well built.

One said, "Sir, my name is Joe Oliver and my partner here is Rod Moss. I know you are holding a gun on us under the towel, and I don't blame you. Please ask your wife to call General Perry on his cell, and ask him to give you a password for me to say?"

Behind the door with a gun in her hand, Bo walked over to the sat phone and called Perry.

Bo said, "General?"

He didn't even wait for her to ask but said, "Bo, are they both African American, good-looking guys?"

"Yes, sir," she responded.

He said, "Ask them what did Satan say to Saddam Hussein on his way to hell, and they should answer 'How's it hanging?' Sorry, but we had to hurry."

Bo bid good-bye and hung up, chuckling, and walked up behind Bobby, saying, "What did Satan say to Saddam Hussein on his way to hell?"

Joe grinned and replied, "How's it hanging, Saddam?"

Bobby and Bo both laughed, and Bobby tossed the towel aside and stuck his Glock into the back of his waistband. Then he put his hand out to shake.

"Hi, Bobby Samuels," he said. "Pleased to meet you, Joe. Rod. This is my wife, Bo."

She shook with both men and invited them into the suite, and they all took seats.

Joe said, "We're with the Central Intelligence Agency, but are on loan to the Department of Homeland Security. We came to help both of you maintain surveillance and just got the suite next to yours. We will relieve you so you don't have to do twelve-hour shifts."

Bobby said, "God bless you. Do you guys know what he looks like?"

Rod said, "Affirmative. We have photos and have looked at video."

"How about Nguyen Van Tran?" Bo asked.

"Yes," Joe answered, "we have pictures and video of him, too."

The four set up a stakeout schedule and watched the building. Finally, after only one day, Rod spotted Muhammad entering the building the following morning.

Bobby said, "Have you guys been monitoring the camera and mike I planted in the Fair Weather conference room?"

Joe said, "We haven't. The NSA has."

Bobby said, "I need you to call it in. Ask if they have any eyes or ears on him in the conference room, and also if there is any new intel on Tran."

"Will do," Joe said.

Bobby and Bo dressed in business suits. Bobby poured out the contents of the two briefcases on the bed, and started putting weapons inside, including his MP5.

Bobby picked up the sat phone and called General Perry.

After greeting him and asking if he could talk, Bobby said, "General, we have got to prevent another 9/11, sir. I need your help right now."

"What do you need, son?" the general replied.

Bobby said, "Sir, I need you to call the president and ask him to call Manila and use whatever political pull he has to allow us to enter that building and take down Muhammad and whoever else we need to find out what the attack plan is on the U.S."

"You got it, Bobby," the general said. "You do whatever you have to do. The president already told me this morning to tell you he has got your back, no matter what. You know how he is about keeping his word. He will back whatever you need to do."

"Thank you, sir," Bobby said. "Also, can you have a team from CAG taken by fastest means possible to California and have them standing by?"

"You got it," the chief of staff replied. "Any thing else you and Bo need, son?"

"Prayers, sir," Bobby said.

General Perry said, "Bobby, you have had those on a continuing basis, and I will put out the word, including to the president, to pray for you right now."

"Thanks, sir," Bobby said. "My dad had a friend who always said, 'There is a time for talking and there is a time for doing,' and this is a time for doing. I'm out."

General Perry said, "Do it, Colonel. Perry out."

Bobby finished dressing, and Bo went through her

briefcase checking her weapons and seeing what Bobby packed. Joe came into the room smiling.

"Bobby, you need to come in here," Joe said.

Bobby and Bo went into the other room, and Rod was looking through the U.S. Army M144 spotting scope and chuckling.

Joe said, "Tell them, Rod."

Rod said, "Colonel, I don't know what's up over there, but it looks like they are having an al Qaeda-Vietnamese summit convention going on. Haven't seen Tran but several Vietnamese men and a couple women have gone into the building in the past half hour, also, a lot of Mideastern-looking gents. Two I know are Arabs because they both wore checkered chemaghs."

Joe added, "Plus, NSA reports that the conference room is full and they are talking about a ship headed toward the Port of Los Angeles. Hang on, I wrote it down."

Joe ran over to the desk and returned with a piece of paper. "They have a container ship headed to Los Angeles called the MV *Fairweather*."

Bobby asked, "What size is it?"

Joe said, "Hang on."

He ran over to the desk and his own sat phone, picking it up.

Prior to the days of container ships, all cargo was carried on what is known as general cargo ships and the cargo was known as break-bulk cargo. Cargo ships are much slower to load and unload, so if a ship is not carrying things like a load of coal, they go with container ships.

A 40-foot container was 39 feet 4 inches long, 7 feet 6 inches tall, and 7 feet 8 inches wide inside. The container holds 2,261 cubic feet of area or about 84 cubic yards. In the cargo business, ships are divided into 20-foot container units known as TEU (20-foot equivalent units).

Container ships are also called "box" ships. The "boxes" they carry are containers that generally are found in 20- and 40-foot lengths. They can be filled with just about any type of cargo, from television sets to fruit or meat. The containers that carry frozen or chilled food are know as "refers," or refrigerated containers. The capacity of a container ship is measured in TEU (technical equivalent units). So a freighter carrying 1,600 TEUs is relatively small compared to many of the larger container ships.

The MV *Fairweather* was much bigger, carrying 4,500 containers and was 1,000 feet long, which is 100 feet longer than a football field.

Bobby ran into his room and grabbed his own sat phone.

He called General Perry again.

"Sir, do you have Weatherford on ice or is he still being questioned?"

Perry laughed and said, "Under the bright lights."

Bobby said, "I have to know if he tried to run interference on a ship out of Manila called the MV *Fairweather*. Did he try to use any influence to get it to port unabated anywhere, especially the Port of Los Angeles? It is steaming for the U.S. right now."

General Perry said, "Stand by. I am calling on another line."

He came back in a few minutes saying, "In fact, he did. Weatherford made a special call to the coast guard and customs. He told them he wanted them to allow that ship to come into port at Los Angeles without inspection, because it was carrying containers filled with supplies for AIDS victims as well as housing kits for those who were still homeless from Hurricane Katrina."

Bobby said, "Bull! If I am correct, General, that ship is a floating atomic bomb and has forty-five hundred forty-foot-by-about-eight-foot-by-eight-foot containers carrying explosives. With the right type of explosives, it could wipe out a good chunk of Los Angeles. The coast guard has got to stop that ship at sea and inspect the containers."

Perry said, "Your hunch is good enough, Bobby. You do your thing. I'll do mine. Bye."

Bobby and Bo gave each other one of those "I'm ready to rock and roll" looks.

Samuels said, "So, Joe and Rod. Are you guys investigatory only, or do you like to rumble, too?"

Rod started laughing and walked over and punched Joe on the shoulder.

Rod said, "Sir, Joe is medically retired from the Marine Corps. Force recon. He received the Navy Cross and three Purple Hearts in Iraq and had three tours there under his belt. The shrapnel he carries literally sets off alarms in airports."

Bobby grabbed Joe's hand and shook with him, saying, "Semper fi, Joe!"

Joe said, "He forgot himself, Bobby. Rod was a detective with the New York Port Authority and rescued I don't know how many people out of Tower One before it collapsed. He got knocked cold himself by falling debris, and they took him out by ambulance before the buildings collapsed."

Tears in her eyes, Bo came over and threw her arms around Rod and held him. He gave Bobby a helpless look. Bobby smiled and winked, then shook hands with him when she stepped back.

"Boys," Bobby said, "and I don't mean that in a racial way." They chuckled, and he went on, "We're headed to the O.K. Corral. You want to mosey over there, too?"

Joe jumped up, enthusiastically saying, "Does Pinocchio have a wooden pecker?"

Then he got embarrassed looking over at Bo and said, "Oops! Excuse me, ma'am."

Bo picked up her briefcase, saying, "That explains it."

Joe was shaken now and said, "Explains what?"

Bo said, "Oh, I saw a sequel to Pinocchio called *Pinocchio, the Teenage Years*, and he always had splinters in his right hand."

Bo opened the door and walked out into the hallway and heard the three exploding with laugher.

Rod looked at Bobby and said, "You wife is totally cool, sir."

They followed her out the door still laughing.

In the lobby, Bobby stopped them and said, "You two need to come in after Bo and me. There is a sofa in the center front in front of the guard's station. Sit down on that and tell the guard you are waiting on a Pearl 2 Bamboo executive who is meeting you there. If he asks who, say Clay Allison, because I remember seeing that name in their brochure, and it was the gunfighter's name, and then I heard the receptionist tell someone that he was on a trip to Hong Kong and would be back in a week or so."

They all shook hands and Bobby and Bo went out the door.

Bobby looked over at Bo and smiled, then said, "I love you."

Bo felt warm all over and said, "I love you, too. From now on, I don't want to kick in any doors without reminding you of that first."

It gave Bobby a grim reminder of what their work was like. They were adrenaline junkies and always facing danger, but on any given day, they could go through a door and get blasted, either one. They accepted that.

They went out and crossed the street, then went down a short distance to the modern-looking skyscraper and entered. Bobby and Bo waved at Rufus, who gave them a big smile. He walked out from behind the security console and handed them both security badges.

They thanked him and put them on.

Rufus said, "You said that you both would be back."

They headed toward the elevators, and Bo grabbed Bobby's arm.

She said, "You want me to trust your vibes, honey. Now, I need you to trust mine."

Bobby said, "Always."

"Good."

Bo followed by Bobby walked up to Rufus and said quietly, "Rufus, you are a good cop, aren't you?"

He threw his shoulders back and said, "Yes, I am. When I can be a real cop and not a rent-a-cop."

Bo said, "So are we."

He said, "Huh?"

Bo continued, "Being a good cop, you had to have noticed all the al Qaeda types coming in here today?"

Rufus said, "I do not racially profile people, ma'am."

"Nice company line, Rufus," she said, "but you did say you are a real cop."

He said, "Yeah, they all give me the creeps. I don't mean profiling anybody. Every one of those Arabs today were all real unfriendly and arrogant."

Bobby picked up on what Bo was doing and said, "They are all al Qaeda."

"What!" he said, astounded but not really that shocked.

Bo pulled out her badge and showed it to him and said, "We are cops, and, Rufus, I am telling you because I like you. It is time to go home. Forget the submissive little wife dream and catch the next plane back to the States. This job will be gone tomorrow."

His mouth was hanging open as Bo pulled out a business card.

She said, "You have much family stateside?"

He said, "No, ma'am."

"Go to Canton, Ohio, and look up the Stark County sheriff," she said. "I have worked with him before and tell him I sent you to work for him. You become a cop again and the woman will come after, naturally. Be patient."

He said, "This job will be gone tomorrow?"

Bobby replied, "This whole business will be gone tomorrow. She felt for you and does not want you involved in this."

Joe and Rod came in the door, and Bobby signaled them over.

Bo said, "They are cops, too, Rufus. They need visitors passes, too."

Rufus got tears in his eyes and wiped them away. He handed Joe and Rod passes and shook hands with each.

Bobby explained, "Rufus has been working for us here undercover."

Rufus looked at Bobby with wonderment and then Bo. He stuck out his hand and shook enthusiastically.

He said, "The first jet I can get out of here on. I promise. Thank you. Thank you both."

He went out the door, tossing his badge on the desk.

They smiled and the four of them headed for the elevators. They went up the first one, and Bo explained the floor plan to the other two and told them to let Bobby do the talking.

They went down the hallway toward the conference room, which had the doors shut. They stopped and set the briefcases down, and Bobby pulled out his MP5 and slammed a magazine in place and jacked the first round in the chamber. Then he pulled his Glock 17 out with his left hand. The others armed themselves, too.

Bobby nodded and Bo reached out with her left hand, and they went through the big door and spread apart.

Immediately, Muhammad's biggest bodyguard screamed, *"Allahu Ahkbar!"* and yanked out a sawed-off pump twelve-gauge shotgun.

Bobby's burst of fire from the MP5 almost ripped the big man in half. The shotgun went off and blew the leg off a Vietnamese terrorist two chairs down. Several women screamed, one man started whimpering, and all raised their hands. Bobby looked at one of the Vietnamese near the wounded man.

He said, "Speak English?"

The man said, "Yes."

Bobby said, "Go ahead and put a tourniquet on his leg."

The man dropped down to tend to his fallen comrade.

Bobby looked at a distinguished-looking American and said, "Are you James Weatherford's brother?"

He replied, "I damned sure am, and you wait until he hears about this."

Bobby said, "Maybe he'll hear about it in his prison cell at the Supermax federal pen in Florence, Colorado, but he'll only be able to commiserate with his cellmate, Brutus. He is out of business, and so are you, as of today."

The man started to speak, and Bo interrupted him with a well-placed bullet that went into the table and shattered his drinking glass all over him. He was drenched with a couple of slivers of glass sticking in his face and hands. He started picking them out.

Bo said quietly, "Shush. You are done talking. Unless you are spoken to."

Bobby was bothered by one very pretty Vietnamese woman at the tray of coffee who kept smiling at him, and even winked one time.

Rod's gun barked and a man next to Muhammad grabbed his chest, a pistol falling from his hand. He had slid it up behind his glass and Bobby and Bo both missed it.

Without looking back, Bobby said, "Thanks, Rod."

Bobby turned his attention to Muhammad Yahyaa.

He said, "Muhammad Yahyaa, head of al Qaeda for all of Southeast Asia. What is packed in the containers aboard the MV *Fairweather*?"

Yahyaa hissed at him, *"Ya l'aahira!"*

Bobby said, "Yes, I'm a bastard and a mean one right now, because I will not let you or anyone commit another 9/11 on my soil. I will do anything I need to, to prevent that. Now, what is in those containers?"

Muhammad stared defiantly, and Weatherford's brother said, "He will never tell you."

Bobby said, "Good point."

He raised his MP5 and aimed it directly at Muhammad Yahyaa's face and saw the man's eyes open wide with terror and Bobby opened fire. Brains and blood went all over several people and Muhammad's other bodyguard screamed and raised a folding-stock AK-47 up from under the table and took three sets of simultaneous double taps from Bo, Joe, and Rod.

Bobby pointed his MP5 at Weatherford's face saying, "Last time. What is in those containers?"

The man's eyes opened very wide in fear, and he held his hands protectively over his face.

He shrieked, "Please! Please! I swear I don't know. He

told us they were going to make a statement and blow up some boats and docks in Los Angeles, but that is all I know. I swear!"

Bobby turned the MP5 quickly and many rounds went through the giant coffeepot drenching the pretty Vietnamese woman, and he pointed his weapon at her.

Bobby said, "Speak English?"

She said, *"Titi."*

He said, "Good, really cute disguise, but the next time, Nguyen Van Tran, you want to try to pass yourself off as a woman, wear a scarf to hide your Adam's apple. Women don't have Adam's apples."

Joe looked at Rod and shook his head, grinning.

Bo smiled with pride at her husband and partner.

Tran yelled, *"Choi oi! Choi doc oi!"* which means "sun rock" but is really cursing in Vietnamese.

He raised an MP5 himself and shot Bobby in the same arm that was slashed. Bo hit him with a double tap center mass, but he was wearing a Kevlar vest with a heart plate, under his *ao dai,* or dress. She dropped as he fired at her, and Rod's shot in the heart plate threw his aim off.

Bobby and Bo, under the table, opened fire on his legs, and he went down like a shot, and they emptied their magazines into his legs and groin area. He was screaming and suffering from several arterial hits.

Joe screamed at everybody in the room to lay across the table, hands out.

"You no speaky English, you die right now."

Everyone complied.

Rod ran to Bobby and grabbed a necktie off the man by him to make a quick bandage for Bobby's arm.

Joe yelled, "Rod, her, too."

Bobby and Rod looked and saw that Bo was bleeding from her right triceps. Rod got another tie and bandaged her. Bobby and Bo, using their good hands, covered the people across the table while Rod and Joe quickly frisked everybody for weapons. They recovered several.

Then Joe looked at them and laughed, saying, "Do you

two shoot and kill all your suspects before you question them, or is this just a bad day?"

Just then Bobby's sat phone rang. He answered it.

It was General Perry.

He said, "Bobby, are you two okay? NSA has been watching the whole episode with the camera you planted. In fact, so have I and the president. By the way, the tape is going to be destroyed, but we have enjoyed the hell out of it. Do you remember the nasty fertilizer bomb that Timothy McVeigh and his cohorts made to wipe out the Murrah Federal Building in Oklahoma City?"

"Yes, sir," Bobby replied, "I sure do."

General Perry said, "Well, that was what was in all forty-five hundred containers on the MV *Fairweather*. Imagine a bomb going off in the Port of Los Angeles with forty-five times the explosive power of the Oklahoma City bombing, and that is what you just prevented."

Bobby said, "We did. How?"

The general replied, "Good idea on asking for the team from CAG. The coast guard got fired on when they approached the cargo ship. Lost two and had several wounded. The Delta Force team never even landed. They flew on out and the whole team HALOed in and landed on containers fore and aft, and shot the hell out of the crew. The ship was searched and was a floating mega-bomb. How bad are your wounds, seriously?"

Bobby replied, "Neither of us had a bone or artery hit, sir."

General Perry said, "Well, you two will get checked out and patched up and are flying back here on Air Force One. The president wants to have a talk with you. First of all, you are killing my budget on Purple Hearts. Then I want to talk to you both about Command and General Staff College and the U.S. Army War College. I want you to get your full-bird promotion as soon as possible, so I can have somebody take over command of maybe the Fifth Special Forces Group at Fort Campbell or the Third or Seventh at

Fort Bragg, and of course Bo will be commanding an airborne unit on the same post you end up at."

Bobby said, "I don't know what to say, sir."

General Perry said, "I do. God bless you and Bo, Bobby."

Bobby smiled and replied, "No, sir, God bless America.

Don Bendell is the author of twenty-four books and a motion picture with more than 1.5 million copies of his books in print worldwide. As an enlisted man, he served as an MP at Fort Dix, New Jersey, and as an officer, he was a Green Beret captain and served on a twelve-man A-team in Vietnam in 1968–1969, as well as the top secret Phoenix Program and three other Special Forces groups. Two of Don's sons are Green Beret sergeants serving in the global War on Terrorism. A seventh-degree black belt master instructor in four different martial arts, Don also owns karate schools in southern Colorado and was inducted into the International Karate Hall of Fame in 1995. Don's political editorials have been published far and wide, and he has been interviewed on *Fox News Live* and many other national radio shows. A real cowboy with a real horse, Don, and his black belt master wife, Shirley, live on a large mountain ranch overlooking Cañon City, Colorado. He has four grown sons, two grown daughters, and five grand-children.

Watch for his upcoming Combat Application Group series about the modern-day army's Delta Force, coming soon from The Berkley Publishing Group.